AS -FATE- DECREES

by
DENYSÉ BRIDGER

EDGE SCIENCE FICTION AND FANTASY PUBLISHING
AN IMPRINT OF HADES PUBLICATIONS, INC.
CALGARY

As Fate Decrees
copyright © 2007 by Denysé Bridger

EDGE

Edge Science Fiction and Fantasy Publishing
An Imprint of Hades Publications Inc.
P.O. Box 1714, Calgary, Alberta, T2P 2L7, Canada

In house editing by Kimberly Gammon
Interior design by Brian Hades
Cover Illustration by Geoff Taylor

EDGE Science Fiction and Fantasy Publishing and Hades Publications, Inc. acknowledges the ongoing support of the Canada Council for the Arts and the Alberta Foundation for the Arts for our publishing programme.

Library and Archives Canada Cataloguing in Publication

Bridger, Denysé, 1960-
    As Fate Decrees / Denysé Bridger.

ISBN-13: 978-1-894063-41-8
ISBN-10: 1-894063-41-4

    I. Title.

PS8603.R527A8 2007   C813'.6   C2007-903451-9

FIRST EDITION
(x-20070724)
Printed in Canada
www.edgewebsite.com

This novel is
dedicated
to my father,
in loving memory

ARES

THE COY MISTRESS

Thracian filly, why so heartless?
Why, so shyly sidelong glancing,
Hold me ever at a distance,
like a fool with wit untried?
I could clap a bridle on ye, very well,
for all your prancing;
Down the course I well could rein ye,
make ye wheel the way I guide.
Yet a while, across the pastures,
go your ways with light feet dancing—
You have still to find the master
that shall curb ye and shall ride.

Anacreon of Teos
(c. 570-c. 485 B.C.)

PROLOGUE

The slavers had chosen a true hovel to conduct their illegal commerce in this day, he thought as he surveyed the dilapidated structure that barely stood before him. Theseus had outlawed slavery shortly after the people of Athens had made him king; which perhaps added to the appeal of this particular market. His mouth twitched with distaste he made no attempt to conceal and his eyes flickered shut briefly before he strode into the shabby building.

Inside, it was no more pleasant. The cramped quarters were filled to capacity as the potential customers milled about, all anxious for the day's business to get underway. Shadows kept identities safe, or at the very least ambiguous. The smells of too many people and too much decay mingled with other distinct scents, livestock, waste of all types, and indiscernible to most, the rich, underlying tang of bloodshed. He moved deeper into the throng, alert eyes missing no detail, however insignificant.

The stranger walked among the buyers at the slave market, his identity concealed beneath the full length cape that swirled dust and dirt around his feet as he moved. He was regal in motion, head held high, broad shoulders easily clearing a path as he strolled amid the nobility and commoners who were equal for the brief span of time that it took to trade in life. The slavers were a hard lot, and they laughed openly as they wagered on which prize would fetch the highest price.

He was nearing the front of the room, within easy view of the auction platform when he was stopped. The hand that grabbed his arm and tried to push him back was heavily weighted with jewels. He smiled inwardly and turned toward the man who had dared to touch him.

"There's plenty of space at the back, stranger."

"Then I suggest you move," he replied, gravelly voice pitched to dangerous quiet.

The nobleman's face quickly distorted into comical ire, his pasty skin suddenly florid as he sputtered in outrage. Two bulky figures appeared on either side of him and the shrouded stranger sighed inwardly.

"Think carefully before you incite something that will cost you your life, Poias," he advised softly, voice absurdly pleasant and reasonable.

The man paled further as his name was spoken so casually, and so openly. Automatically his gaze darted to the throng around them, desperate to note if any had heard the stranger's address. Low laughter made his stomach knot and he glanced warily at the dark man who towered before him.

"Who are you?"

Within the cowl, a flash of teeth preceded deeper laughter. The men fell back at a look from Poias, and relief was tangible when the stranger continued his walk through the people.

Grimy slaves moved about in the crowd, pouring wine for the customers, their eyes downcast, bodies thin and aged. Looking at them, he knew they were barely into their adult years, yet all appeared ancient from their servitude.

He listened with a mixture of curiosity and contempt as the marketplace quieted and the bidding began on the unfortunate souls captured by the slavers. He appraised each new prize carefully, growing steadily more irritated as his admittedly short patience began to wear thin. *Something* had drawn him to this underground cesspool, but his determination to discover precisely what it was had dimmed considerably.

The comments and plans of the new owners passed through his consciousness without note. Human life was of no consequence to him, and he had little tolerance for those who refused to fight for their freedom.

As the auction carried on, he turned to leave. A rumble of dark mirth stirred the buzz of the crowd, and his attention was arrested. Standing at the far edge of the gathering, he still had a clear line of vision to the makeshift platform. The captain of the slave ship hauled the captive into full view of the room.

He smiled inwardly as the prisoner lashed out at the man, her foot catching him firmly at the back of one knee. The enraged captain growled in fury and backhanded her when he regained his footing. Several men came onto the platform and quickly had her ankles shackled, as well as her wrists. When they dragged her back to her feet, the slaver stepped closer to her again. She spit at him and he took her hair in one fist as his other hand stripped away the rags of her clothing.

The stranger's interest was piqued. Clean and groomed she would be beautiful. At a glance, she could be mistaken for an old woman; her hair was silvery white, and her skin ivory pale. Even her eyes, a faint gray, seemed remarkably colorless, yet vivid at the same time. Around her neck, suspended from a thin strip of black leather, was an intricately cut pendant; two blood-red rubies molded into the form of a heart. The thread of silver that held them into their shape made the heart appear broken.

"She calls herself Amarantha," the slaver announced.

A tingle of response coalesced at the base of his spine, and he stepped forward, ignoring the mutters and curses of those he pushed aside.

The captain grabbed the pendant and yanked it from her neck.

"This doesn't go with her," he informed the bidders with a leer.

Amarantha made a lunge for him, heedless of the chains that bound her.

"That is mine, pig!" she snarled.

When he would have struck her again, a voice from the crowd stayed his hand.

"Leave her be, and let's get on with it. Damaged she isn't going to be worth much to anyone."

The stranger glanced at the man who spoke, saw the lecherous gleam in the nobleman's dark eyes. Bidding began without warning, and he listened intently as the sums escalated to preposterous amounts in minutes. The comments were as wild as the bids, many of them blatantly sexual as the crowd incited itself to a lusting frenzy over the exotic creature all suddenly coveted.

Disgusted, he stepped forward, stopped at the edge of the raised platform. He pulled a bag of gold from his belt and tossed it at the feet of the slaver.

"The bidding is ended," he stated quietly. Behind him, the crowd gradually murmured to an uneasy silence.

"The bidding stops when I say it stops," the captain shouted.

"Not this time," he answered and tossed back the hood of his cloak. He smiled, and the slaver stumbled back a few paces.

ϒ ϒ ϒ

Amarantha stared at the man who stood before her, oblivious to the disquiet of the assembled men at his back. He was terrifying and alluring at the same time; handsome beyond most men, tall, with shoulder-length black curls, and jet dark eyes. His face, lean and sculpted, was shadowed with equally dark hair; mouth defined and shaped by the moustache that merged with the inky blackness of his beard. Beneath the cloak, she sensed broad shoulders, lean, well-muscled chest, and long legs. When he lifted his arm and held out his hand, she glimpsed smooth, contoured muscles.

"The necklace," he demanded.

She turned to look at the slaver, curious despite the fear that still coursed through her veins. He was gawking openly at the stranger, but there was sincere terror in his slitted eyes. His gaze darted furtively to the restless patrons of the auction; he saw only his fright reflected in most faces.

"Now!"

He flinched at the sharp order, then hurried forward to drop the pendant into the outstretched palm. He backed off instantly.

"Release her," the stranger ordered quietly, and waited, dark eyes glittering dangerously within the heavy cowl he'd pulled over his head again.

Amarantha's smile was derisive as two men rushed forward and unlocked the chains, then quickly backed away with them. Their fear, and the unfurling terror of the gathered Athenians, came to life as an invisible mist that snaked through the crowd, touching them, tainting them with the contagion of dread as all considered flight. They knew who walked among them, it seemed. Amarantha did not.

"Cover yourself," the stranger directed and swept his cloak from his shoulders to offer it to her.

She met his steady stare, but didn't move. His smile was sardonic, amusement and faint disdain in his eyes. He shrugged indifferently and dropped the heavy cape at her feet. For several moments she remained motionless, agape as he turned his back and walked toward the exit. When he didn't hesitate, she heard the whispers begin anew. The wisdom of leaving spurred her and she scooped up the cloak, then ran after the mysterious man who had just bought her.

Amarantha caught him outside the slaver's hut. She touched his arm, and he halted, but made no move to look at her. She walked around him, looked up into his eyes.

"You have something that belongs to me," she said, and held out her hand.

For a second there was silence, then his laughter rang out. In spite of herself, Amarantha smiled, his laughter was very pleasant to the ears.

"Your courage will serve you well," he remarked and stunned her when he inclined his head in a tiny bow of respect. He dropped the pendant into her hand and gestured for her to go ahead of him.

Amarantha tied the precious piece of jewelry around her neck and pulled the rich cloak closer as she walked at his side. They reached a nearby stable without further exchange of words and she waited when he went inside, then returned a few minutes later leading a midnight black stallion of exceptional beauty and breeding. She stepped forward, stroked the animal's shining coat with open appreciation.

"He's magnificent," she murmured, her gaze darting to the dark man who watched her. He nodded, and indicated that she was to mount the splendid animal. Amarantha did as he requested, and shivered inwardly when her new master mounted and sat at her back, uncomfortably aware of the strength and power that emanated from him.

"Why did you buy me?" she asked once they were well away from the squalid slave market.

"To teach you."

She glanced over her shoulder, scepticism and irony in her features.

"I doubt you'll find me an apt pupil for—" Abruptly, she turned away from his glittering dark eyes, uneasy with the renewed laughter she glimpsed in their inky depths.

"For what, Amarantha?" he asked, voice low and rough with combined sensuality and amusement. He tightened his loose hold on her, pressed her back against the broad expanse of his chest as he guided the horse toward the waterfront. "You might enjoy all the lessons I could teach," he taunted softly.

She tried to pull away from him, cursed under her breath when she was held firmly by arms that felt like steel bands.

"I am neither slave, nor whore," she hissed in fury.

"If you're not careful," he warned, tone suddenly edged with distinct warning, "you *will* be both."

Wisely, she refrained from comment.

"Why is the pendant so important to you?" he questioned after another short silence. "Borias might have killed you when you fought him over it."

"It was a gift," she confessed after several seconds of hesitation.

"From a lover?" he speculated.

She made no response, and appeared oddly saddened by the assumption, leaving him to wonder if he'd been correct, or completely mistaken.

They reached the waterfront without further conversation, and he nudged the stallion toward a large ship moored at the northern end of the long pier. She scanned the vessel with curious eyes when he reined in and dropped from the horse's back, motion carelessly graceful.

He kept a firm hand on the reins and led the animal to the plank that would permit them to board. Amarantha bent to touch his arm.

"We are bringing him aboard?"

"He's yours," the dark stranger said casually.

"I have no desire to own this animal," she replied gently. "He is amazing, but—"

Deep black-brown eyes bored into her, a gleam of annoyance in their expression.

"There's something you don't like about him?"

She almost winced at his displeasure, caught the response and quelled it before meeting his candid stare.

"I will not ride a black mount by choice," she stated. "Black is the color of night... and death." It was an aversion she'd had since her childhood, and she loathed it. Inwardly, she shuddered as she looked down at him, frightened by the fire in his eyes. This man who had bought her life was dressed totally in the cast she feared and hated. Yet, on him, it seemed the only *right* shade he could have worn.

He surprised her when he shrugged and lifted her from the stallion's back as though she were made of air and had no substance of weight. He handed the horse to a beggar who wandered the pier, then laughed openly when the wretched man backed up, terror on his face.

"You are not like the others who would have owned me," she observed cautiously.

He smiled, a disarming change in his fierce visage. She was forced to concede that he was exceptionally handsome as men went; the kind of master to whom many women would willingly bow.

"My reasons are not theirs, Amarantha," he assured her. "Never think otherwise."

"Yet you will not tell me why I am now your property," she said, bitterness and anger unmistakable.

"When we reach Thrace, you can choose the mount you want," he told her, and led her directly to the only private quarters on the square-rigged, three masted sailing ship, the Captain's.

When they were inside, she looked around, curiosity and suspicion in her eyes, her entire body tense with wariness.

"Relax," he laughed. "I have no intention of raping you."

"Then what do you want?" she retorted, irritated that he could read her thoughts so effortlessly.

"Your lessons will begin tomorrow," he announced. "At dawn. You'll find clothes, and food. I expect you'll want to rest until morning."

"And where will you be?"

He crossed the space that separated them, towered over her as he pondered a reply to her insolence. He touched her chin, forced her to meet his frank gaze.

"Wherever I choose to be," he answered softly. "For now," he paused and smiled, "that is not in your bed."

"I was wrong about you," she snapped, tone low and derisive. "You want what they all want."

He grabbed her arm when she would have turned away from him, and his grip tightened until she cried out.

"What I want I take, little one," he whispered. "What I expect from you is not what you fear so obviously." His look swept her, his expressive features giving the appraisal a faint tinge of contempt. *At least not yet*, he amended silently. He released her, and would have left if she hadn't halted his departure.

"Is this ship yours?"

"*The Halcyon* is one of many vessels at my disposal," he responded, answering without revealing anything of real value to her.

"And we are going to Thrace?"

He nodded and turned to face her again, his back braced casually on the closed door. He folded his arms across his chest and waited for the rest of her questions.

"What am I to call you?" she wondered, manner still distrustful. He was overwhelming in all aspects, and his physical presence made her feel both afraid and safe, despite the obvious absurdity of the paradox. Yet, deep within his brilliant black gaze, she knew there was a great deal about him that was not at all what it seemed on the surface.

"Master will do," he smirked, clearly sensing that she would rebel against the title, but equally sure it would be used, however unwillingly.

She scowled, then turned her back to him.

He waited, but she made no further attempts to question him. He left her.

ϒ ϒ ϒ

Amarantha woke with a jolt, her heart pounding wildly within her as she fought her way back to awareness. She'd spent most of the night watching the door, waiting for him to return, despite his assertions to the contrary. All she'd gained was cramped muscles and little sleep for her vigilance. She threw back the blanket that she'd finally wrapped herself in, and took another look around the cabin. At some point, she'd had a visitor; food waited on the table, also fresh water. She rose and quickly washed, and ate. Once her stomach felt less empty, she opened the small chest he'd shown her the previous day. There, she found clothes, a loose, pale blue tunic, and pants of a deeper blue. There were white underthings, and leather sandals. All fit as though made for her, making her wonder how he could have known her so well when they had met less than a day earlier. Fully aware that she was deliberately avoiding him, and that it would be tolerated for only so long, she tied her hair with a thin length of leather and braced herself as she left the relative haven of the cabin. With a sense of growing trepidation, she forced herself to walk up the steps that led to the main deck of *The Halcyon*.

Sunshine was muted by a thin layer of gray cloud cover. The sea air was tangy, salt and warm wind giving it a distinct flavor as she breathed deeply. A surreptitious glance at the vessel's company surprised her; no man looked at her.

"They've been warned," a soft, mocking voice close to her ear noted.

She bit back a cry of fright, spun, and glared at him when he laughed at her. She was preparing a scathing response to his amusement when he took her by the arm and led her to the aft section of the ship's deck. She jerked away from his hold, and was rewarded with a tighter grasp as he placed her where he wanted her to stand.

"Fight with me and this will cause you a great deal more pain than is necessary," he reprimanded casually.

"What, precisely, is it you intend to do with me?" she snarled quietly.

"I'm going to say this to you once, and once only," he stated with obvious reproach. "You are here to learn. I am your teacher," he smiled; the same heart-stopping change of expression that had unnerved her the previous day. "Your mentor. You *will* learn," he assured her.

"Learn what?" She didn't wait for an answer. Amarantha spun on her heel and took a single step away from him, anger and humiliation making her reckless. She had taken less than a half dozen steps when she was sent sprawling across the wooden deck floor. Stunned, she rolled over and stared upward at him. Furious, she vaulted back to her feet and launched at him. Usually, her opponents fell back in the first wave of her assault; this time, she met resistance that made her efforts seem ludicrous. Enraged further by his obvious amusement, Amarantha attacked him with greater ferocity. He dodged her kicks and swings, occasionally landing a solid blow to her whirling form as he goaded her to indignant frenzy.

She managed to gain a small advantage and quickly knocked him flat on his back. As she grinned in triumph, her master lashed out, his foot connecting with the back of her knee. She cried out in real pain as the fire tore up her leg and made her gasp. On her knees, she backed up when he stood over her, his features a study in profound fury.

"Your first lesson," he ground out harshly. "Humility before a superior skill. I could kill you," he informed her with icy disdain. "I could have done so at any time. Take advantage of what I am offering, Amarantha." He smiled, though the shift of expression lacked any warmth. "Attack me again, and you will die, little one." For several moments their gazes remained locked, and when she finally nodded in defeat, he resumed the interrupted lesson that had begun the day.

He glanced skyward, eyes narrowed in concentration, then nodded.

"Feel the sway of the ship beneath your feet," he said softly. "Let it guide your body, make the motion your natural rhythm."

Amarantha stared at him, motionless. She yelped in fright when he turned his attention back to her and his glare darkened dangerously.

"Do it!"

She scrambled to her feet, calmed the roar in her ears and closed her eyes. She sensed his watchful gaze, and gradually blocked her consciousness of his presence. The gentle rock of the ship lulled as it had the night before, but she didn't feel the lure of sleep this time, merely the relaxing swell of the waves that lapped the sides of the vessel. She opened her eyes and saw his nod of approval, absurdly pleased by the wordless support.

Her eyes widened when he passed her a bow, and a quiver of arrows. He pointed toward the target that had been placed near the front of the ship.

"That is your goal," he informed her. "Use the motion, let it guide you."

"You expect me to hit a target that appears to be moving?"

"Most targets are moving," he replied derisively. "Usually running for their lives."

She hesitated, then nocked an arrow to the bowstring. With a silent prayer to Artemis, she lifted the bow and took aim. The lurch of the ship was no longer soothing, and her stomach knotted with apprehension as she tried to focus on the weaving target.

"Move with the currents!" he snapped.

Startled, she let loose the arrow. It flew wild and she shuddered when a yell of pain broke the crash of the waves that buffeted the ship. She saw a crewman sprawled on the deck, the arrow protruding from his back, and her horror threatened to empty the contents of her breakfast onto the wooden planks beneath her feet.

"Concentrate," he ordered, and walked around her to stand directly at her back.

"We have to help him," she said, shaken. "I may have just killed him!"

He shrugged and lifted her arms again, guided her aim.

"Stop it!" She tried to break free of him, only to discover that she was immobile.

"He's of no consequence," the harsh voice ground out, his tone low and furious in her ear. "Already dead."

"What?"

"I said concentrate," he repeated furiously. "If you take this long with everything, you may be old before our task is complete."

"I have no task with you," she shouted and pushed at him with all her strength. He didn't move.

"Aim."

She shook her head, but the defiance was futile. He placed his hands on her hips and twisted her toward the side, then covered her hands with his as he took careful aim.

His proximity was as disturbing as the wavering perception created by the increasingly turbulent sea. Amarantha tried to ease slightly away from him, and he hissed a soft warning in her ear.

"Focus," he demanded. "If you continue to fail, I'll take your breast to see if that improves your accuracy."

She bit her bottom lip to control the fear and sickness that was cresting in her throat, and peered intently at the target. His arm was strong and reassuring, despite her terror at causing the crewman's death. She mimicked his easy movement, allowed her body to move with his. When he freed her abruptly, she loosed the arrow.

He nodded, and she stared in shock at the mark she'd hit.

"Now, do it without me," he instructed.

"I can't," she murmured automatically.

"Do it," he directed, and softened the order with a smile of encouragement.

Amarantha subdued the tremors that plagued her, and forced her concentration to remain fixed on the target before her, while the motion of her body merged with the rise and fall of the deck upon which they stood.

ϓ ϓ ϓ

"How many more days to Thrace?" Amarantha asked when her master entered the cabin that had been her home for weeks. He often came to join her at the end of a day, to discuss the progress she made, or simply to talk. She had been wary in the first long days of their journey; now she looked forward to his company, though she would never admit it.

"Several more weeks," he answered. "We'll be in port in a few days, a stop for supplies. I expect to be no longer than a day."

"Am I to be permitted a look at the marketplace?"

He laughed. "I'll go with you, and if you behave yourself, I may even buy you a gift."

She felt the almost foregone resentment resurface at his casual words; it surged back into her heart with shocking swiftness, and she rose from her seat.

"I want nothing from you ... Master." She deliberately made the title a sneer of insolence, all but guaranteeing his anger.

He surprised her with mocking laughter instead of anger.

"What you want is of no consequence to me, little one. You deserve a gift. You're making excellent progress."

She glowered at him.

"You tell me nothing, no matter the volume of words you sometimes speak. Why is that?"

"I tell you what you are required to know," he responded, and the fire in his eyes flared with warning that she leave it at that.

"What I *require* is truth," she prodded, knowingly ignoring the temper that was flashing in his dark gaze.

"Truth is subjective," he snapped. "When you need to know more, I'll tell you. Until then, do as you're told."

Amarantha stepped toward him, then ground her teeth in frustrated annoyance when he rose from his casual seat on the edge of her berth. As always, his height and bearing unnerved her. There was something in his manner that deterred more effectively than weapons or words ever would; she was not afraid of him, not truly, but she did know that he would only allow so much defiance before he'd exact punishment for the disobedience. It was that potentiality that had smothered her wrath more than once, and did so again now.

ϒ ϒ ϒ

Amarantha deflected another of the endless series of parries that he'd directed at her throughout the morning. His gift had been a specially tailored outfit of leather and armor, something she was gradually getting used to. It was slowing her, and he was relentless in forcing her to maintain her defense.

"Please..." She stumbled beneath the impact of his great sword clashing with her lighter weapon, and her knees buckled as her grip gave way and the sword fell to the deck. She knelt before him, gasping and weakened. "Enough!"

"Do you think an enemy is going to give you time to catch your breath?" he snarled angrily. "Get up!"

She shook her head.

"I can't!"

He landed another glancing blow, pleased when she automatically moved to deflect the strike with the heavy leather wrist guards he'd fashioned for her. She rolled away, grabbed the fallen weapon and tried to regain her footing, only to stumble and slip to her knees again. She dropped the sword and glared at him.

"If you intend to kill me, do it!" she yelled, anger and weariness in her rasping voice.

He shrugged and stepped closer, his sword raised to deliver the killing blow. He laughed when she yelped in shock and dove for her sword. As his blade descended, she raised the gleaming length of the finely honed sword, caught the arc of his swing and scrambled to her feet as sparks showered from the clashing weapons.

Fear motivated her now, and she was inwardly shaking with combined terror and rage. His skill was always a marvel, but today he matched it with ferocious, unrelenting determination. She began to believe that he did, in fact, want to kill her with this session.

The battle had reached a standstill, neither gaining advantage, yet he continued to attack, repeatedly forcing her to defend herself. Amarantha's muscles were aching, her grip growing slippery with sweat; she ignored the blazing sun, no longer blinded by it as she had been earlier. It was difficult to hear even the waves above the roar of heartbeat and labored breathing; he was calm and relaxed, a thing which frequently infuriated her further.

He landed a flat-sided strike to her back and she fell face down on the deck. Exhaustion settled on her as dead weight on her limbs. She waited, certain he would make the final strike a smooth, honorable death. She rose stiffly, muscles screaming objection to the imposed movement as she prepared to face him.

"You prove me right yet again," he told her with a small bow of his head. "You should be pleased."

She stared, disbelief making her gape at him. If she planned a response, it faded as the afternoon sun suddenly turned to gray haze before her eyes. Her body was liquid, and she knew she was fainting in spite of her efforts to prevent revealing the weakness. An instant later, she was taken aback completely when he lifted her into his arms and carried her down to the cabin that was her sanctuary.

He stayed at her side long after she'd fallen into spent slumber, and was still present when she woke. Instead of the wariness that his presence would once have evoked, Amarantha appeared genuinely pleased to find him with her.

Behind his careful smile, he dared to believe that he'd been right in choosing her.

ϒ ϒ ϒ

Thrace was a wild, primitive country, and the men who greeted the vessel as they docked made her wonder what her chances of survival truly were now that they had reached their destination.

"Master?"

She was no longer awkward or angry when she used the title, and he smiled slightly as he stopped at her side.

"Why Thrace?"

"Here we can finish what needs to be done," he replied enigmatically. "Without the interference of," he paused, considered, then laughed softly, "my family," he concluded.

"Your family would object to you training a slave?" Amarantha looked closely at him, then touched his arm. "Or is it the owning of a slave that would displease them?"

He laughed with genuine amusement, and brushed her cheek with surprisingly gentle fingers. "No, owning slaves would not offend their sensibilities, little one," he assured her. "But my reasons for wanting you might not be welcomed by all."

"You will not explain that, will you?" she asked, and followed him automatically when he stepped onto the plank that would allow them to again stand on firm ground.

When he ignored the query, she nodded and continued to trail after him. The attention she garnered kept her close to him, and she was inwardly fascinated by the combination of fear and reverence with which he was greeted, and avoided.

They reached a stable and he was immediately brought the most magnificent stallion that she'd ever seen, a horse even more beautiful than the one she'd ridden in Athens. The animal's coat gleamed blue-black in the afternoon sunshine, and he was as regal as the rider who presently stroked his sleek neck.

"You can choose the mount you wish when we reach the castle," he informed her, then placed her on the stallion's back before she could object. A moment later, his arms encircled her as he mounted and sat at her back.

The castle wasn't far from the dock; she spotted it looming in the distance long before they ever reached the uneven road that led to it.

"This is your home?"

"It's to be your home from now on," he stated quietly.

Puzzled by the vague reply, Amarantha held her tongue and enjoyed the savage beauty of the land as they drew ever nearer the brooding palace.

ϒ ϒ ϒ

He watched, hidden in shadows, as she waded into the pool and permitted the crystalline waters of the fall to pour over her. Even with the distance, he could feel her weariness, the ache in her muscles that had lessened over the past years' training, but never abated entirely. She'd been an apt pupil, as he'd known she would be. Shortly after their arrival in Thrace, he'd given her this garden paradise as a reward for her skill and diligence. She came here often, and he watched each time. The waters were warm, clear, and soothing; the only touch she would allow in the wake of their grueling practice sessions.

He smiled. She would, in time, desire other caresses from him. He'd sensed their entwined destiny for many, many years; yet it was only chance that had driven him to seek the slave markets that day. Apollo's Oracle spoke truths to Gods as well as men, and Ares, proud God of War, was no exception. Amarantha was an instrument of Fate, and she would, one day, serve him willingly — in all ways.

The War God maintained his secret observance, his body caught in the thrill of anticipation, savoring the expectations and the possibilities. He preferred to ignore the deeper knowledge he held in his mind; the awareness that another would hold her long before she would accept him. A God owned her — but a mortal man possessed her woman's heart. Ares was a jealous lover, and it took all his restraint to resist the temptation to simply kill his rival before he would take the warrior's innocence. Ares was also a patient God when it suited his need; he would wait.

Past the passions that had grown and been nurtured in utmost secrecy, reason was stemming the God's rage in a way that he rarely employed. If Zeus knew, too soon, he could conceivably alter the course of his son's destiny and desire.

Ares would permit no one to change what the Fates had set in motion.

PART ONE

CHAPTER ONE

The sounds reached Amarantha long before she caught sight of the campaign that raged. Screams and curses mingled, distorted in the uneven terrain; yet the horror was easily discerned. Deep within her, a familiar, long-suppressed anger stirred, against every effort she made to quell the rash battle-lust. She'd spent most of the past few years training with a master who demanded absolute control, and she had eventually won his praise. She did not want it undone mere days after leaving him.

She closed her eyes, breathed deeply, sought for the inner core of discipline. It came, slowly. His voice, a gravelly purr of teaching cadence, filled her mind with the calm that he imposed. She shook off the lure of her impetuous nature, and continued her trek through the heavily wooded forest. Unconsciously, she stroked the neck of her beautiful white mare, Furey. She calmed the animal's agitation with soft words as well, spoken in a voice that lulled, a direct foil to her inner turmoil. Furey knew the moods of her mistress as intimately as the master who had given the horse.

Minutes later, still wary and watchful, she was almost run down on the path. Cursing softly, she quieted the rearing mare, steadied her, then dropped lightly to the ground. Swaying when the man clutched desperately at her, she groped for a tree trunk and kept her balance. The stranger crumpled at her feet. He was badly injured and a single glance made it clear that he had little more than moments of life remaining to him.

"Please... You must... deliver... the message."

She stared as he pulled a scroll from his belt, and held it toward her. She took the blood-stained missive and knelt beside the stranger. He was dark, and young, barely more than twenty seasons, she guessed. He had the look of a farmer, but in his eyes was a sadness that spoke of too much knowledge of death and destruction. He was dressed in rough, worn clothes, and carried no visible weapon.

"Where are you from?"

"Pheneüs," he gasped softly, wide eyes darting wildly as he tried to see if they were about to be attacked.

"You are safe," she assured him. "Who are you running from, and why?" She was steadfastly ignoring the fear that woke at the mention of Pheneüs.

"Give the scroll to the King," he pleaded.

"The King?"

"Corinth..."

She opened her mouth to question him further; then realized it was futile when his eyes rolled and he drew his final breath.

She tucked the scroll in her belt and glanced around. The forest was no longer a sanctuary, the reverberation from too many soldiers rapidly descending on her location was making itself felt in her bones. The heavy scents of crushed wildflowers and trampled undergrowth created a pleasing perfume in the air, despite the danger its cause presented. Birds flew, and small animals scattered before the intrusion, she could hear their escape and feel their fear seeping into her mood. Sighing heavily, she caught Furey's reins, left the dead messenger from Pheneüs, and quickly slipped away.

She had ridden little more than a few yards when the first wave of soldiers came upon her. She smiled inwardly as she assessed them. They halted, surrounded her, and their thoughts were as easily read as their thirst for blood.

"Well, what have we here?" the captain drawled, circling her.

"I am an outlander," Amarantha said softly, her nerves drawing taut as she faced them in seeming innocence of their intentions. "Simply seeking the road to Corinth."

"We'd be happy to escort you, once we've concluded our business," the captain offered. "Have you seen any other on this trail?"

"No," she shook her head. Of them all, the captain was the most pressing threat. He was a large, dark man, with cruel eyes and a leering smile. He was also heavily armed, and the thick muscles of his forearms told her he was well-versed in the use of his arsenal.

"You carry fancy weapons for a woman," another soldier pointed out.

"A gift," she smiled without warmth.

"More likely you are a thief, and these fine weapons the fruits of your skills," the captain proposed.

"Are you always this eager to make false accusations?" she wondered, her gaze searching constantly for an opening in the ranks of men. They were only a small unit, less than a dozen in number; she could defeat them.

The first blow took her by surprise, coming from her left when she was facing the captain. The forest spun erratically as she tumbled from her horse. Regaining her feet almost as she hit the ground, Amarantha swatted the mare's rump to send her running, then drew the sword that was sheathed at her back.

The captain grinned at his men and slid from his horse, drawing his weapon as he did. Amarantha raised an eyebrow and smiled with feigned sweetness.

"Are you very certain you wish to die today?"

The soldier laughed merrily and swung at her as his men surrounded them. He was genuinely startled when she side-stepped his thrust and gracefully whirled out of reach. His amusement faded when she struck a quick blow and blood began to trickle the length of his arm. He cursed, tone low with wrath, and his rage was repeated in his eyes when he turned the full force of his glare on her.

She smiled again, unknowingly echoing an expression her master had perfected and defined lifetimes before her birth. Amarantha knew the others were beginning to dismount and were preparing a full attack; she had to defeat their leader or risk losing her life to a coward's ambush.

Amarantha's sword twirled easily in her hand as she leaped into the air to avoid a low swing aimed to slice her legs from beneath her. He dodged, not swiftly enough, and she aimed downward. The finely honed blade glided through sinew and bone effortlessly, and the captain shrieked in agony as his sword dropped to the ground, his hand still clutching the hilt. He backed up, cradling his gushing wrist to his chest as he issued orders for her death.

Tossing her head to clear her vision of the impediment of loose tendrils of long, silvery hair, Amarantha mentally calculated her chances of surviving this skirmish. She breathed deeply, focused intently on the lessons she'd learned. A second soldier fell before her, his life's blood spurting over her bare arms as she disemboweled him with a casual ease that would later sicken her. In her head, she heard the voice of her mentor, and she listened with her mind and her body as he guided her.

Fresh scarlet warmth streaked her sword arm, rapidly followed by fiery lances of pain. She'd been injured, though the gash was not serious. It angered her and she glared at the man who was attempting to land another strike, one that would rip her in half if he was lucky. He wasn't.

Amarantha's expression became blank, and she gritted her teeth against pain and rage. The fury rose to taunt her, and his laughter incited greater speed to her parries and thrusts. On the fringe of her vision, she caught a glimpse of chestnut; an armored soldier escaping. Yelling furiously she attacked with the full force of her anger and skill; the unit, diminished already, were finished in minutes.

Breathing heavily, Amarantha bent over, dragged in great gulps of air as she fought down the desire to pursue the captain and silence him. If this was a scout unit, he would warn the rest of whatever army he served in, and she feared that Corinth would be under siege in days.

The concern for Corinth reminded her that she now had an unanticipated mission to complete. She glanced around, winced at the jolts of pain her motion created, then whistled sharply. Furey trotted into view a few minutes later, and Amarantha sheathed her sword as she walked to the mare's side. She touched the flowing white mane and grimaced when she left behind a stain of crimson gore.

"If we are to meet the king, Furey, I'm going to need a bath." Weary, she led the animal along the trodden path that now bore the mark of the soldiers' passage. Before too long, she found a tiny stream; not large enough for a proper bath, but it would have to do.

Amarantha tossed the reins over the saddle and left the horse to drink her fill. She dropped to a seat on the bank of the brook and closed her eyes, tired and sickened now that her mind was clear of battle-rage. She'd taken lives with an ease that was horrifying.

Before tears of grief could find their way into her eyes, she leaned forward; then fell back instantly. The face that looked at her from the water was a nightmare; her own, savage in aspect, streaked with blood. After drinking in several deep, calming drafts of air, she inched forward again. This time, she ignored the rippling image that accused her of murder, and quashed the tumult of sobs that rose inside her. The water, crystalline moments ago, ran scarlet for a long time before she finally rose and turned away from the site.

As she went to the mare's side, she shook off the droplets of water that clung to her skin. Stopping again to rinse the blood from Furey's mane, Amarantha wondered what awaited her in Corinth. Jason was king; she'd met him once, years earlier, when he had been renowned for his adventures aboard *The Argo*. Heracles had been with him then. She deliberately veered away from remembrances of the demi-god; they inevitably led her to a place that would fill her with anxiety and loneliness.

She secured her weapons and mounted the fitful horse. Smiling, she patted the animal's neck and leaned forward in the saddle.

"Let's get this over with, Furey," she murmured, tone warm with affection. The mare whinnied softly, then stepped onto the path that would take them to Corinth.

ϒ ϒ ϒ

"I am here to see the king," Amarantha repeated to the guard who stood before her at the palace entrance.

"State your reason, woman," he snapped back.

Amarantha smiled, an expression that was forced. The man was well suited to his job, he was six and a half feet tall, and built like the wall at his back. Dark eyes glittered with annoyance as he scowled at her.

"I have told you already," she replied patiently, and slipped from Furey's back, motion carelessly graceful. She wasn't unaware of the attention she was receiving from others who waited for the outcome of this confrontation. "I have a message that must be delivered to the king. Will you allow me to pass?"

"What message?"

"I carry a scroll from Pheneüs, the original messenger was killed. It was his dying request that I take it in his stead." She watched closely as the man responded to her words, and trepidation settled in the pit of her stomach when his previously belligerent expression altered to reveal a genuine concern for the news she had just imparted.

"Follow me," he directed. "Leave your horse with Dacius, he'll see that she's looked after."

Amarantha handed the reins to the man who stepped forward to accept them. She lifted the scroll from her saddle, and tucked it into her belt as she followed the Captain of the Guard.

The palace of Corinth was a magnificent place, a true palace. The two men who stood on either side of the doors to the castle nodded curtly to their comrade, then held the massive double panels open. She passed into the palace and her breath caught at the grandeur of the large entrance hall. Floors gleamed, marble polished to flawless mirror-like shine; tapestries covered the stone walls, vividly depicting the glories of the Gods and their escapades; and the silence that permeated the huge building was not stifling, but the quiet of peace. As she trailed after the Captain, she found herself wondering if the tranquility would survive whatever message she was bearing.

"Wait here," the Captain directed, then spoke to another nearby guard.

As she watched, he nodded, then disappeared behind another door. He was gone only a few minutes.

"The king has agreed to see you," he announced when he had returned. "He's in the garden, just beyond that door."

"Thank you," she inclined her head and made to leave him. A hand on her arm halted her momentarily, and she looked up into his wary gaze, mildly chilled by the threat in his dark eyes.

"There are men close by," he warned. "If you attempt to harm any of the family, you *will* die."

Startled, she merely nodded once, then went through the door that was being held for her. As she walked the sunlit path into the heart of the garden, she had a few minutes to ponder the loyalty of the guards. Jason must be a fine ruler to inspire such staunch support, she decided.

The garden was a glory of scents and colors, all vivid and filled with life. She breathed in the aromatic fragrances, occasionally stopping to touch the silken petals of a particularly dazzling bloom. She could happily have lost herself for days in such surroundings.

As she rounded a bend in the pathway, laughter drifted toward her; laughter, and a small body running at full speed. For the second time that day, Amarantha was almost run down. She grabbed his arms to steady him when he would have fallen backward in reaction to ploughing into her. Her heart stopped beating for an instant as she stared into the deep blue eyes of the boy, and his responding smile was one of pure innocence.

"Who are you?"

"I'm here to see the king," she answered. "Would you like to show me where he is?"

"I'm Iolaus," he told her, tiny face suddenly serious as he looked at her.

"The Prince?" she wondered as she scooped him up and went in the direction he indicated.

He nodded and pointed, "They're over there."

The prince was barely two, she estimated, but oddly old for a child. She smiled, and turned the final corner. As she spotted the boy's parents, she froze. The couple were on the lush green grass, the king lying on his back as the queen sat demurely at his side. She smiled, expression loving, and touched his forehead, brushing aside a lock of hair. The warmth of the afternoon sunshine grew chill, and the brightness dimmed to gray haze. Amarantha swayed, unaware of the sudden loss of strength in her limbs until Iolaus' childish squeal of concern reminded her that he was still in her arms.

The couple rose instantly, and the king stared back at her; she saw her own shock mirrored in his handsome face. Against her will, she let herself truly look at him, her gaze caressing the shining dark hair that fell to his shoulders, skimming invisibly the smooth, contoured planes of his face, and stopping briefly over the full curve of his mouth. His dress was casual; earthy brown tones that complemented him to perfection. He was taller than she remembered, and much broader through the shoulders. Everything about him made her feel self-conscious and vulnerable.

At his side stood his Queen, one hand resting lightly on his arm as she watched them. She was lovely, delicate of features, and fair-haired, as her son was; she was a full head shorter than her husband, and dressed in flowing lengths of pale blue. Amarantha thought her to be the most beautiful woman she had seen in many years. As striking as his mother had always been.

Iolaus squirmed and shook her a little.

Swallowing convulsively, Amarantha smiled weakly and set the boy down. He ran immediately to his father's side, was once again lifted off his feet, then they came to greet her.

"My lord Iphicles," she whispered and bowed her head in obeisance.

Iolaus leaned close to his father and whispered into his ear.

"My son thinks you're very pretty," Iphicles informed her, his eyes drifting over her familiar, well-remembered features.

Amarantha's eyes blurred with sudden tears and she tried to smile as she pretended indifference to the flicker of concern in King Iphicles' eyes.

"Thank you, little Prince," she murmured, and kissed the small, soft hand that reached to touch her hair.

Prince Iolaus caught a handful of the silky silver tresses and he began to chew happily on his prize while Iphicles and Amarantha stared at each other. The spell broke a moment later when the Queen, Automedusa, joined them and nodded a greeting as Iphicles introduced the women.

"You've been hurt, Am," Iphicles noticed, his tone filled with unmistakable concern.

Amarantha glanced at her arm when he touched her, the angry gash forgotten in the unexpected shock of seeing him again.

"It's nothing, really," she murmured, and gently eased free of his light grasp. "I encountered a troop of soldiers. They tried to persuade me not to see you," she added with distinct irony.

"We'll have it looked at immediately," Iphicles replied, dark eyes narrowed to a frown. "Tell the physician to join us," he requested of his wife.

Automedusa nodded, her light hazel eyes appraising the visitor for a moment before she smiled again at her husband. She took the toddler from his father's arms, hushed Iolaus when he objected, then left.

"It's been over ten years," Iphicles observed quietly when he'd led her to a stone bench in the garden.

Amarantha nodded, nerves making her restless. She didn't sit, instead she paced, agitation creating greater levels of static within her.

"Why are you here?"

"I was asked to see that this was delivered to the King," she replied softly, pulling the scroll from her belt and handing it over to him. "I had expected to meet Jason. I did not know that you were Corinth's new ruler."

Iphicles looked closely at her.

"Would it have made a difference?"

She considered his words, then shrugged.

"How?"

She wasn't surprised when he understood the precise point of her cryptic query.

"Medea's wedding gifts to his new wife made him unpopular, to say the least."

Amarantha looked closer at him, saw the disquiet in his eyes.

"Do you fear for your family?"

He looked skyward for a moment, then shook his head.

"I had no desire to be King of two cities," Iphicles murmured.

"You will be a very good king, Iphicles," she replied with a smile. "It was your destiny."

He didn't look convinced, and she dropped the discussion in favor of more immediate concerns. As she watched, he unfurled the scroll and read it, his face bleaching free of color, then slowly growing dark with rage. Amarantha went to his side, and accepted the missive when he passed it to her, his gesture indicating that he wanted her to know its contents.

"What do you intend to do?" she asked once she'd read the message and returned the parchment to him.

"I don't know yet," he answered with his customary, direct honesty. "While I consult with my advisors," he smiled wryly as he spoke, "I'll see that Automedusa attends to your comfort. Once you're settled, the physician can look at that arm." He started to turn away, then halted, his dark eyes locked intently with hers. "I hope you'll stay for awhile, Amarantha," he said quietly. "I've missed you."

She was surprised, and it showed.

Iphicles laughed. "I didn't know it myself until I saw you again."

"I'd like to help you, my lord—" She stopped abruptly when he held up his hand.

"We know each other far too well for that kind of formality, Am," he intoned, his husky voice suddenly revealing a weariness that she had never before heard in him.

"Iphicles?"

He smiled. "We will talk later, I promise." He held out his hand and was silent as they walked into the castle.

ϒ ϒ ϒ

"You've known my husband a long time?"

Amarantha was startled by the unanticipated presence of the queen. She'd bathed, and was now being attended by the palace physician. The clothes that had been placed on the bed were loose, flowing garments of the palest gray, the material rich, finely woven silk.

"Since childhood, my lady," Amarantha answered. The physician finished the bandage and left them without a word. Amarantha stood and indicated the lovely gown she wore, her fingers a graceful arc that encompassed the clothing with a single, eloquent gesture. "This is beautiful, my lady. I thank you for your generosity."

The queen smiled, though the expression lacked warmth.

"Iphicles chose it," she observed coolly. "He said you hated dark colors."

Amarantha's eyebrows rose and she felt decidedly awkward.

"He seems to know you very well," Automedusa continued.

"As I said, we have known each other since childhood. Your husband was one of my few friends. As was his brother."

"Heracles, as well," the queen noted with a nod.

There was an undercurrent of knowledge in her eyes that made Amarantha edgy. Her anxiety intensified and she remained silent for several minutes, uncertain of what the other woman wanted from her.

"Iphicles has asked me to show you to the war chamber," Automedusa advised her. "Your weapons have been cleaned and are here," she lifted a length of white linen to reveal the sword and daggers that had been the gifts from Ares. Her staff was standing next to the table that held the other things. "Your armor and leathers will be brought here as soon as they've received the same attention."

"You are very kind, my queen," Amarantha whispered.

"Somehow, Amarantha," Automedusa remarked, "I don't think that I will ever be your queen," she paused, met the pale, silvery eyes of the stranger. "Though I suspect that my husband has always been your king."

"A long time ago," Amarantha stated. "When we were children."

Automedusa nodded, her expression sceptical.

"Perhaps," she murmured, and they left the chamber in apprehensive silence.

When they had reached their destination, the queen indicated the doors, then left Amarantha.

The warrior hesitated, unnerved beyond reason. Irritated with herself, she nodded and the guards held open the heavy doors. Iphicles' head turned instantly, and his smile was welcoming. He came to greet her and drew her into the room, to a place at his side.

"This is Amarantha," he told the assembled men. "It was she who bore the news of Pheneüs."

"What else can you tell us?"

Amarantha glanced at the man who spoke, and her spine tingled in warning.

"I can tell you nothing," she said firmly. "I was asked to deliver a scroll. The man who could have answered your questions died and entrusted me to complete his task."

"Iphicles?"

"Lyaeus, I didn't ask her to join us so that you might interrogate her," the king reproved.

"Then why is she here?"

"This is my chief advisor, and war strategist, Am," he told her. "Lyaeus, Amarantha is an old friend. She is also more familiar with Pheneüs than anyone in this room; she was born there. Melaneus has grown powerful over the past years, but he is an outsider."

"A stranger, one who clearly knows little of the people of Pheneüs," Amarantha interjected. "They are a loyal and fierce people," she told the gathered men. "If they have chosen to accept Iphicles as their king, they will honor him as deeply as he does them. You will have an army with spirit to lead in this battle with the warlord."

"Can you show us the best route into the city?"

She smiled at Lyaeus' dubious tone.

"I can map you a way into Pheneüs that will enable an army stealth and surprise," she laughed. From the corner of her eye, she caught Iphicles' smile of approval.

ϒ ϒ ϒ

"I want to go with you, Iphicles," she said when they were alone much later in the night. The conference with his advisors had been a long, draining discussion; frequently deteriorating into loud, heated arguments when she clashed with one of the men over strategy. Iphicles had handled the potentially disastrous confrontations with admirable aplomb and diplomacy.

"No," he shook his head. "I can't risk your life in a battle that is my responsibility. You've helped already, Amarantha."

They were alone in the throne room, and he rose to walk to the window, face a study in thoughtful speculation. Amarantha wanted to put her arms around him and forget that they were talking about a war that could end his life. The mere thought of that possibility turned her blood to ice in her veins.

"I am a skilled warrior, Iphicles," she reminded him. "And you know I could be of use to you."

"No."

She bristled slightly and went to his side. When he refused to look at her, she touched his chin and forced him to face her.

"Why? Because I am a woman? Or, because your men dislike your trust in me?"

"Both," he admitted. "Mostly I just don't want to see you die."

"That's my choice to make, isn't it, my lord?" she enquired with obvious annoyance.

"No," he denied with a smile that belied his anger. "If you accept me as your king, then the choice is mine. If you still call me friend, then I am right twice in my desire to leave you behind."

"That's not fair, Iphicles," she snapped. "You are both king and friend, as you have always been. But I want to go with you."

His response was forestalled by the arrival of his wife. She glanced at Amarantha, hazel eyes cool and watchful, then went to Iphicles' side. He placed his arm around her shoulders and kissed her temple.

"Are you coming to bed?"

Amarantha turned away, stared blindly out the window, oblivious of the glittering blanket of stars that winked overhead; and the luminescent moon that bathed the grounds in shimmering silver-frost hues.

"We will discuss this further, my lord," she stated softly, but didn't look at him. She heard his sigh of resignation, followed by the quiet footfalls that told her she was being left alone.

For a long time she continued her vigilant watch, blind to the present as the past held her in its spell.

ϒ ϒ ϒ

"Am, please," Iphicles asked gently. "This is not going to change my mind."

"We shall see, my lord," she replied briskly. She was again dressed in her armor and leather; polished and honed sword held easily in her right hand. "You think I am less able to defend you than others who will ride with you. I intend to prove you wrong."

Iphicles looked at her, dark eyes alive with conflicting emotions. He did not like that she had goaded him into this challenge, and less appealing was the thought that his child would witness it. Above the private courtyard, watching them, stood Automedusa and their son. Iolaus was quiet, an oddity in itself, as he awaited the outcome of the argument with the mysterious and beautiful stranger.

The king knew already that the boy thought her someone special, and Iolaus rarely liked outsiders.

"Test me as you would any man in your army, Iphicles," she taunted. "I have been taught well, I assure you." Before he could launch into another debate, she backed up a few paces, and raised her sword.

Iphicles' anger rose to his expressive features, and she smiled as he made a half-hearted thrust at her. When she defended against the strike, motion agile and seemingly effortless, he began to warm to the mock battle.

Amarantha let her mind blank, opened her thoughts to the lessons of her master, and slid into the rhythm of the dance of death he'd taught her with such determination. Control was among the most difficult of the things she had learned, and she employed every aspect of her discipline while engaging the king. Iphicles was a skilled swords-man and she quickly discovered that the exercise was one she could truly enjoy. He attacked with renewed fury when she slipped past his defense and landed a glancing strike to his side. Not enough to hurt him, but firm enough to make him acquiesce to her ability.

"You're very good, Am," he smiled.

She nodded, then launched a true attack, one that had them circling each other in the open courtyard. The clang of clashing steel echoed as they met and fell back repeatedly. Iphicles brought her to her knees at one point, and was shocked when she nudged his ribs with a dagger.

"You'd be a dead man if this was real, my lord," she assured him.

The king whirled away, his sword arcing smoothly through the early morning sunshine. He grinned, and they met again, blades gleaming brightly as they carved pat-terns of silver in the air.

The battle went on for some time, each gaining small advantage only to lose it moments later. As the combat-ants grew tired, Iphicles' guard slipped, and Amarantha stepped up to face him. She refused to humiliate him before his son, and cleverly twisted so that only he would see that once again, his life could have been hers.

"Concede, my lord," she whispered sweetly.

Iphicles' grin was accompanied by genuine laughter, and he nodded as he stepped away, his breathing harsh.

"You're as good as you claim," he admitted. "And, since I need my energy to battle real enemies, I am forced to accept your offer to ride with me."

"A wise decision, Your Majesty," she grinned, pale gray eyes sparkling with humor and gratitude. "Thank you, Iphicles," she added, her low, rich voice alive with unintentional seduction.

He shook his head and glanced upward to where his family watched.

"Thank you," he said softly, his tone unconsciously responding to the erotic intimacy of hers. "For allowing me to retain my pride."

Amarantha's gaze followed his, and she smiled when Iolaus waved to her. The child's dark blue eyes seemed piercing, even with the distance that separated them — as though he knew what had just occurred.

CHAPTER TWO

"We'll be in Pheneüs tomorrow," Iphicles said when Amarantha came into the tent that had been erected in the center of the traveling army's camp. She glanced around, wry humor irrepressible when faced with the extent of luxury accorded the Royal presence.

"What's so amusing?"

"This," she shrugged. "You know that without asking, Iphicles. We're going to Pheneüs to fight a war, quite probably, yet your aides deem all this necessary for your comfort."

He laughed, and rose from his seat amid an array of plump pillows placed on a long couch.

"You're the only one who'd dare suggest this was foolishness," he smiled. He picked up a pitcher of wine and she nodded when he silently offered her a cup.

"That looks good on you," he murmured when he'd handed her the wine and indicated that she should join him on the couch.

"It feels lovely after days in leather and armor," she agreed. "Your wife didn't seem overly pleased that you requested it be given to me."

His eyebrows rose in mild surprise.

"She wonders at our knowledge of each other," Amarantha continued with a ghost of a smile. "At the intimacy of it."

He nodded. "She did ask," he informed her, laughing when Amarantha's pale eyes rolled back and she shook her head. "So have my men," he added as he watched her sit, pull her legs up, and settle casually on the opposite end of the couch. "I don't think they believe it's your skill with a sword that warrants your presence."

Amarantha's eyes flashed dangerously and she frowned. "Oh, they know it's my skill with a sword that influenced your decision, Iphicles. They're simply inclined to think it's not the one I carry at my back."

Iphicles hesitated, then decided against attempting a reply to her suggestive assumption. She was, he knew, correct in the observation. "Why are you here, Am?" he questioned when the silence threatened to become awkward.

"To help you," she replied instantly.

"Why?" he repeated more firmly.

"Does it truly matter so much?" she countered, suddenly uneasy. "I am here. It is where I choose to be. Why make it more than that?"

"Because I know you too well to presume anything can be that simple for you," he answered softly.

"Then perhaps you think too much," she stated, unable to keep the annoyance from her tone.

"You used to trust me," he murmured, dark eyes wary as he watched her.

"Trust?" she whispered in a near gasp. "Iphicles, trust is not what we are discussing. I have trusted you, implicitly, from the moment we met."

His smile softened, and he didn't respond to her words. When the space of time lengthened, she stood and paced the tent. Finally, she spun around and faced him again.

"What are you thinking about?"

"The first time we met," he replied, and this time there was something enigmatic within the shaded brown depths of his eyes. He stood and went to stand before her; he raised his hand and with the backs of his fingers stroked the smooth curve of her cheek. "You're even more beautiful now."

"Iphicles. Don't." She took a step back, the reaction involuntary. "Please."

Before he could deny or accept her request, the shout of one of his guards heralded the arrival of Lyaeus.

The advisor looked unhappy and suspicious to see her with the king; a situation made worse by Iphicles' insistence that she remain with them during the strategy planning for their entrance into Pheneüs the following day.

ϓ ϓ ϓ

Shock was the easiest reaction to define. Amarantha rode beside Iphicles, discreetly observing his response to the devastation that greeted them. They had reached Pheneüs quickly, infiltrated the city via an old, forgotten underground passage. It was with their emergence into the open main street of the kingdom that they had seen the true extent of the incursion.

Miraculously, they had escaped the attention of the invading warlord's men; something that worried her more than the death that presently surrounded them.

"Iphicles?"

It took several seconds for him to acknowledge her with his look, and she winced unconsciously at the outrage she read in his dark eyes.

"It's too quiet," she said softly. The words sparked greater anger and she wondered if it was wise to continue toward the palace. "We may be too late," she offered, ignoring the disdain in Lyaeus' sour expression when he overheard her observation. For an attractive man, he could look surprisingly unappealing a great deal of the time, she thought absently, her attention erratic as she scanned the area.

"That doesn't negate the need to continue to my palace," Iphicles snapped.

"It does if the purpose of this slaughter is to lure you to your death, my lord," she retorted hotly, her eyes suddenly intent on the king. That possibility frightened her deeply, though she took care not to reveal it to his men. "Iphicles, listen to reason," she begged quietly.

There was no time for further talk as the area came to life with the warlord's soldiers. They'd been lying in ambush, and now attacked with a ferocity that made her blood run cold for an instant of abject terror. When Iphicles slid from his mount, rationality and purpose overrode her desire to flee.

Amarantha drew her sword and dropped easily to the ground, gritting her teeth as she met the first of the warriors. Motion became instinctive and she forced her fear for the king into a dark corner of her mind.

"Am!"

She sliced through the midriff of the soldier in front of her, the finely honed metal of her sword finding the weakness in his armor. In the same spin of movement, she twisted adeptly and thrust the bloodied weapon into the throat of the man who had launched at her back. Iphicles' dark eyes held hers for a moment, shock and something indefinable in their depths; then he was running to the aid of another of his men who was fighting a losing effort against several adversaries.

Amarantha tried to keep sight of him even as she dealt death to more men than she would ever want to remember. Her arms ached, yet the outsiders continued to pour into the central square of Pheneüs. She took a glancing blow to the upper part of her leg and winced as the flow of warm blood made her stomach twitch. She waited for the soldier to take advantage of the strike and smiled inwardly when he came at her, sword poised to run her through. She ducked, slid free the dagger that was sheathed inside her boot, then began to stand, driving the gleaming silver blade deep into his gut. She yanked the weapon free and wiped it clean on his back, then dashed to the center of the diminishing fight.

As she reached the pith of the assault, she spotted the king. Rage blinded her a moment later when he was struck from behind and fell to his knees. Iphicles' sword skittered away and he rolled, quickly regaining his feet, but no longer armed.

"Iphicles!"

He glanced in her direction and held out his hand as her sword went sailing toward him. Iphicles deftly caught the weapon and on the downward arc of motion, he decapitated the soldier who was attempting to drive a blade into his heart.

From the corner of her eye, she noticed Lyaeus pale at
the evidence of the king's fury and deadliness. She dismissed the advisor from her mind and stumbled to a halt
next to Iphicles. He passed her the sword and bent to
retrieve his weapon. They were safely flanked by the Royal
Guard, and the remaining invaders were fleeing the site.

"What awaits us at the palace?" she queried in an
undertone that was meant only for the king's ears.

"I'm sure we can count on you to protect our king's
back," the chief advisor said with no small amount of snide
insinuation.

"Lyaeus," Iphicles warned softly. He turned his attention
to Amarantha, and startled her when he went down on
one knee at her side. "You've been hurt again," he observed,
worry in his gravelly voice.

"It's nothing, Iphicles," she assured him. "Please, don't
bother with it. I am not in pain."

He nodded and stood. "I'll have it looked at when we
retake my home," he stated firmly. He faced Lyaeus, "Leave
the injured, and a physician. We'll come back for them, and
make arrangements for the dead later."

The horses had been brought, and the king himself
handed Furey's reins to her before he mounted and led
toward the palace those men who remained able to fight.

ˠ ˠ ˠ

Another battle met them at the gates of the royal palace of Pheneüs; though the number of men who engaged
them was considerably reduced. Once the gates had been
smashed open on the king's order, Amarantha sensed a
new presence among them — one that filled her with dread.

"What are you doing here?" she demanded when her
Master strolled into the fight, his austere features reflecting
amusement.

"Pheneüs is a decoy," he told her, and casually took her
by the arm to lead her to the edge of the battle. "Tell him
to return to Corinth, quickly."

"I can't *tell* the King to leave a city that is under siege,"
she snarled. "He is the king!"

"Then watch him lose everything, and know you could have prevented it," he replied, deep eyes glittering with rage. She stared at him, confused, and inwardly afraid of him.

"What is it I am supposed to tell Iphicles, dear Master?" she asked sardonically. "That a man whose name is unknown to me has advised me of his Fate?" She laughed, the sound a low bark of bitterness. "A king pays little enough heed to the words of a slave," she spat viciously, "Iphicles is not a fool, nor do I wish him to think me one."

"Would you rather watch him mourn the loss of all he holds dear?" Ares mocked. She turned away, too swiftly, and he grabbed her arm, made her face him. "*Is* that what you want, Amarantha?"

"No!"

"You lie, little one," he sneered. "Badly."

"What do you know of this war?" she challenged, deliberately avoiding the unwelcome awareness of her selfishness with regard to Iphicles.

"I know it's a farce," the God answered, schooling his tone to indifference rather than expose the resentment that seethed within him. "Designed to entertain one man's vanity, and another's desire for power." He shrugged, and his expression shifted to jeering disdain. "Which makes it no more important than any other of its kind."

"Are you telling me that Iphicles may die for something so petty as another's..." She stopped speaking, absolute fury lighting a trail of fire in her veins. "Who—?" The question sputtered to silence when she saw that she was alone again.

"Amarantha!?"

"Tell him to return to Corinth..."

She shivered involuntarily as the whisper of his warning taunted her. She was still rooted to the spot minutes later when Lyaeus and Iphicles approached her.

"We've retaken the palace," Iphicles informed her, his look watchful, worried.

"Without your aid, I might add," Lyaeus remarked coolly. "Did you find the bloodshed not to your taste, Lady? Or did you simply have your fill of death?"

"Enough!" Iphicles snapped icily. "I want a physician sent to my chambers immediately."

"Are you hurt, Iphicles?" Amarantha asked instantly.

Lyaeus snorted, but refrained from comment as he strode off to fulfill the king's order.

"This is the second time your blood has been spilled because of me," Iphicles said softly, his gaze focused on the scarlet trail that ran the length of her leg.

"You are not making it easy for me to go unnoticed by your men, Iphicles," she chided softly.

His head rose and she caught the glitter of something dark and defiant within his earth-colored eyes. He nodded, then took her arm and walked with her to the palace gates.

"How long will you remain in Pheneüs?" she asked as they headed directly for the king's chambers. She had seen the looks they were given and resigned herself to the scorn and derision of his men.

Iphicles didn't answer her immediately. When they entered his private rooms he began issuing orders, and Amarantha waited. The time gave her pause to look around, and to recover her shaken composure.

The palace was not as grandiose or luxurious as the castle in Corinth. The king's private chambers here were furnished much simpler; tapestries decorated the stone walls, told the stories of the Gods; the coverlets on the massive bed were subdued, but richly woven; a huge fire-place dominated one wall. Off to the side, a bathing pool was being filled with hot, steaming water. Servants hurried about, nodding quickly as Iphicles issued his instructions in a voice that was much less haughty than it might have been.

After several minutes, they were alone.

"Iphicles?"

He turned, almost startled to find that she was still with him.

"Your room adjoins this one," he told her and indicated the door at the far end of his bedchamber. "Unless you prefer something more remote?"

"I don't really care," she said, voice vaguely impatient. "We need to talk about returning to Corinth."

"Why?" he countered, and walked toward her until they were eye to eye. "I need to remain in Pheneüs," he stated. "At least for a few weeks."

"What about—"

"Amarantha! If you have something to say, simply say it."

"I feel that this threat is not the real one," she began, choosing her words carefully, fully aware of the evasiveness of them. "I think Corinth is the real target," she repeated, unable to look directly into the shrewd gaze that suddenly locked on her.

"What do you base this on?"

She closed her eyes, drew a deep breath.

"Instinct," she offered.

"No," he shook his head and touched her chin so that she had to look at him. "What will you not speak?"

"I am afraid for your family," she replied.

Iphicles' expression softened slightly and he nodded. When he spoke again, his voice was pitched to a low, almost sensual murmur. "I know you love my son already," he smiled. "He was equally charmed by you. But, this is not simply concern for my family. What won't you tell me, Am? I need you to be honest with me."

"No," she shook her head, unwilling to fall into the trap he was unknowingly setting for her. Her master had been right, the king would demand truth, and her pride would not allow it. "You need to learn trust, my lord Iphicles." She backed away when he would have held her in place, then spun on her heel and left him.

When she reached the room that was adjacent to the king's, and slammed the door behind her, she was further angered to discover she was not alone. He turned and smiled.

"What do you want now?"

She winced unconsciously at the darkening of his eyes, sensed the rage that woke when she spoke so carelessly. She bowed, fully aware that her obeisance was the only apology he would accept; and the only way to prevent him from hurting her. She'd learned her lessons well at his hands, and the respect he demanded was one of the most painful of those teachings.

"Why are you here, Master?" she questioned again, this time in a tone that was weary and discouraged.

"Have you advised him to go back to Corinth?" Ares wondered.

She nodded.

"And?"

"And he ignores me, as I told you he would!" She paced, furious with him, and with Iphicles. "Why won't you tell me why he has to leave here? If I could give him a reason he could understand—"

"I've given you reason," the War God explained with forced patience. "It's your pride that places the lives of his family in jeopardy." He walked to the window where she stood, then turned her around to face him before he continued; "Your disregard for his Queen is worthy of a tavern slut's ambitions."

Amarantha's hand rose without thought of her action, and she almost succeeded in striking him for the insult he'd just used to wound her heart. Ares' grip tightened and she shook her head, pleaded without words.

"If I'd wanted to train a harlot, I'd have chosen better than you, Amarantha," he declared icily. "This is a small part of your destiny, something I am forced to accept. I will not permit your foolishness to destroy my plans."

She hauled free of his grasp, fully aware that the only reason she could step away was because he allowed it.

"Sit down," he directed. She hesitated and he flung her onto the nearby bed. He knelt beside her, one knee braced on the edge of the bed as his hand skimmed the injured surface of her thigh. She winced, and he smiled at her, the expression altered completely from moments earlier.

"How bad is the pain?"

"Not bad," she answered, and sat, curious eyes locked on the elegant hand that brushed over her skin. She stared in wonder as warmth seeped into her flesh, then the wound knitted together and smoothed as she watched.

He stood, passed his hand over the partially healed gash on her arm, and it too vanished.

"How?"

"Never mind," he evaded the query. "Let him stay in Pheneüs," Ares decreed with an eloquent shrug of one broad shoulder. "I want you to come with me, tonight."

"What?" She shook her head. "I can't do that," she said firmly. "I have given Iphicles my word."

"The word of a slave is worthless, Amarantha," Ares reminded her, voice icy with derision.

"He doesn't know I'm a slave to you," she snarled, sudden fury rising within her again. "I won't leave him."

"If I give you no choice?" the War God speculated.

"Unless you want to end my life, this is one choice you will not take from me."

Ares contemplated her decision, and the strength she exhibited in defying him so openly. He laughed, then nodded.

"You can stay," he told her softly. "For the moment."

The condescending tone rankled her further and she rose from the bed, anger radiating from her in near-visible waves.

"You infuriate me," she whispered recklessly. "I am sick of you! My life is my own. No matter what you think." Inwardly she was equally vexed with the king, and his unwanted hold on her.

Ares laughed again, truly amused by the defiance, and the enraged beauty of the woman he owned.

Amarantha scowled and began to walk from the room. She was steps from the door when her blood froze and her heartbeat began to roar in her ears.

ϒ ϒ ϒ

Iphicles peeled off the last of his clothing and stepped into the steaming bath that had been filled. He gestured the servants away and groaned quietly when his body was immersed in the warmth of the water. He closed his eyes, let his mind wander as his muscles slowly relaxed.

Amarantha was not to be dismissed lightly. If she was this adamant in her need to return, Iphicles knew she had reasons that were valid; even if she chose not to share them. That she would not open her heart to him was the real core of his objection; alone with his thoughts, he was honest enough to concede to that. He was torn between loyalty to the woman he'd chosen to be his wife, and curiosity about the girl he'd been so enchanted with as a child. She'd grown more exotically beautiful over the years, and he'd forgotten how deeply attracted to her he'd been, until the moment he'd looked up to find her holding Iolaus in her arms. In a single instant, he'd discovered that his son had been born to the wrong mother.

He scrubbed his eyes in frustration and weariness. Amarantha was a complication his life didn't need. Alcmene was fond of Automedusa, had been pleased by his decision to marry. Heracles had been wholly approving, as well, which meant more to Iphicles than he'd ever openly admit. The striking, frost-haired woman in the next room was little more than distant memory to his family.

The rustle of motion near the pool made him sink deeper into the water, and he gestured absently for the servant to pour in more hot water. He roared in outraged fury seconds later as icy water flooded over him. He stood, his voice ringing through the chamber as he glared at the pretty girl who hurled fervid, incomprehensible accusations at him.

The doors to his chambers burst inward from two directions, and Iphicles had a combined awareness of Amarantha, sword ready, coming through one entrance, while several guards came into the room from the main doors.

ϒ ϒ ϒ

"Iphicles?" Amarantha halted, her eyes riveted unwilling to the king, her body suddenly, acutely, responding to the shock of his nakedness. He gleamed like a beautiful god, water still running over smooth muscles, his damp, dark hair brushing his shoulders. She forced herself to look away, focus on the cause of his present anger.

She sheathed her sword, and stepped forward when the girl tried to run. Amarantha caught her, and held her.

"If you continue to fight," she said quietly, close to the girl's ear, "I will have no choice but to give you to the men."

The reed thin girl stopped fighting and stared at the white-haired warrior woman who maintained a loose, but casual hold on her.

"Are you unharmed, Highness?" Amarantha questioned, careful to keep her tone free of the laughter that was bubbling up inside her.

Iphicles frowned, catching the nuance in her tone.

"Get her out of here," he snapped.

"Take her to the throne room," Amarantha directed when the guards came forward. "Do not hurt her," she added softly, the warning implicit.

They looked to their king, saw him nod his acceptance of the order, then they took the girl away.

Amarantha faced Iphicles again, and this time her smile was permitted to surface.

Iphicles, abruptly recalling his state of undress, slid back into his bath. His expression mutated into a scowl of irritation when Amarantha laughed quietly and went to fetch a bucket of steaming hot water. She dumped it into the pool, and sat at the edge; a respectful distance from him.

"What do you want me to do with her?"

"Find out what she wants," he growled, his mood darkening further in the face of her open amusement.

"And if she wants you, my lord King?" Amarantha questioned sweetly.

"She was babbling something about her family," he snapped.

Amarantha nodded and rose. When she would have left him, Iphicles' voice halted her departure.

"We'll leave in a few days, Am."

She heard the reluctant acquiescence in his voice, and glanced over her shoulder, gratitude genuine.

"Thank you, Iphicles."

He held her gaze for several moments, then leaned back in the tub and closed his eyes, listening intently to the barely audible sound of her footfalls as she slipped from the room.

ʏ ʏ ʏ

The night sky was alive with glittering, ice-white stars; a veritable tapestry of winking fire drawn against the background of jet-black velvet. Amarantha was alone on this section of the castle battlements, her mind determinedly blocking the sounds of activity from the courtyard. She leaned on the stone wall, stared upward at the infinite display of diamond-bright brilliance that shone on the shadows of earth. The moon was equally luminescent, a radiant sliver of silvered-ivory, ducking periodically behind the gauze of light clouds that drifted aimlessly in a sea of air.

"Lyaeus said I'd find you here."

She smiled, the response just beyond her conscious control, then she turned to see him stepping toward her. In the pale light, Iphicles was a shade against the deeper blackness of night, and it wasn't until he stood in front of her that she saw he was without armor, or sword.

"You should not be outside unarmed, Highness," she observed, faint worry easily read in her tone.

Iphicles smiled. "I think I am safe in your company, Am," he answered blandly.

She wasn't mollified by the quiet amusement she heard in his voice. When he continued to stare at her, expression unreadable in the murky illumination, she turned her back to him, unreasonably afraid.

"You won't explain why you chose to come on this campaign."

"What is there to explain, my lord?" she countered softly. "I did not come upon this war by design, I stumbled into it quite by accident. That you are Corinth's king was an unforeseen complication."

"Complication?" He was annoyed, and it echoed in his tone.

"Yes, Iphicles," she said without apology. "A complication."

"Do you intend to clarify that statement, Amarantha?"

She laughed, without humor. "What isn't clear, my
king?"

Iphicles grabbed her arms and whirled her around to
face him; shocked by the rage that burned from her pale
eyes. She tried to free herself, and he held her more firmly
in place.

"What's happened to you?" he asked, his anger fading
rapidly in the face of her fury.

"Nothing that matters." She rejected him with words,
and waited while he made a decision to accept her choice,
or press her for answers. The set of his jaw a few seconds
later warned her before he spoke again.

"It matters, Am," he denied. "We've not seen each other
for over ten years. What has your life been in that time?"

"I am no one's queen, I assure you," she snapped,
inwardly appalled at the bitter rage of her tone.

You're wrong, a voice inside his head protested, but he
held his tongue and waited for her to go on.

"Why do you want to know things of no consequence,
Iphicles?" She was pleading for a reprieve he wouldn't
grant, and she knew it. He maintained his silence, and she
sighed heavily, then drew away; this time he permitted
her to step back and turn toward the wall.

"My mother died a few years ago, and I headed for
Athens after I buried her." She paused, chose the most
succinct words she could find, then glanced at him. "En
route to the city, I was captured by slavers. I did make it
to Athens, but only as far as the slave market; where I was
bought for a flatteringly high price."

Iphicles' eyes sparked with indignation and undiluted
rage. He touched her hair, drew her close to him, realizing as he did that he was lying to them both about his
reason for the comfort he offered. He kissed her temple
and pulled her against him, cherishing the feel of her finally
pressed close to him. He wanted to keep her there for an
eternity. He drank in her scent and the lush curves that
fitted so naturally to him. Amarantha had been his dream

as a boy. He'd woven fantasies of her coming to him, giving herself to him; all the while denying that it was the truest desire his soul would ever know. Now, he held his dream within his grasp, and she was more unattainable here than she had ever before been to him.

"I'll buy your freedom, Amarantha," he vowed. "You are not a slave, to anyone. I won't allow it."

She was too comfortable in his arms, too intoxicated by his closeness. And, too reluctant to leave the shelter of his embrace. It frightened her. Forcing her body to wholly false indifference, she shrugged and lifted her head from his shoulder so she could meet his gaze.

"That is not necessary," she informed him with a lazy smile. "I am free to go where I will, when I will. My Master is a most undemanding man when it suits him."

"Who—"

"How did you become King?" she interjected, changing the topic abruptly.

"I told you," he began, absently, "Jason was meant to be king, before Medea..." He stopped speaking and held her face between his hands, his eyes locked with hers. He bent, fully intending to kiss her. He wanted to know her taste. He wanted to lose himself in the madness that holding her would incite within him. He'd lusted after women before, knew all too well the foolishness that could overtake a man determined to bed a beautiful wench. In Amarantha, he knew he would know passion unlike any he'd yet experienced. He wanted that madness. The sheer, all-consuming force of his desire shocked him on some level. And died a moment later when she smiled before their lips could touch.

"You have a queen, Iphicles, and it is not me." She managed, barely, to keep the words steady and lightly uttered. Inside, her pulse throbbed an erratic pace, and her heart mocked her. He would have ignored her rebuff, but the voice of his chief advisor made him release her.

"She's given that impudent brat sanctuary in the palace," Lyaeus snarled when he joined them, his glare settling on the woman at his king's side.

"Am?" Iphicles prompted, finding it difficult to make his mind function smoothly beyond the thwarted needs of his body.

"Her name is Maia," she supplied sweetly. "An orphan of this war. She has no one, Iphicles," Amarantha whispered, pitching her tone to a low that could only be heard fully by the king. "I know how that feels. Another servant in your palace will hardly make a difference to you, but it gives her a life to cling to. A life to replace the one she blames your absence for taking from her. It seemed a fair trade, Highness," she concluded, eyes warily shifting from Iphicles to the advisor who had come close enough to catch her last words.

"She may be a spy left by the warlord," Lyaeus proposed.

"She's a terrified child, with no family," Amarantha countered instantly. She looked closely at the handsome man who sparked such dislike within her. Lyaeus was easily as tall as the king, broader through the shoulders, and his face was defined by even, sculpted features which were dominated by palest blue eyes. His hair was braided in the fashion of warriors; unbound it would fall in deep waves to the middle of his back. He chose dark colors, wore them well in contrast with his fair hair. She would have found him desirable, had he not been so obstinate and narrow-minded.

"Let the girl stay," Iphicles instructed the man. He glanced at Amarantha, saw her nod of appreciation, then moved to catch Lyaeus as he strode from the battlements.

Amarantha watched them leave, her spine tingling with chilling apprehension. She glanced around, seeing only shadows and darkness. Inside, her heartbeat roared for an instant, then slowly evened. She felt Him watching, and dread blossomed to life within her; dread, and paralyzing fear.

Shivering violently, she fled the heights of the wall, and sought refuge in her chambers.

She lay awake all night, waiting.

And remained alone.

ϒϒϒ

The familiar disciplines of training were helping to clear her head of the day's long, often tiresome, strategy sessions. Iphicles had asked for her presence during the meetings with his advisors, and she wasn't immune to the jeers and snide remarks to which he appeared oblivious. His men were unhappy with her inclusion, and they saw his dependence on her as a weakness; even if it was far from the truth. She knew what they didn't — Iphicles depended on no one, man or woman.

She spun her sword in graceful, precise arcs, gleaming silver picking up the last rays of the day's sun as it set. Tongues of illusory flame licked at the polished metal, threw off sparks that danced wildly on the stone walls of the courtyard. She knew the guards watched her, and blocked their presence with the will her Master had forged within her through his exacting lessons. The patterns of her practice flowed naturally, and she began to relax. Her solitary peace shattered minutes later when the sound of hands clapping together drew her angry gaze.

"Lyaeus," she purred, and permitted faint contempt to color the word. "Tell me, how is that you bear the name of a God?"

He was startled by the question, but smiled.

"I am the only progeny of parents who thought they would never have a child. During a festival honoring Dionysus, that changed, and to thank Him for the gift they believed was bestowed by his generosity, I was given one of his lesser names."

"Then you chose the path of a warrior. Hardly an honor to the God whose name you carry."

"Perhaps not, but Dionysus appreciates the sensual pleasures of this life, and you do make swordplay look as seductive as lovemaking," Lyaeus noted, tone textured with amusement, and, surprisingly, sincere appreciation.

Amarantha bowed, the gesture a mocking acceptance of his compliment. She twirled the weapon she held and spread her arms, the invitation implicit.

Lyaeus laughed, considered her stance, then nodded as he drew his sword. He tossed aside his cloak, and began to circle her, seeking an opening.

Amarantha smiled slightly, her focus narrowing to the man before her. On the periphery of her vision, she sensed the presence of the guards, curiosity bringing them to the edge of the yard.

"Would you like to make a wager on the outcome of this contest, Lady?"

She chuckled softly, and backed away a single step.

"Can you defeat your king, Lyaeus?" she wondered, tone light, faintly taunting.

"It's not the king I've engaged in combat," he returned with a broad smile.

Amarantha inclined her head, thoroughly amused, though none of that humor reached her expression. He had answered her question.

Lyaeus lunged unexpectedly, and she dismissed from her mind everything but purpose. Her body flowed into the movements, swords clashed periodically, then she would whirl from range. She was faster, and lighter than Iphicles' chief advisor, something she used to full advantage to tire him. His color was ruddy, and his breathing growing louder when a shout from above them halted the spurious battle.

Amarantha dropped her guard, and was furious when Lyaeus' arm snaked around her neck and a dagger was placed against her throat.

"Concede, Lady," he snarled.

"I said that's enough!" Iphicles shouted, his tone filled with unmistakable fury.

"You cheat," Amarantha gasped, rage tempting her to take his life while the king watched. She could do it; she'd been trained in an impressive array of dirty tricks, though she rarely employed them.

"I'll collect my prize later," Lyaeus promised, then released her.

She turned, silver-gray eyes slits of wrath as he presented her with a jeering bow of false deference. He glanced upward, and she followed his gaze to the tower window where the king observed.

"She fights well, Highness," he announced, loudly enough for all to hear his parody of respect.

"I want to see you," Iphicles directed. "Both of you," he clarified when Amarantha began to leave the courtyard.

ϓ ϓ ϓ

"King Iphicles appears to rely heavily on your wisdom," Lyaeus observed carefully.

Amarantha sighed inwardly, weary of the day's constant mental manipulations, and the thinly veiled interest Lyaeus had suddenly taken in her. She'd sought refuge in the huge kitchen, and the servants had given her a wide berth, going about their work as though she were not present.

Maia was the only one who spoke to her, and she'd quickly reassured the girl that she would not be thrown into the streets once Iphicles left Pheneüs again. Mollified, Maia had left Amarantha to her solitude. She was silently polishing her weapons, and reviewing their strategy sessions when the advisor found her.

"The king relies on his own wisdom, Lyaeus," she warned quietly. "I would suggest you bear that in mind, and not imply otherwise to your men. I've had more than enough of their pettiness and insolence when they think I am not listening." She smiled, without warmth, then added, "Or, when they think Iphicles is not able to hear them."

"My men are men," he shrugged, pulling up a stool to sit in front of her. "They see a beautiful woman, so loyal to the king, and they assume..."

"They assume far too much," she snapped, voice low, icy.

Lyaeus leaned back, his gaze bordering on brazen as he perused her in thorough appraisal.

Amarantha rose abruptly, let her sword begin to slide to the floor. As she'd anticipated, Lyaeus made a grab for it. As he bent forward, Amarantha's foot caught his shoulder and she tossed him backward, the throw effortless.

Before he could regain his posture, she stepped over him and left the kitchen area.

She was nearing her chambers when Iphicles entered the corridor from one of the battle rooms. He stopped and waited for her, his scrutiny as blatant as his advisor's had been, though vastly different in attitude.

"What's put that look on your face?"

"Not now, Iphicles," she hissed, her rage making her voice a rasp of sound that was forced from between clenched teeth. She continued past him, and almost screamed in frustration when she realized he was following her into her rooms.

"Iphicles! By the Gods, isn't there a place in this palace where I can find peace and solitude?"

His dark eyes glinted in the low flares of candle flame. He caught her arm when she would have left her chambers again.

Instinctively, Amarantha's hand lifted, and she was stunned when Iphicles' fingers wrapped around her wrist and he jerked her toward him. Stumbling, she was stammering an apology, unaware of anything beyond her inner horror at almost striking him. Her awareness altered radically when her head was drawn back and Iphicles' mouth covered hers. The kiss was unexpected, and as her body shuddered to life at his touch, the pressure of his lips changed from ruthless to seductive.

Your disregard for his Queen is worthy of a tavern slut's ambitions...

The mocking, purring memory of her master's taunt cooled the wild hunger that had exploded within her, and she forcibly freed herself from his arms, gasping slightly.

"Am..." His body shook with the depth of his disappointment, and the shock of how suddenly and vividly passion flared between them.

"No!" She shook her head and backed away a few paces. "I will not be a substitute for your queen, my lord Iphicles," she said, her tone shaken but firm.

"I was not seeking a substitute for the queen," he snarled, voice eerily soft, but with the impact and fury of a shout.

"I am *not* a whore to be used by you, or any man in your army," she stated, her head clear of the rush of passion he'd incited in her veins.

Iphicles looked closer at her, sensed the conflict of emotions that plagued her. He nodded, unwillingly accepting her decision.

"Who has tried to bed you, Amarantha?"

She laughed at the outrage in his eyes.

"Aside from you, Highness?" she responded, the insolence her only defense against the desire to succumb to her longing to throw aside honor for the pleasure she'd never experienced with any man; because none were the proud king who stood before her now.

She saw the set of his jaw and knew she'd pushed as far as he would allow.

"It doesn't matter, Iphicles," she relented.

"Lyaeus," he stated, correctly guessing. He'd seen his advisor's interest in her grow from resentment to want; he intended it to go no further than it had already.

She refused to answer him.

"He's staying in Pheneüs," Iphicles informed her.

"Because of me?" she asked, eyebrow raised in surprise.

Iphicles didn't answer, he stared at her for several moments, the silence strangely soothing after the erratic tensions of the past few minutes. That she was right didn't seem a thing that required confirmation, so he ignored the question.

"Goodnight, Am," he said, and bowed his head briefly. A moment later she was alone.

ϒ ϒ ϒ

"You look worried."

Amarantha started at the unexpected voice, then glanced over her shoulder to see her Master striding toward her. As always, she was shocked by the raw sensuality of him. Her thoughts had veered toward the erotic far too often in the past few weeks, and his physical presence was overwhelmingly intense.

"Where have you come from?"

Ares' dark eyes narrowed slightly and he peered closely at her, then laughed, genuinely amused.

"You haven't taken to his bed, have you?"

Her features twisted into a scowl, and she resisted the urge to slap him for his temerity — she was all too conscious of how futile the gesture would be, and how painful the consequences.

"Why do you care whose bed I share?"

Ares' handsome countenance transformed to swift, lethal anger, and he controlled the recklessness of his rage with real effort. Reaching past his emotions, he walked to her side and stared down at her.

"You've lingered too long," he warned. "Corinth has been under attack for most of the past week."

"What?!" She shivered, chilled to the core by his words. And his knowledge.

"He's going to need you, Amarantha," Ares taunted. "More than he presently does."

She chewed her bottom lip thoughtfully as she watched the subtle shifts of his mood, revealed so clearly in the dying light of day.

"Why does it not bother you to have me at Iphicles' side?"

His expression darkened at the wholly mistaken assumption, but he refrained from comment.

"There's a traitor in his company," he imparted softly.

"Who?"

Ares smiled, the humor in his eyes bitter, ironic.

"Now that would take all the fun out of finding him, wouldn't it?"

"Please," she begged, her grip on his arm desperate. "Tell me who is betraying him, Master!"

Ares removed her hand from his forearm, and kissed her fingers in mock gallantry.

Iphicles' voice broke the strained silence, and Amarantha turned toward it.

"Tell me," she pleaded as she spun back to her Master. Ice flooded her veins when she saw that she was alone again.

"I've been looking for you since sunset," Iphicles announced when he reached her.

"Why?" She spoke vaguely, her eyes searching the area for some trace of him; uneasy when she understood that she could no longer recall the detail of his face or form. All that remained was the distinct sense of his presence resonating in the dusky night air.

"Have you been here all evening?"

She made herself focus on the king, hearing his concern amid the demand in his tone.

"Yes, I have. I am sorry if my absence caused you any," she hesitated, sought for a word, then settled for, "inconvenience, my lord Iphicles."

"Am, I wish you'd stop treating me like the enemy," he snapped.

"We have to leave at first light," she told him, her pale eyes narrowed with fear. "I hope we're not too late," she added, voice barely audible.

"Amarantha?"

She stared up at him, her look caressing the impossibly handsome face she had adored since her childhood. She wanted him with an intensity that frightened her.

"The army must be prepared to move quickly, Iphicles," she emphasized. "I'll see that everything is arranged." Afraid to linger, she left him standing in the shadows, confusion the most readable emotion in his features.

ᚷ ᚷ ᚷ

Iphicles watched her all but run from him, and he sighed heavily. He'd seen the longing in her eyes, was beginning to understand that it had always been there, had he not been blind to it. She possessed a warrior's honor, and he knew that it would forever stand between them now. His men talked, and wagered on whether she was his lover; he let them guess because it kept any one of them from trying to claim her.

It was a delicate, and decidedly uncomfortable balance. It was also unfair; to Am; to him; and to his wife.

His heart betrayed his good intentions, though, and
Iphicles knew he'd continue to keep her too near for his
sake. Even if she refused him; he could not accept her in
another man's embrace.

Her mysterious Master was out there, he knew. She'd
told him theirs was not a relationship of lovers, and he'd
been too happy with the news. He'd see his wife within
days now, and for the first time since their marriage, he
dreaded the return home. Almost as much as he resented
the responsibility of his crown, and the sacrifice he'd be
forced to make when Amarantha left him again.

CHAPTER THREE

Outside Athens, Corinth was the center of Greek culture; a seaport teeming with life, and constant activity. As the returning army entered the city, Amarantha's senses reeled with too many emotions to easily define a single, dominant response. Pheneüs, devastated as it had been, was left intact when compared to Iphicles' principal kingdom.

Fires sputtered erratically, the smell of burnt wood mingling with the more potent and repugnant odor of charred flesh. People cried, the wails and screams of mourning penetrating the inner armor of the soldiers who were returning home to greater horrors and fear than those they'd witnessed in Pheneüs. She knew Iphicles was raging beneath the carefully cultivated façade of composure with which he faced his people; she could feel his anxiety and turmoil rising and ebbing like a tide, battering her heart as though she lived within his body.

"You couldn't have known, Iphicles," she offered, then fell silent when he shot her a look that was consummate rage.

She twisted in the saddle to widen the scope of her vision, and froze. Walking among the dead and dying was her Master. He was regal in a fashion that defied the king's presence, his dark, fierce visage grim. He turned, a graceful arc of motion that made her breath still, then he smiled at her, his head inclined in a mocking bow. Cold, unyielding fear paralyzed her movement; Furey whinnied softly, and she stared.

"What's wrong?"

An icy shiver caressed the length of her spine and broke the terror that had seized her. She swallowed hard, then

shifted her attention to the agitated king who had come
to a halt next to her.

"Amarantha?"

His impatience shattered the last residue of fear, and
she shook her head to clear it of the chaos that had been
unleashed in her mind.

"Have you seen someone you know among the dead?"

This time Iphicles' query was kinder, and she glanced
back over her shoulder. Her Master stood, watching her,
arms folded across his broad chest, smile faintly amused.
She knew in that instant that no one was aware of his
presence — only she could see him as he walked among
them.

"Am?!"

"No," she answered automatically. "It's nothing,
Iphicles," she assured him quickly. "Just too much grief."

He motioned for her to ride at his side.

"I've sent the captain ahead," he told her, voice low,
tension and worry in his tone. "To the palace."

"You should have gone yourself," she murmured.

"No," he denied. "I have to be seen by my people. They
need to know that I'm back, and that I intend to find who
is responsible for their losses."

And what of yours, she wondered silently, eyes on his
rigid profile, heart aching already for the loss she sensed
looming before him. There was no logic in her knowledge,
only an instinctive certainty that what awaited him at his
home would defeat him as nothing yet had.

They continued their meticulous, outwardly composed
ride into the heart of Corinth. Iphicles stopped often, spoke
to his people as he offered his strength to those who had
been so badly hit in his absence. To the credit of both people
and the monarch, there was no anger, no accusations hurled
to injure Iphicles' already battered spirit. The citizens of
Corinth cared for their ruler, and in this difficult time, they
recognized his pain as he did theirs.

At his side, Amarantha was consumed by the helpless
rage that burned within her. She was weary to her very
soul, and swayed as she rode, wave after wave of shock,
loss, and despair assaulting her mind in a way that drained

her life's energy from her. She knew the anger would come from the populace of Corinth before long. Once they'd tended their wounded, buried their dead, and could think past grief again, they *would* blame their king for not protecting them. Would he, in turn, blame her for not telling him all that she might have?

The sun was setting when the small company finally reached the palace gates. On the western boundary of the wall, fiery color slashed the sky, painted everything in bloodied scarlet. The image chilled her.

Iphicles halted at the open gates, and his gaze came to rest on Amarantha. Even with the short distance that separated them, she could see the tremors that shook him. It was not fear, she knew; not in the sense that so many would suspect. She nudged Furey closer to the king's mount, nodded her support, and they passed through the damaged entrance to the palace.

She faltered for an instant when she saw the ruin of the courtyard. The servants had been ill-used, many were dead, others injured to the point that they would soon join those already walking in Hades' realm. Animals wandered, seeming dazed. Amid the living wreckage were the scars that ravaged the palace itself.

The silence was terrifying, and contagious. No one spoke; even the horses went still in the ghastly atmosphere. Amarantha turned to look at Iphicles, her eyes awash with tears that she hadn't been aware of until that instant. As she watched, he dismounted and began to run. Without thought, she followed him.

The palace Honor Guard appeared to be dead to the last man. Bodies littered the corridors, and as she ran after the king, she noticed that many had died of horrible, slowly inflicted wounds. The warlord who had taken the palace enjoyed killing. She caught a glimpse of Iphicles' cloak as he charged into his private chambers; she continued along the hallway.

The prince's rooms were only a short distance from his parents', and she didn't hesitate as she all but stormed into the suite. The shock of sudden silence was again painful, and panic increased the roar within her head.

"Iolaus!"

She whirled when she heard the muffled cry of a child. It took only a few moments to locate the frightened boy, and she grabbed him as soon as he stumbled from his place of concealment. He'd been hiding in a wardrobe cabinet, and she hugged him tightly as he clung to her, his small arms choking her with their surprising strength.

"Father..." His voice broke, and he began to cry into her shoulder.

Amarantha soothed him, stroking the soft, fine hair of his head as she peered into the room. Someone was close to them, she could sense the other presence though she saw no visible trace of another person.

Vaguely uneasy, Amarantha turned to the door, intent on taking the boy to his father. She felt the tingle of warning a second before she was struck from behind; a firm blow that lashed across her shoulder blades and made her stumble.

She spun around, awkward with the prince still wrapped in her arms. The girl, for she was little more than a child herself, launched another assault on Amarantha. She had only a blunt, heavy stick but it rained several painful blows on the warrior woman before Iolaus' screams stopped the girl's attack.

"Father is back," he told his defender when she backed up a few steps and stared. The girl's eyes were swimming with tears, and she trembled with the intensity of her fright. "This is Amarantha, a friend," he added, his young voice kind and older than his years should allow.

"The king is back?" She gazed at Amarantha, hope and wariness in her hazel eyes.

"Yes," Amarantha answered gently. "You have done well in protecting our prince," she added with a smile. "What is your name?"

"Evadne," the girl replied. "The queen..." she paused, drew a deep breath, then continued, "she told me to keep him safe, hidden."

"You've done well, then," Amarantha assured her. "Something the queen will know, Evadne."

At the mention of Automedusa, the girl's tears flowed more freely, and Amarantha experienced a new wash of foreboding. She looked at the fair haired prince in her arms, saw the sadness in his small face, and knew.

"Iphicles!" she breathed softly, and ran from the room, Iolaus still in her arms. Behind her, Evadne chased after them.

"How long were they here?" Amarantha asked before they reached the king's quarters.

"Several weeks," Evadne responded. "They left two days ago, after a messenger arrived. They killed the last of the guards before leaving the palace."

Amarantha burst into the king's rooms, half-afraid of what she would find; certain on another level that she knew what to expect. She closed her eyes, swayed with shock, and felt the prince squirm out of her suddenly lax grasp. When she dared to look again, she saw Iolaus at his father's back, his tiny hand on the shaking shoulder of Corinth's king. Iphicles' low groan of sorrow broke the horror that held Amarantha, and she slid to the floor, her back to the wall. Iphicles turned to gather his son in his arms and they shared their pain as they stared at the body of the queen.

Evadne knelt next to Amarantha, her features alive with concern.

"Are you all right, lady?"

Amarantha felt bitter mirth crest in her throat, but she subdued the desire to lash out at this girl for her ridiculous enquiry.

"We must talk, Evadne," Amarantha whispered, anxious to leave the chamber and its agony of loss and despair. She wasn't ready to look into Iphicles' eyes and see the hollow echo of his loss staring out at her. She felt guilt, and resented it; if she'd pushed him harder, been less eager to savor the joy of his company, could they have arrived in time to prevent the Queen's death? Questions that lacked answers plagued her, and she needed a distraction.

"The King—"

"Needs to be alone," Amarantha interrupted brusquely. She climbed to her feet, unnerved at the deadened weight of her limbs in the aftermath of the day's shocks. "Go!" she whispered harshly, and gestured for the girl to precede her.

ϒ ϒ ϒ

Less than an hour later, Iphicles joined her in the throne room. Amarantha was alone in the large chamber when he entered, and she turned immediately. The desire to go to him was unbearable, and she averted her eyes when he stared at her, afraid that her treacherous heart would betray her thoughts.

"I've sent messengers to Alcmene and Heracles, as well as arranged for the funeral games." she told him quietly, once he'd slumped on the throne and closed his eyes. His absent nod told her he hadn't really heard her.

"I want to know what you knew, Am," he said eventually, his fatigue unmistakable. Despite the echoes of loss and exhaustion, his tone was firm and demanded an answer.

"I *knew* nothing more than what I was able to tell you, my lord Iphicles," she assured him, keeping her words even and reasonable.

His haunted, dark eyes flashed with fury and she held her ground when he rose from his seat and crossed the room to stand in front of her, the action swift and fluid in its grace and its intent. Iphicles grabbed her chin in a grip that was meant to cause her pain.

"I want an answer from you, Amarantha!" he spat softly. "No more evasive non-responses. An answer I can understand."

"I knew nothing," she replied simply, and met the tumult of his rage glaring back at her from his deep brown eyes.

"You knew we should return to Corinth. How?"

"Instinct," she charged. "Nothing more mysterious than that. We found destruction in Pheneüs, my lord," she went on, "but no one who would have given the orders for such waste. The attack was meant to get your attention. It did." She paused. "And that left Corinth open to plunder."

Iphicles released her and paced the confines of a suddenly claustrophobic room. He wanted to scream his wrath to the Gods; and knew it would only amuse them. His family had long been plagued in ways that others were not; paying eternally for the tryst that had given the world its champion, Heracles.

"Would you have me make the burial arrangements?" Amarantha ventured when his incessant motion had burned itself out and left him gazing blindly out a window.

"Do as you see fit," he stated bitterly.

ϒ ϒ ϒ

The funeral was another nightmare, and Iphicles kept Amarantha close to his side as he accepted the condolences and sorrow of the people of Corinth. His mother and brother were present, having arrived the previous evening. He had spoken only briefly with them. He felt the weight of Alcmene's stare as he lit the funeral pyre and Iolaus' muffled cries told him that the boy had turned to Amarantha again, seeking comfort in her arms — as the king wished he could do.

While the fire blazed, the slow procession began to wind its way back toward the palace. Iphicles rode at the head of his diminished guard, his chariot drawn by the powerful white mare Amarantha called Furey. She had given the horse for this somber occasion, and he hadn't done more than nod his acceptance. It was as though she shared his shame; despite the lack of sense in his assumption. They had done nothing to warrant their guilt, yet it was there, an invisible barrier that kept them from all but formal conversation. In spite of that, Iphicles refused to allow her to leave; he used his son's need to mask his own, knowing she would not deny the young prince who adored her as she did him.

Amarantha watched his back, focused intently on the sun-sparked glimmer that was his crown. She would have given much to ease his pain and torment, yet she could do nothing, only watch his agony and curse herself for a fool. She should have left Corinth the moment they'd returned. Somehow, Iphicles had made it impossible.

"Ammy?"

"Yes, little prince," she murmured, and kissed the boy's forehead.

"You're going to stay, aren't you?"

Startled, she lifted her face from his head where it rested beneath her chin. He looked up at her, blue eyes serious and inquisitive.

"Of course," she whispered. "As long as you need me."

Satisfied, Iolaus snuggled close to her again and tried not to cry further tears. He was safe, and his father was home. Amarantha would stay. For now, it was enough.

ᵞ ᵞ ᵞ

Heracles and Alcmene awaited Iphicles when the king and Amarantha entered the private chamber that adjoined the throne room. Amarantha felt acutely the near-anger her attendance was evoking in the demi-god and his mother, she had said as much to Iphicles when he requested that she meet them at his side.

"It is good to see you again, Heracles," Amarantha greeted the tall, tawny-haired hero. She was mildly shocked by the stature of Iphicles' brother, then laughed inwardly at herself; Heracles had always been a rather awesome figure.

"Amarantha," he smiled and bent to kiss her cheek. "You're the last person I expected to see here."

"Six months ago, I would have agreed with you," she smiled slightly, then shrugged one shoulder in dismissal of the notion. "Iphicles has asked that I stay."

Alcmene had been silently watching the woman who had come from the past and taken a very solid place in the present life of her oldest son. It had not taken long to see that both Iphicles and his young son leaned on the frost-haired woman; Iphicles had always been drawn to Amarantha. Alcmene had hoped it an infatuation left behind with his youth — a wish she now recognized as futile.

"I'd like to speak to you, Iphicles," Heracles said quietly, his eyes straying from his brother and back to Amarantha. "Alone."

Watching, Amarantha felt the flare of anger in the king. She shook her head, pleaded wordlessly with him for peace. His brow furrowed, but he refrained from responding to his brother's lack of prudence in speaking so plainly.

The men left them, choosing one of the ante-chambers frequently used by Iphicles' advisors.

Amarantha felt the weight of Alcmene's stare, and she braced herself to face the displeasure of the former Queen of Tiryns. Alcmene surprised her with a rather sad smile.

"Your mother told me you were in love with my son," Alcmene observed softly, her sapphire eyes sharp and knowing. "All these years, I thought it was Heracles."

Amarantha laughed, the sound a quiet murmur tainted with bitterness and irony. "No one asked me. Everyone just assumed it had to be the son of Zeus." She peered intently at the older woman and smiled, expression forced and shaky. "Why is that?" It was a whisper.

Alcmene shrugged. "I don't know," she replied honestly. "Amphitryon laughed at the idea of you loving Iphicles. Perhaps I merely listened too easily?"

Amarantha nodded, then her expression grew distant and thoughtful.

"I met your sons when I was five years old, Alcmene. I was being tormented by the other children because of how I look. *Iphicles* was the one who stopped them." Her voice roughened with the memory as tears blurred her vision, but she went on. "He was the first person who ever told me I was pretty." She smiled again, melancholy and self-deprecation in the shift of her features. "Can you imagine that, Alcmene?" she wondered softly. "Your handsome nine-year-old son told the village freak she was pretty, and that the other kids were jealous because I was so different."

Against her best efforts to remain detached from the childhood pain, Amarantha's tears escaped her and she cried silently as she faced the lovely former Queen.

"I probably fell in love with him that very moment. Gods know, I can't remember a day in my life when Iphicles didn't own my heart."

"Why didn't you tell him?" Internally, Alcmene was surprised by the surge of empathy she was experiencing; all it would have taken to have radically altered the course of her son's life was that simple admission from this strange, exotic woman who had long owned his heart and his allegiance.

Amarantha wiped away the wetness on her cheeks and slowly shook her head. With a defiance that had been her shield throughout her life, she met the unexpected kindness in the eyes of the king's mother.

"Tell him what? That I adored him? That I wanted to serve him, and love him with every breath of my life? I'm nothing, Alcmene," she whispered fiercely. "Less so now than then. I was... I *am*... a slave. Iphicles is a king, and that destiny was something I saw in him even as a child. Just as Heracles is meant to be the champion of people everywhere. What would a king want with a slave?"

"Shouldn't you have let him decide that, Amarantha?" Alcmene questioned with quiet dignity. "My sons are both men of integrity and honor, they judge no one, lover, friend, or even enemy by the threads woven by the Fates."

"It is not Iphicles' judgement that I fear," the warrior replied blandly.

"Then what?"

"Fate itself," Amarantha uttered, voice barely audible. She turned away, relieved, when the king returned, his brother a few paces behind him.

"Heracles, I need to speak with you, if I may?" Amarantha requested softly. She was aware of Iphicles and Alcmene watching them closely, and waited for the demi-god to reply. He was thoughtful, then shrugged broad shoulders and held out his hand. Smiling, Amarantha bowed briefly to the king and his mother, then slipped her hand into Heracles' and followed him.

The late afternoon sun blazed down on them as they walked in the palace gardens. The silence between them lacked rancor or tension for the first time since he'd arrived to find her in Corinth.

"I believe there is a traitor in the king's personal guard," she stated when they had reached the outer edge of the garden and stared at the gleaming Gulf of Corinth. Sunbeams dappled the azure water with silver and gold, tiny currents tipped with diamond sparks as the Gulf stretched and breathed as Poseidon himself.

"Why?"

She smiled at the succinct, unemotional query. Heracles had grown circumspect in the years since she'd last seen him; now he thought before reacting.

"The strike on Pheneüs was preemptive, meant to take us from Corinth. The warlord responsible for this was told precisely when we would return. What else is there to think?"

Heracles smiled, expression ironic.

"I can think of a few possibilities," he murmured darkly.

Amarantha's eyebrow rose and she turned to look fully at him.

"Why would the Gods interfere in Iphicles' reign, Heracles?" she enquired quietly. "He's simply another ruler of Corinth; one of many who will hold that title."

"He's my brother, too," the demi-god noted dryly. "That distinction is not one shared by other rulers."

"Then what have you done that would cost your brother his family and his people?"

"He chooses the Guard carefully," Heracles said, ignoring the impudent query.

She was thoughtful.

"Yes. But none of the servants in Corinth could know exactly when we would return. Iphicles meant to stay in Pheneüs; I persuaded him to return quickly."

"What did you know that he did not?"

There was no challenge in the question, yet Amarantha bristled slightly as she stared into his unexpectedly shrewd hazel gaze.

"Nothing," she repeated for Alcmene's other son. "Merely an instinct."

"You never did lie well," he noted diffidently.

"Nor did I appreciate being called a liar," she retorted. "That has not changed, Heracles," she added softly.

He nodded, but made no apology. For several minutes the only sound to be heard was the lulling whisper of the Gulf. Amarantha sensed when his attention shifted again to her, and she looked up to meet his direct gaze.

"We're going after Melaneus, Amarantha," he announced, watching her closely for reaction to the news.

A deep-rooted sense of dread and despair held her for a moment, then she strode away, putting several paces between them. Looking out over the Corinthian waters, she eventually nodded.

"I had thought Iphicles would do so," she forced the words to formal, even cadence; betraying none of the agitation that raged within her.

Heracles said nothing. For indeterminate minutes he watched her rigid profile, then he left her without further comment.

ϓ ϓ ϓ

"Do you think it wise to leave Corinth so soon after an attack? You have enemies, my lord Iphicles," Amarantha reminded him cautiously. "This would be the time for them to make a move against your reign."

She'd been startled to receive a summons to the king's chambers very late in the night, despite her awareness that it was highly probable he would consult her. She had not anticipated his next request.

"That's one of the reasons I want you to remain here in my absence," Iphicles informed her. He came to stand in front of her, hands resting lightly on her shoulders. "My son trusts you, and I trust you with his safety."

"Iphicles..."

"Please, Am," he murmured softly. "I cannot be in two places, and I need to find the man who killed my wife, and all but destroyed two kingdoms."

"I do understand, my—"

"Leave the formalities outside this room, Am," he directed. "We are friends, and it's your friend that is speaking to you now, not your king."

In a distant corner of her mind, Amarantha remembered Automedusa's assertion that Iphicles had always been her king; the memory suddenly seemed oppressive and placed another layer of guilt on her heavily burdened conscience.

"Iolaus needs you," Iphicles stated, his voice a low, persuasive purr of sound. "I need you to do this," he added, seeing her resolve weakening, and playing on it shamelessly. The truth was, he didn't want to return to Corinth and discover she'd vanished from his life again.

Reluctantly, Amarantha slowly nodded. She was hardly aware of his smile as her mind whirled in frenzied, chaotic fear. She was becoming too involved with Iphicles' pain, too entwined in his life. If she continued to remain close to him, she would never be free. The knowledge came with panic, and undeniable allure.

CHAPTER FOUR

Lyaeus perused the courtyard of the palace in Pheneüs with little satisfaction. Work was finally underway, and the yard was beginning to again look like the residence of royalty, but it wasn't happening quickly enough to suit him. Nor were a great many other things.

"You appear to be enjoying yourself."

At the unexpected voice, Lyaeus whirled, hand dropping automatically to the hilt of his sword. He relaxed, outwardly, when he saw who had entered the throne room, unannounced.

"You shouldn't have come here so openly," he noted, careful to keep his tone neutral.

The visitor laughed heartily, swept past the advisor, and peered into the busy courtyard.

"King Iphicles is busy burying his dead and avoiding his own demise," he commented blandly.

"You underestimate him, Melaneus," he addressed the warlord from a safe distance, fully aware of how tenuous his position was in the treachery of which he'd so easily become a part. "He has a new advisor. An *unofficial* advisor who wields a great deal of influence with him."

Melaneus looked interested for the first time, and he turned his mocking countenance from the courtyard at last. He indicated the war chamber and they went into the room.

"I've heard rumors about the King's companion. Who is she?"

Lyaeus snorted softly and poured a goblet of wine. He handed it to Melaneus, took a second for himself, and sat at the long table that dominated the room.

"She calls herself Amarantha," he began after a moment's pause. "Apparently she was a childhood friend of the king."

He hesitated, took a large swallow of wine, then met Melaneus' piercing stare. "She fights better than any soldier in his legions, and would die for him in an instant. Iphicles will hear nothing against her, and keeps her at his side in defiance of anyone who speaks against the action."

Melaneus looked unsurprised by the news, and nodded thoughtfully.

"Some say she is the protégé of Ares," he informed the nervous Corinthian lord.

Lyaeus paled slightly and went for more wine.

"She's simply a woman with a sword, nothing more," he decreed sharply.

Melaneus laughed again, this time the sound filled with mockery and disdain.

"You fear her."

Lyaeus' eyes narrowed and he glowered at the other man.

"She can't be bought, or persuaded to leave Iphicles," he retorted hotly. "And she's too smart for a woman."

"And too smart for most men, I would guess," the warlord observed. "Not smart enough to stop his death, though." He made the statement slowly, with theatrical flourish, and smiled when Lyaeus stared at him in confusion.

ϒ ϒ ϒ

The days had passed quickly as the King of Corinth prepared once again to leave his palace. Raising an army to pursue and destroy those who had invaded the city was not a task that posed great difficulty; most of those who were able to fight were more than happy to seize the opportunity to strike back for those they'd lost.

Amarantha dreaded the arrival of each new recruit, knowing that as the army grew, Iphicles' departure drew nearer. He had asked that she take part in training the men, and she had chosen a background role in acquiescence of his request. She quietly instructed his newly appointed captain, then watched as he carried out the meticulous teachings in less than admirable fashion. She refused to allow Iphicles to force his men by royal order to accept her.

The weeks had dulled the pain and guilt that plagued her; yet little was spoken between Amarantha and Iphicles. His family tolerated her presence, and she knew it was mostly for Iolaus' sake; the young prince was her constant companion, even when she walked the courtyards to observe the training.

It was late in the afternoon, the one time of the day that Alcmene insisted Iolaus spend in the company of other children, and not the warrior woman his father had entrusted with his safety. Amarantha strolled the practice yard, wincing occasionally when one of the new soldiers blundered badly, or fell too easily for Sceiron's liking.

Her attention was unintentionally captured when she saw the captain grab a young boy and fling him to the ground. He raised his sword and she felt the arc of his rage whisper against her before the sword began to descend. Reacting without thought, she drew her own weapon and darted into the sunlit yard. She deflected the blow inches from the boy's throat, used the momentum to continue the loop and disarm Sceiron. He glared at her, surprise and anger distorting his hard features.

"You have been asked to train these men," she snarled softly, "not kill them."

"He can't keep up," Sceiron spat contemptuously. "He's insolent, defiant, and reckless."

"Then dismiss him," she replied icily. "His life is not yours to take."

"We'll see," the captain sneered.

Amarantha smiled, an expression that was devoid of warmth or humor.

"I am not a pleasant enemy, Sceiron," she warned quietly.

"The King's whore is no threat to me," he answered.

She laughed and raised her sword.

"Perhaps not," she agreed sweetly. "But I am not the king's whore, and I am a very real threat to you now."

Before anyone could anticipate their actions, the two unexpected combatants engaged in battle. Amarantha had finally found an outlet for her rage and frustration, and she allowed her body to move as her Master had taught it to. The dance of swordplay was, as Lyaeus had once pointed out, as seductive as lovemaking. She whirled easily out of harm's way when Sceiron lunged, his strike clearly meant to kill. Forcing her mind to accept that this was not supposed to cost a life, Amarantha slapped his exposed back, hard, with the broad side of her sword.

Fury and humiliation blazed from Sceiron's baleful glower as he spun back to look at her. She knew it would no longer be enough to best him; if she tried to avoid killing him, he'd take her life when she was least ready to defend herself. Iphicles' guards, those who had been with him longer, stirred restlessly. All knew that the King would be unwilling to forgive any man who permitted her death.

"Sceiron, that's enough!" Tatius was a new member of the Guard, and had spent time with the King and Amarantha. He knew she was the real force behind the training, and her skill was far superior to the brash Captain who took orders from her. "This is supposed to be a training exercise, not a death-match. Show the students your abilities, and your honor. Is an insult to your pride worth dying for, man?" he added quietly. He stepped into the dusty yard, one hand resting casually on his own sword. The implication was less than subtle.

"It is not necessary for you to be involved in this, Tatius," Amarantha assured the man. "Sceiron has been finding it... *difficult* to accept the King's wishes when it comes to the training of his army."

"Then perhaps he would do better to seek his employ-ment elsewhere, lady?" Tatius suggested with a smile.

"He is skilled and courageous," Amarantha said, her pale eyes serious and genuinely respectful when she looked at the man who stood a short distance from her, his sword held in a steady hand. "And, like the rest of us, eager to avenge the deaths of so many.

"I have no desire to do battle with you, Sceiron," she added after a brief pause. "Iphicles wants an army willing to fight for his people. Train them; you have the knowledge to keep them alive and able to fight for him. I merely ask that you not kill those who are less apt pupils."

The small interruption Tatius had provided had cooled tempers and rash judgements. Amarantha inclined her head in a small bow, turned away, and held her hand out to the boy Sceiron had been about to kill.

"Let me help," she said softly, her spine tingling with uneasiness as she feigned indifference to the very real threat still there. She was placing her trust in Tatius' ability to warn her if Sceiron planned to attack. The boy in front of her stared, his erratic gaze shifting from Amarantha to Sceiron, and back again. He didn't move from the spot he was presently rooted to by his fears.

"Sceiron, continue instructing your men."

She controlled the sigh of relief that coursed through her veins when Iphicles' voice issued the order from the walkway high above the courtyard.

She glanced up, saw Heracles at his brother's side. The demi-god's smile was speculative, and she looked away again.

"Pick up your weapon," Amarantha directed. "What is your name?"

"Naxos," he murmured.

"Let me show you something that may save your life, Naxos," she smiled.

♈ ♈ ♈

Watching the activity in the spacious courtyard, Heracles grew uneasy. Iphicles was measuring the readiness of the new recruits, but his attention was cursory; his real interest was in the smooth, flowing motion of one figure in the compound.

"There's something decidedly familiar about the way she moves, isn't there?" Heracles mused quietly.

Iphicles laughed and turned to look at his brother.

"We've known her since childhood," he grinned. "She's changed very little."

"It's more than that," Heracles stated. "She's been taught to fight, and whoever her teacher is, I've seen the style before."

Iphicles' expression changed, grew introspective and brooding. He suspected the teacher was her mysterious *Master*, and that thought never ceased to infuriate him.

"Who?" It was a question he didn't really want to ask. He couldn't *not* ask.

Heracles' frown was thoughtful as he tried to bring the vague sense of memory into clear focus. Perversely, it remained out of immediate reach.

The training session was reaching an end for the day. The sun was beginning its arcing descent in the western sky, fading rays painting the landscape in a fiery array of golden hues. The palace courtyard was slowly emptying of tired young men, yet Amarantha remained.

"What's she waiting for?" Heracles wondered.

Iphicles smiled; then pointed.

Tatius came forward when the area was clear, drew his sword, and bowed before her.

Heracles shared his brother's admiration long minutes later as they watched the graceful sparring that went on below them.

"How long will she last?"

Iphicles laughter was low, and a hint of pride was easily read in his voice when he answered the demi-god.

"What you should be asking is, how long will Tatius last before she bests him?" the king replied.

ϒ ϒ ϒ

Ares stared into the scrying glass that stood in the middle of her garden retreat. When she was present, this fountain was decorative; in her absence, it was his link to all she said and did. At the moment, what he witnessed stirred both rage and worry within his ancient heart.

Heracles was close, and that was never a good thing. She was falling more in love with Iphicles. And Ares knew her thoughts were often of finding a way to escape his claim

on her. He had trained a champion for the Gods, and she
now used his teachings to help mortal men win petty wars.

The Temple in Thrace was a dark, turbid place; befitting
the God it stood to honor. The taint of blood and war was
in every ancient stone. Ares felt more comfortable here
than he did when looking down from the great heights
of Mount Olympus.

He reached out to ripple the waters with one long,
tapered finger. He could end the mock battle he was
observing; end it with bloodshed and triumph for her.

"She is not yet yours to command, Ares."

The War God whirled, sword in hand, ready to slay
whoever dared to come upon him and speak. He sheathed
the weapon and spun away an instant later, enraged
further.

"I've waited long enough, Father," he ground out from
between clenched teeth. "I *will* have what is mine."

"You chose to do this thing, Ares," Zeus replied with
false mildness. "The Fates decreed the cost, and she is not
yet yours to command. Only when her mortal existence
has been served will she be in your hands."

Ares' rage intensified, blinded him for several minutes
as he accepted that he must bow to the law he had sworn
to accept.

For a long time, there was silence. Father and son stood
motionless, neither testing the limit of the other's patience
nor intent. Finally, it was Zeus who broke the impasse.

"Do not be blinded by your jealousy of Alcmene's sons,
Ares," he advised. "What you have begun will last far
beyond their lives and mankind's memory of them."

It was an unusual, and wholly unexpected, kindness
from the King of the Gods; from Ares' father. The War God
merely nodded, then felt the whisper of power that stirred
the air and told him he was alone again.

ϒ ϒ ϒ

The palace in Corinth was quiet in the darkest hours
of the night, only the occasional stir of a guard could be
heard within the vast labyrinth of corridors. The upper

wing housed the royal family's residential chambers; and was less heavily guarded than other areas of the palace. Iphicles had often stated that he would not live with every movement he made observed by another presence. Automedusa had reluctantly accepted the order; despite her fear that they might well be vulnerable to attack.

Tonight, the halls were still and silent as a figure moved deep into the home of Corinth's king. Chosen for his stealth and skill, the outsider smiled as he neared the room where the ruler slept. He knew every inch of the palace; had spent many hours studying its layout.

The stillness was mildly disturbing. Something should have been moving, and the silence felt tangible as he walked, keeping hidden in the shadowy spaces that the torchlight never quite reached. Perdix waited near the room he knew belonged to the King. Iphicles was a man possessed these days, and no one knew for certain that he slept at all. He couldn't afford to confront the ruler with Amarantha close enough to hear any disruption in the palace's tranquility. The problem of Heracles had been solved for him when the demi-god had unexpectedly announced that he would be gone for a few days.

Perdix had joined the household staff amid the turmoil of Iphicles' return from Pheneüs; so far he'd managed to avoid drawing attention to his presence. Even with that slight reassurance, Perdix's nerves were taut — the warrior woman missed nothing, and he'd seen her taking note of all the new palace servants, as well as the soldiers.

Drawing in both courage and a deep breath, he took the final step that would place him at the King's door. Poised to bolt in the event Iphicles heard him, Perdix began to inch the door open. The chamber was dark. He slipped into the small crevice of the open door and pushed it shut, freezing when the heavy wooden panel heaved a low thud as it closed.

Again, nothing moved within the murkiness of the room. Waiting precious moments for his eyes to adjust fully, he finally dared to look at the massive bed that dominated the chamber. There was at least one person buried beneath the rumpled linen; he assumed it was the King.

Drawing his dagger from a hidden sheath in his tunic, Perdix went forward on noiseless feet. The familiar calm of detachment washed over him when he neared the bed. This was what he did, he thought with macabre humor. He had no feelings at all for the man he had been ordered to kill; Iphicles' death was merely the result of war and deceit.

Perdix raised his knife, and felt the ice of terror sweep through him. Pain shaped an abyss; a dark, bottomless chasm that loomed before him. He fell, and deeper agony rose to sear his soul. The bed moved beneath him, shouts came from a long distance, and the dagger dropped from his numbed fingers as he saw the edge of the void draw closer.

ጥ ጥ ጥ

"What...?" Iphicles' voice stammered to a halt before he could form a single question. His shocked gaze moved to the sprawled figure on his bed; the figure bleeding all over his bed at the moment, some deviant corner of his conscience reminded him.

Amarantha swept past him and shoved the body over to see precisely who it was she had just killed.

"Perdix!" she snarled, her voice a rasp of anger and disgust. She yanked her dagger from the center of his back, wiped it clean on his tunic, and tucked it into the slender sheath at her belt.

"Am?"

"By the Gods! You are no longer safe in your own home, Iphicles," she said sharply and turned to look at him. He was shaken, but calm.

"What are you doing here?" he finally asked.

"I heard a noise in the hall," she confessed. "I sleep very little these nights," she added with a wry smile. "I was, honestly, expecting something like this, my lord. When I saw him, I entered your room through Iolaus'. Since he has been sleeping in the adjoining chambers, it was not a difficult thing to accomplish."

"Who is he?" Iphicles questioned, deliberately avoiding the other part of her statement. It was not comforting to think that he was a target within the palace walls.

"He arrived shortly after our return," Amarantha replied. "He has been working in the palace since. Always careful to stay in the background." She was furious with herself now that the fear for Iphicles had passed, and reality and logic were slowly emerging.

"I am sorry, my king," she murmured, head bowed.

"Sorry?" he was confused, and it was clear in his voice.

"If I had acted less... rashly, we would have been able to discover who hired him to commit this treachery." That was simple truth. She had been terrified when she saw the figure skulking in the king's rooms. She knew there would be an assassination attempt; it would be a reasonable course of action for anyone who wished to take control of Corinth and Pheneüs.

"I should have been better prepared," she concluded quietly. If her Master had knowledge of this failure, he would have been harsh with his ridicule; and intolerant of her lack of discipline.

Iphicles watched her closely for several moments, both curious and affronted by her manner. She was distant in those seconds; a stranger who berated herself not for killing, but for killing too quickly.

"I will see that he is removed, my lord King," she said eventually, once again controlled and at ease.

Iphicles didn't know what to say. He nodded, and went to check on his son. When he returned a half hour later, the room had been cleared of the dead assassin, and his bedding replaced. There was no sign of Amarantha.

ϒ ϒ ϒ

Heracles spotted her first when she entered the war chamber, and his dark hazel eyes narrowed speculatively. Iphicles noticed his brother's shift of attention and turned to look toward the door. Amarantha bowed slightly, waiting for permission to enter.

"Am?" Iphicles gestured for her to join them, inwardly irritated that she was forcing these small formalities between them.

"I have come to say goodbye, my lord king," she said quietly, her gaze darting to Heracles for an instant, registering his surprise before meeting the anticipated enmity in the king's dark eyes.

"Why?"

The single word had a glacier quality, and the impact of a sword thrust into her heart. His look screamed betrayal.

"It is best that I leave, my..." His expression grew more dangerous, and she relented. "Iphicles, I have no place here. We both know that. Will you truly ask me to explain my reasons when you already know them?"

"I need you here, Amarantha," he said quietly, voice belying the turmoil he was feeling. If he confronted her with his anger, she would leave simply to defy him. "My son needs you."

She felt a stab of pure resentment when Iphicles made the one statement that would weaken her resolve. Iolaus. *Iphicles'* son. The child she would never have herself.

"Iolaus needs his father," she said softly. "*You*, Iphicles. He does not need the presence of a stranger."

"You are *not* a stranger, Am!" He almost shouted the words, only controlling his fear-induced exasperation at the last second as he spoke. "He loves you."

"Iphicles, if she wants to leave, it might be for the best?" Heracles interjected, fully aware that he was inviting his brother's wrath.

"Best for whom?" Iphicles snapped instantly.

"Best for everyone," Amarantha smiled. "I suspect your mother would agree with him."

Iphicles' fury all but arced across the room at her.

"This is between us, Amarantha," he growled. "It doesn't involve Heracles, or my mother."

"I have told you that I think it best," she replied with a shrug. "You are the only one who objects."

For several minutes there was an impasse; the kind that made everyone present uneasy and restless. Finally, the king nodded.

"You are free to go," he stated firmly. "Iolaus will return to Tiryns with my mother. Go safely, Am. May the Gods be with you."

Tiryns. A shudder gathered at the base of her spine and she stared at the two brothers. Iphicles had turned his back to her, but Heracles watched her for reaction to the curt dismissal. Her stomach tightened with fright; a panic that held no logic, simply instinctive fear.

"Do not send Iolaus to Tiryns, Iphicles," she said, voice little more than a whisper.

Surprised, the king turned to look at her again. Dark eyes narrowed with suspicion, and a hint of fear.

"Why?" He walked to her, stood so close that she had to lift her head to maintain the contact with his intent gaze. "And I will have an answer this time, Am," he added in overt warning. "You fear something. What?"

"I do not know that, Iphicles," she said quietly. "It frightens me. I can explain it no more clearly than that."

"And if I choose to not believe you, Am?" Iphicles proposed softly, his voice a breath of air that stirred the fine tendrils of silver hair that brushed her forehead. "If I send my son away against your advice, what will happen to him?"

"You are asking me for answers I do not have, my lord," she responded, her tone even and falsely calm. "He is your son. The choice belongs to you."

Iphicles' smile was cruel as he nodded.

"Which makes it convenient if I disregard your counsel and lose him."

Fury woke within her and she forgot for that second that he was a king, and she was a slave. Her hand rose and she landed a slap to his face that made him stagger back a couple of steps, then stare at her.

"You have no right, Iphicles!" she charged, shaking with her anger and the very real pain his accusation had cut into her soul. "Who are you to judge me?"

"A man who fears losing you," he replied, completely candid with her for the first time since their return to Corinth. "It's not only my son who needs you, lady," he added with a hint of wistful, bitter irony.

Amarantha spun on her heel, turned her back to him for precious moments as she tried to find composure.

"I will stay with Iolaus until your return, my lord king," she whispered into the heavy silence. "But then I *will* leave."

It was a small reprieve, one that would give him time to persuade her when he was free again. Before he could offer his thanks, she was gone.

"That was a mistake, Iphicles," Heracles said into the uncomfortable quiet that followed her exit.

The king glanced over his shoulder and shrugged.

"Can you think of anyone more able to protect our mother, and my son?"

"That's not why you want her here."

Iphicles ignored the challenge in his brother's tone, and indicated the maps they had been studying.

ϒ ϒ ϒ

"Heracles tells me you will be staying with us."

Amarantha looked up from the sword in her hand. She set the sharpening stone aside and let the weapon rest across her legs as Alcmene took a seat on the bench opposite her. The fading rays of day caught sparks of gold in the Queen's hair, and Amarantha waited for her to say what she needed to say. The courtyard was free of activity for the first time that day, and the peace had been welcome. She sensed that it was also at an end; this woman could unnerve her as no other person had ever been able to do. She saw too clearly, and that made her a threat to Amarantha's carefully constructed shield of composure.

"He thinks Iphicles has made a mistake asking you to stay in Corinth."

"He is probably right," Amarantha conceded with a polite smile.

"Yet you will remain here."

"Yes," the warrior nodded slightly. "The king has asked it of me."

"If he hadn't?"

"I would have been gone weeks ago, Alcmene," Amarantha said with an ironic smile. "This is not a comfortable place for me, either."

The queen smiled and nodded.

"Iphicles is not indifferent to you, Amarantha. Quite the opposite."

"Is that why you and Heracles want me to leave?"

"No," Alcmene denied softly. "Heracles thinks Iphicles should have married you years ago."

Amarantha was sincerely surprised.

"A king does not marry a slave," she noted, again with the bitter irony that conversing with Alcmene stirred within her. "He beds her if he wishes, but he does not make her his wife."

"You weren't a slave in Tiryns," Alcmene returned.

Amarantha shrugged one shoulder.

"No. But even then I sensed our lives would be very different. Your sons are destined for greatness, my queen," she bowed her head respectfully. "That has always been so."

"Iphicles is a good king," Alcmene agreed with gentle pride. "Heracles is less thoughtful, and more confident. But he sees something in you that you do not see in yourself. A greatness you have yet to realize."

"The son of Zeus is a superb champion, but a terrible oracle," Amarantha laughed. "I may not have been a slave when you last saw me, Alcmene; but I am most definitely one now. Iphicles knows this. Why should I believe he sees more than the property of another man when he looks at me?"

"Because he has loved you from childhood," Alcmene said with faint regret. "Something we should never have denied. I hope one day you will both forgive me for that."

"There is nothing to forgive, my queen," Amarantha said, suddenly angered. She rose and slid her sword into the sheath she carried. She bowed, formal and cool, then walked away.

ϒ ϒ ϒ

The war rooms were closed again, and Amarantha paced the hallways of the palace. Iolaus was with his teachers; Alcmene was surrounded by Automedusa's ladies; and the warrior who had no true place was forced to suffer her own company. She could have gone into the practice yard, but teaching men to die was not appealing to her. She knew, having watched the training sessions, that many of the young Corinthians would never return. They were not seasoned fighters, and the warlord had a formidable army for them to face.

This was a war that should never have involved her. She did not belong in Corinth, nor in the affairs of Iphicles' kingdom. Alcmene was ambivalent, at best; disapproving most of the time. Heracles had accepted his brother's choices, but Amarantha knew her presence was not welcome to him.

And what of her own desire? Was she staying because she had begun something honorable? Or was she staying because she now loved Iphicles more than she had as a young girl? Iolaus was the excuse they used, to themselves, and each other; but the lie was growing less plausible as the weeks passed.

Her mind in chaos, Amarantha left the palace and headed for the stables. Twenty minutes later, Furey was saddled, and they sped through the gates. She gave the mare freedom to choose the pace and direction of their journey; and smiled a short while later as the lovely animal took her out of the city limits and into the tranquility of the coastal landscapes.

ϒ ϒ ϒ

When she returned to the palace several hours after nightfall, there was a summons awaiting her. Steeling herself for the news she dreaded, Amarantha went to the king's private quarters. A light knock on his door, and moments later she was face to face with Iphicles.

"Come in," he requested, and stepped aside to give her admittance to the room. The door closed solidly and she walked to the window, staring out at the night.

"I wasn't sure you intended to come back," Iphicles began softly.

"I would not leave without telling you, my lord," she replied with a smile. "And, I have given you my word that I will act as guardian to your son. Did you think I would not honor my promise to you?"

He didn't answer the challenge in her words. When the silence lengthened, Amarantha turned her attention outward again. It was easier than trying to look at Iphicles and hide what she felt for him. She sensed more than saw when he joined her at the window. She was unprepared for the fear that assailed her a minute later. He placed his hands on her shoulders and made her look at him.

"We leave Corinth tomorrow."

The panic grew to agonizing proportions in the space of seconds as Amarantha stared into his shaded eyes. For several moments she was certain she'd faint, then the terror passed and in its place was weary resignation. She had known the time for departure was drawing near; she had merely been avoiding thoughts of it.

"Tomorrow," she repeated, tone schooled to neutral softness. "I wish you success, my lord king," she added with a slight bow of her head.

"Success?" Iphicles repeated, and the lack of discernible emotion in his voice made the quiet utterance feel like a shout.

Amarantha's head lifted and she looked closely at him.

"Let me go with you, Iphicles?" she asked earnestly. "There are a hundred men who could be left here with Iolaus and your mother."

"And none I would trust as I do you," he assured her.

For several minutes the silence between them was uncomfortable. Amarantha finally walked away from him, imposing physical distance as she tried to impose emotional detachment.

"You know what I am, Iphicles," she said, choosing her words with care. "If you do not return, I cannot stay in Corinth forever."

Her master, he realized.

"Will he claim your loyalty so quickly?"

"It is not loyalty that we are discussing!" Amarantha shot back angrily. "My loyalty is to you, as it has always been. But he owns me, my king. And that is not a thing that either of us will be permitted to forget so easily."

"I'll buy your freedom," Iphicles said rashly. "Every man has a price."

She smiled. "I do not think this man will be bought by a king's wealth," she whispered. "But I do thank you for the intent of your offer."

"Will you stay?"

"I have told you I will," she replied, startled when he came to stand in front of her, dark eyes locked intently with hers.

"I meant will you stay with me," he corrected, gravelly voice rougher, yet smoother than its normal tone.

Amarantha felt the vaguest sense of panic wake deep within her; panic and uncertain excitement. What *was* he asking from her, really?

"You have told me to stay in Corinth."

It was a coward's statement, and she accepted it as such. As did Iphicles.

"Then tonight we'll be in the same place," he commented, voice pitched low and enticing.

"Will we, my lord king?" she wondered, cool irony texturing the words. "If we share your bed tonight, it will still be as king and slave. Is that what you want of me? To be slave to you as I have to no other?"

Iphicles' eyes lit with fury and offence.

"I have never taken any woman to my bed by order or royal decree, Amarantha," he uttered softly, dangerously. "Why would you believe that I would dishonor you in such a manner?"

Shamed, she bowed her head.

"Forgive me, Iphicles," she requested in a whisper. "Forgive me, please?"

Iphicles smiled, a slow, warming shift of handsome features. He touched her face and made her meet his eyes, gazing at her in silence for several minutes. When he bent to kiss her, he felt more than heard the breathless "no" she offered as objection. He ignored it, trusting his instinctive understanding of her rather than listen to her misplaced guilt.

The kiss was tentative, experimental as the young King of Corinth finally felt a dream he'd thought truly lost finally come within his reach. He controlled his desire, let her find her own understanding of what she wanted and needed. Only when Amarantha's arms lifted to wrap around his neck did Iphicles pull her to him fully. Her body softened against his, smooth curves fitting to him as he'd always imagined they would.

When he broke the kiss to look at her again, he saw the fiery glitter of passion burning in the darkened silver gaze.

"Are you certain, my king?" she whispered, pleading without words as she stared at him.

Iphicles smiled.

"Shouldn't I be asking you that, Am?"

She hesitated, then her smile turned to low, purring laughter.

"I have always been certain, Iphicles," she assured him, her smile radiant. Her happiness dimmed moments later as she considered all that had happened during the months that she had been with him again. He had been married and quietly ruling one of Greece's busiest cities. Now, he was alone and about to go to war. Time had never been with them. Not as children; nor, it seemed, as adults.

"This may be the only time we have, Amarantha," he said, eerily reading the shift of her thoughts and the turmoil it stirred within her.

His arms shifted around her, and his hands began to glide over her, persuading her to accept what they both wanted this night.

Ignoring her fears and uncertainties, the warrior closed her eyes, leaned into him, and offered him the only answer that her soul would accept as right. Her body trembled in response to his caressing hands, accepting an intimacy she had never permitted with any man. Her heart felt as though it had grown wings and was beating wildly against her chest, eager to burst forth and proclaim discovered happiness.

She returned his kisses with fervent ardor, learning the
contours and tastes of his mouth and his skin as he taught
her a passion that was not born in battle, nor in desperate fear, but in their total, long denied devotion to each
other. Each piece of clothing was carefully removed, slowly
and deliberately as each savored the delights of this new
dimension in their love.

"Iphicles," she moaned softly as he placed her on the
bed and joined her moments later. He was leaning over
her, features softened with the intensity of his desire, and
she shivered violently as naked skin met naked skin fully
for the first time.

"Amarantha?"

It was a breathless query that hung between them, an
asking as eternal and ageless as the erotic dance of lovemaking. So attuned were they that he felt her uncertainty
within his own muscles, and it chilled him with momentary
apprehension.

"I would not wish to..." She paused, searched for the
simple words that would convey her fears, and not drive
him away. "I have never done this before, Iphicles," she
confessed, and looked away, unable to face him with a truth
that evoked shame and fright in her.

"Look at me, my love," he asked, and waited until her
wide silver gaze swung back to lock with his. "You honor
me as few others ever have," he assured her. "In all ways."
He kissed her, a soft, arousing exploration that made her
arch beneath him, her hips asking for a joining that would
complete a union begun in their childhood. And Iphicles
accepted the gift of his dreams at last being given life in
her arms.

ϒ ϒ ϒ

"How many will die with him, would you guess?"

Amarantha shuddered at the familiar voice close to her
ear. She stood on the wall that overlooked the gates to
Iphicles' city, watching the vast Corinthian army leave. She
had said her farewell to the King in the privacy of his bed
chamber; afraid to see him afterward. Afraid of what his

family would see if she stood next to Iphicles. Her body ached, combined joy and sorrow creating a minor war inside her.

She finally swung her gaze to meet the inky darkness of her Master's eyes. The fury she read there made her tremble with fright.

"Will he return?"

Ares shrugged, disinterested.

"Please," Amarantha's voice quivered with entreaty. "I know that somehow you already know how this war will end. I must know if he will survive?"

"The only thing you *must* know," Ares ground out from between clenched teeth, "is what I deem necessary for you to know."

Shocked, she stared at him; torn as rage and terror vied for dominance of her emotions.

"Why do you hate him?" she finally asked, shaken by the unexpected knowledge she suddenly held.

This time it was the God who was startled, and he looked closer at her, faint admiration in his handsome features.

"Hate him?" he repeated, the flicker of betraying emotion quelled instantly. "Why *would* I hate him, little one?"

She was shaking uncontrollably, but the tumult of her emotions began to coalesce in spite of the panic that seized her.

"You hate him because I love him," she decreed. "It makes no sense, yet I know this to be true. Why?" she asked in desperation. "I am nothing to you. Why can you possibly—"

"Enough!" Ares snarled. "*I* do not answer your demands, Amarantha," he reminded her in a voice gone deadly soft. "*You* answer mine. You would do well to remember that in future."

A scowl transformed her features and she looked away from his mesmerizing eyes.

"I remember, Master," she spat. "Each moment of my life, I recall it clearly."

When she turned to plead again for some reassurance of Iphicles' safety, he was gone.

ϒϒϒ

The dreams were a plague.

A torment that refused to leave her; conscious or not, Amarantha saw the images of death and treachery.

Iphicles' death.

And the face of the traitor who wished to take his throne.

The army of Corinth had been gone less than a month. She had sworn to protect the King's son; but even that oath was becoming less a tie as the days turned to weeks and she continued to see nothing other than bloodshed and betrayal in her dreams.

When she entered the throne room, she saw that Alcmene and Iolaus were doing lessons in the corner that overlooked the expansive palace gardens. To his credit, the young prince managed to stay in his seat when she came into the room. Alcmene shared an amused smile with the warrior woman before her blue gaze grew serious and watchful.

"What is it, Amarantha?" she asked when the warrior was reluctant to speak.

Subduing the panic and the unwelcome and sickening sense of disloyalty, Amarantha took a deep breath and chose to speak frankly with the former Queen of Tiryns.

"I must leave Corinth for a time," she began awkwardly. Iolaus deep blue eyes widened, but he remained silent. Amarantha knew what that small concession cost the boy, and she bowed respectfully to him. "With your permission, Highness," she said softly, "I would leave this day."

Alcmene's surprise was instantly hidden when Iolaus gave the request consideration that was far too adult for such a young prince. He didn't so much as glance in his grandmother's direction. He stood and went to stand before Amarantha. She knelt to face him.

"I would not leave you willingly, my Prince," she assured him. "But there is something which must be done. Something of grave importance."

Iolaus weighed the words in his childlike/adult way, then nodded slowly.

"Will you come back?"

"As soon as I am able," she promised.

Iolaus reached out, touched her hair as he had so often seen his father do, then he threw himself into her arms, a child once again.

Amarantha held him far longer than she should have, then left him in Alcmene's care. The older woman said little, which meant she had much to say before the warrior would be free to leave.

ϒ ϒ ϒ

"May the Gods protect you," Amarantha said formally when she was mounted on her white mare. Alcmene and Iolaus stood in the courtyard, the boy looking frightened despite his attempts to conceal the emotion. Alcmene's eyes blazed anger and disapproval at her. They had been arguing, heatedly, for much of the morning.

"And you," Alcmene replied icily.

Iolaus offered a small smile, then turned away, breaking into a run as he neared the open doors of the palace.

Amarantha's eyes misted with tears as she watched the child, then she wheeled Furey into a sharp turn and gave her free rein. The horse sensed the urgency in her rider and all but flew through the unclosed gates.

ϒ ϒ ϒ

"What is it?" Lyaeus snapped as soon as the messenger was permitted entry to the throne room.

The bedraggled man took several gasping breaths as he tried to pull himself together to speak to the King's regent. After a few minutes, he bowed.

"She... she was due to leave Corinth a few hours after me, my lord," he told the impatiently pacing Lyaeus.

"Who was?" he asked, furious and fearful at the same time. Unconsciously, he went utterly still as he awaited the answer.

"Amarantha."

Dread chilled the blood in his veins and he searched frantically in his mind for an explanation that would fit the breach of promise he knew she'd made in leaving Corinth. Nothing presented itself, except that she had uncovered his duplicity.

"Get out!"

Startled, the messenger stared stupidly for an instant. When Lyaeus drew his sword and began to stalk toward him, the man fled.

ϓ ϓ ϓ

Amarantha was weary to the core as she neared the palace in Pheneüs. She had chosen to linger outside the city for a day, gathering information. Her questions to the local people had supplied her with a terrifying understanding of what had become of the lesser of Iphicles' kingdoms since their departure. Now, as night approached, she hesitated again to enter the palace openly.

The sky was overcast, hiding the eyes of heaven from her, and cloaking her presence as she began to walk toward the imposing castle. She knew Pheneüs and this palace well, choosing an invisible entry was not difficult. The area at the back of the vast grounds was overgrown and wild; a perfect concealment. She tethered the mare in a sheltered cluster of trees, then disappeared into the shadows of night.

Amarantha drew her dagger and kept it ready. There were others in this area who also knew of the pockets of security offered by the anonymity of the forest. Several times as she trekked closer to the palace, she heard the faint murmur of voices. Each time she would wait, ready to dispatch anyone foolhardy enough to attack her. Each time the voices would fade, leaving her free to continue her journey.

Eventually she spotted the back wall of the palace grounds, and smiled as she came up to the solid rock barrier. Long minutes later she located the decayed section that would permit her access to the gardens.

A short while later she knew that Lyaeus had somehow received warning of her intention to confront him. There were guards everywhere; many more than had been left by the king. And, despite the lateness of the hour, they were vigilant in their patrols.

Amarantha lingered in the darkness. She twisted her white hair into a tight knot and unfurled the lightweight cloak she carried. Safely hidden within the folds of the inky material, she ventured into the farthest section of garden.

As she'd suspected, this area was guarded less heavily. Here there would be little need for a large deployment of men; Lyaeus couldn't know about the weakness in the outer wall. One man patrolled the quadrant; an old, battle hardened soldier who was visibly unhappy about his present duty if the perpetual scowl on his scarred face was any indication.

Amarantha approached the farthest corner of this soldier's assigned area, the most distant point from his current position. With a little luck she'd slip past without having to face him. Luck, of course, wasn't with her.

She was nearing one of the rear entrances to the palace when a strong hand clamped over her shoulder. She said nothing, but turned slowly to face the guard.

"Let me pass," she requested quietly, voice a low stirring of air between them.

He smiled, an expression that bore more resemblance to a leer than the amusement it was meant to convey.

"I am here under the king's protection," she said, testing the weight of the still hidden dagger she held. She did not want to kill anyone, but if he made it necessary she was more than capable.

"The king isn't here," he spat. "And my orders are that no one passes."

"Rethink your stand," she suggested, the ice in her tone unmistakable now.

"Why?"

"You will live longer."

She sensed the movement of his hand to the sword at his hip, and reacted instinctively. The dagger slid into his neck, severed the vocal chords as he tried to cry out. Blood gushed, ran in sticky warmth over her hand as she finished

cutting his throat. Before he had settled on the ground, she
was moving. Seconds later she was inside the palace, and
dared to breathe again.

A quick scan of the area told her she was in the servants'
wing. After a short pause to wash the blood from her hands
and the knife, she went in search of Maia.

ϒ ϒ ϒ

"There's no sign of her," Taphius repeated patiently. This
interview with Lyaeus was growing tiresome, as they so
often did nowadays. The descendant of kings, Taphius had
limited patience, and unlimited arrogance. Both had served
him well and brought him to his present position and rank
among warlords. "We have no way of knowing it was
Amarantha. Draco is dead, but there is no reason to suspect—"

"It was her!" Lyaeus snarled, spinning to face the captain
of his guard. "Your men were warned! I want her found."

"We cannot find a ghost, Lyaeus," Taphius tried again
to reason with his oldest friend. He'd advised against this
act of treason, but he owed Lyaeus his life enough times
to make his loyalty to the king secondary to his obligation
to the man who wanted Pheneüs for himself. "Iphicles
cannot possibly know of what has happened."

"Then why has she left his son without protection,"
Lyaeus charged, his eyes alight with the fire of madness
and fear. "She's found out."

"She's found nothing," Taphius retorted. "Unless Melaneus
has been playing you for a fool all along and has given
you to Iphicles for his own reasons."

Lyaeus slid his sword free and covered the distance
between them in several long strides. He stopped with the
tip of the blade at Taphius' throat.

"Find her, Taphius," he whispered. "Or I'll have your
head in place of hers."

Taphius smiled grimly and stepped back. He bowed
once, curtly, then turned on his heel and left.

ϒ ϒ ϒ

Amarantha listened to the exchange from a hidden passageway; the entire throne room could be observed from this place of concealment. Maia, like all servants, had a knowledge of the palace that was much broader than the nobles who inhabited the large castle. The girl had also been only too happy to tell Amarantha of all that had transpired since she'd left Pheneüs. The warrior now knew without doubt that Lyaeus was a traitor to their king.

She found the small triggering device that would open a section of the wall, then slipped into the room with Lyaeus. Still hidden by the curtains hung behind the throne, Amarantha watched him for several minutes. He was nervous, and angry. Off guard.

"Why did you think a warlord would keep his word to you, Lyaeus?" she asked as she stepped free of the shelter.

He whirled, stark fear making his eyes widen as he groped for his sword. He had the weapon free, but made no further move as she came fully into the room. When she stood before him, he smiled, expression mocking.

"You're a bit late," he sneered. "By now Iphicles is dead."

The sound of the doors swinging open was the last noise he would ever hear.

Guided by terror and rage, Amarantha struck without thinking. The blade of her sword slid past lightweight armor as though it were mere linen. Surprise lit the features of Corinth's betrayer; then triumph.

She hauled her sword clear of the body as Lyaeus fell, then whirled gracefully, ready to face the guards who had begun to pour into the room.

CHAPTER FIVE

Sword poised to do battle, Amarantha's eyes were everywhere at once as she watched the men of the guard in Pheneüs enter the throne room. Some were men she recognized as those left by the king; there were more that she had never seen before.

"The traitor is dead," she apprised them with false calm. "I am King Iphicles' justice. Are there any among you who wish to join Lyaeus?"

She was shaking with combined shock and unexpected exhaustion; and knew her words to be bravado. In her present state, she was not certain she could fight this many men. And was very certain that she did not wish to make the attempt.

One of the older men, a man from Iphicles' personal guard, stepped forward and bowed.

"Lady," he said respectfully. "We had begun to fear that our message had not reached the king."

It has not.

She resisted the hysterical impulse to tell him that.

"Your name?" She watched closely as the old guards quickly disarmed those men whom they knew to be fully loyal to Lyaeus. There were unfamiliar faces among the group who were left holding weapons. She was going to trust Iphicles' men to know what they were doing by leaving arms with that part of the group.

"Zetes, Lady Amarantha," he replied. "Is the king with you?"

She didn't sheath her sword, but relaxed slightly.

"No," she shook her head. "He is tracking the warlord with whom this one conspired." She refrained from kicking the corpse, and walked a few paces from the temptation he offered her rage. Lyaeus' last words taunted her and she fought past fury to find reason. "I wish to speak with you privately, Zetes," she stated. "Assign men you trust to confine those who served this traitor."

She turned and walked into an adjoining war chamber. It took several minutes for Zetes to carry out the orders she'd given, and those precious moments were spent in composing herself. She needed to think clearly if she was to discover how much truth there had been in Lyaeus' dying proclamation. She sat at the head of the table, placed her sword within easy reach, and forced order to her racing thoughts.

A knock on the door announced that she was no longer alone. When Zetes stood at the table's edge, she indicated a chair.

"How long has he had control?"

"Since the king's departure."

"Why were we not told sooner?"

"We sent a messenger days after the army left."

"No one has reached Corinth, Zetes," she finally confessed. "Iphicles and Heracles are heading toward Cleonae, then on to Nemea. They have been on that course for many weeks."

"Then how—" He bowed his head in apology before the question could be fully voiced.

Amarantha chose to answer him.

"I have come as a result of my own suspicions," she disclosed. "I was sworn to protect our Prince, and must return to Corinth as quickly as possible."

He nodded gravely.

"If I may be frank, Lady," he said after a noticeable hesitation, "that would be wise."

She was startled.

"Really?" The word held a distinct note of dry irony.

"The people of Pheneüs know you've killed Lyaeus in the palace. They also know he was King Iphicles' chosen regent." Again he paused.

"And?" she prompted impatiently.

"The charge of murder is already being whispered, Lady. They think you mad."

She smiled, genuinely amused.

"Perhaps they are right?" she suggested.

Zetes was surprised, then a slow grin split his face.

"And what will the King's madwoman ask of us?" he wondered solemnly.

"You will be captain and regent until the King returns, Zetes," she told him. "I will not be staying. Keep close to you those men who share your loyalty to Iphicles."

He nodded.

"When will you leave?"

"In two days," she decided.

ΥΥΥ

"Maia?" When she came to her, Amarantha smiled. "Thank you for your help."

Surprise shone in the girl's warm brown gaze.

"Zetes is a good man. He will not allow anyone to harm you." Amarantha finished packing her few belongings as she spoke. "If you need me, have him send a message."

"The captain has asked that you meet with him before you leave," Maia informed her.

Amarantha nodded distractedly.

"Fine. See that Furey is waiting for me in the courtyard."

The door closed a few seconds later.

The sudden stillness was eerie, and unnerving.

Amarantha felt a sense of dread and fear coiling in the pit of her stomach. Something was seriously wrong, and she had no true awareness of precisely what it was that troubled her. Scooping up the small pack that contained her things, she slung it over her shoulder and went to find Zetes.

He was waiting in the war chamber off the throne room.

"Are you certain everything is in order, Captain?" she asked when she had joined him.

He nodded somberly.

"When...?" He hesitated, visibly choosing his words with solicitous care.

"I do not know when Iphicles will return to Pheneüs, Zetes," she replied, answering instinctively what she felt he had wanted to ask. "Corinth is where I must go. From there, I *will* attempt to get a message to the King. I can do no more."

The uneasy Captain accepted her promise in his serious, silent way.

"Do you have men enough that you trust?" she wondered. It was a moot point, regardless; she had no support to offer him if he had felt overwhelmed by his sudden change in status.

"I will make them enough, Lady," he assured her.

"Then I will take my leave, Zetes," she said quietly. "May the Gods protect you."

"And you," he bowed curtly.

Amarantha made her way to the courtyard, pleased to some extent that the palace had begun to look again like a royal residence.

Her horse was waiting in the yard, and she mounted quickly, eager to leave behind the frightened stares that were cast her way. Word had traveled rapidly to the palace servants, and Zetes' assessment of their fear was correct. They looked at her with combined terror and pity; she was a madwoman to them.

A number of miles from Pheneüs, she felt the weight of dread settle on her shoulders once more. This time it was accompanied by an icy chill in her veins. She drew Furey to a halt and dismounted, walking toward a sparkling stream. She gave the mare her freedom to drink, and stood gazing into the glittering waters.

"You were sworn to stay in Corinth," a voice observed, heavily laced with sarcasm and cold amusement.

Suppressing a shudder, Amarantha turned, no longer surprised by his startling appearances.

"I am returning there."

"I don't think so," Ares said casually.

She smiled, no warmth in the expression.

"I have given my word, and I will not break it. Until Iphicles returns, I am Protector to the Prince."

The amusement had shifted to thoughtful speculation. "And when the Prince no longer needs your," he paused dramatically, then laughed, "your *protection*, what do you intend to do then, little one?"

"Stay," she stated firmly, without hesitation. "If that is what Iphicles wishes."

Ares' eyebrow rose and he nodded as he came to a halt next to her, dwarfing her with his height and bearing.

"Iphicles is not the one who decides your future, Amarantha," he warned in a tone that had dropped to an almost seductive purr.

"No," she agreed. "I will decide that." She peered closely at the man she was forced to call Master, remembered Iphicles' promise, and the last night she had spent with him. "I will be with him," she murmured, "as wife, or consort. It matters not."

When the declaration hung between them for several moments, she turned and would have walked away; Ares grabbed her arm and held her in place with implacable strength.

"You're still my property, Amarantha," he reminded her, voice a lethal breath of sound close to her ear. "You'd do well to remember that."

"Are you threatening me?" she countered, angered beyond caring that he could kill her with very little effort if he wished to.

"I've tolerated your infatuation with Iphicles," he growled softly, and yanked her closer, so their eyes were mere inches apart. "I will not permit a marriage to him."

"That is *not* your decision to make!" she snarled furiously.

"Oh, I think it is," he smiled, expression dark, ominous. "I own you. You have no choice that I do not grant. And *this* isn't up for discussion."

Ares released her abruptly and stared as she stumbled, caught her balance, and straightened to face him.

"He will pay for my freedom."

The God laughed harshly.

"You're not for sale."

"No," she agreed. "And I am not a slave. To you, nor any other."

"Don't try my patience," he advised, dark eyes gleaming with reproach.

"Who are you?" Amarantha asked after the silence lengthened and grew oppressive with too many rampant emotions. He refused to answer and she took a step toward him, looking closely at the sensual, handsome man before her.

"I see you, so clearly. I know your face as intimately as Iphicles', yet I cannot bring it to my mind when you leave. You vanish, but you remain within me. How... why?"

Quiet settled again, a tension laden, expectant stillness that made her nerves quiver with alien excitement, tinged by sincere trepidation.

"I'm your Fate," Ares whispered long minutes later, his shadowy eyes becoming less piercing as he chose his course.

"Then let me know you," she challenged softly.

Ares smiled and nodded, and finally permitted the truth to go beyond her visual perception. While he held her pale gaze captive with his, her features became mobile as the enormity of his identity solidified in her mind.

"My God..."

"I intend to be," he murmured, tone laced with faint irony.

Shock gradually faded and she stared at him in abject wonder. Her voice failed her as she tried, several times, to speak; to ask the multitude of questions that begged to be asked. Finally, she turned away from the splendor of his godhood, the dazzling beauty and brilliance that was part of his very essence. Free of that hypnotic magic, she was able to think. Slowly, her voice returned to her.

"Why...?" She put her hands to her mouth, closed her eyes and tried, desperately, to focus on something solid and real. "Ares..." she murmured, tone one of mild despair.

The War God contained his irritation, but took her by the arms and whirled her to face him squarely.

"Your Fate, Amarantha," he repeated ruthlessly. "You have been mine since before your birth. Your mother was mine!"

Shock vied with anger for a few seconds, then her head tilted to one side, tears sliding along her cheeks.

"What are you telling me, Mas... *Ares*," she corrected softly.

He smiled, and she was caught off guard by the glimpse of warmth his changed expression revealed.

"I want you to come back to Thrace," he told her.

"I cannot do that," she objected instantly. "I gave him my word, Ares," she used the name awkwardly, a tremor making it an admission of her unwanted fear. "I need to return to Corinth. Then to—"

"Don't push me, Amarantha," he chided.

"This is a matter of honor," she stated. "And my obligation to a king."

He laughed, genuinely amused.

"Your obligation to a king?" he repeated. "Your life belongs to a God!"

"My life belongs to me," she said firmly.

Ares considered her for several minutes, then nodded. He spread his arms and bowed, mocking her.

"Go to Corinth," he allowed magnanimously. "And tell the king that your Master commands your presence elsewhere."

Amarantha bit back the retort that sprang to her lips. Seething with sudden ire, she lowered her head in a gesture of false deference, heard his amused snort, then felt a shimmer of power arc the air. It died in the same heartbeat of time, and she dared to look.

She was alone again.

But for the first time, knowledge did not vanish with his physical presence.

ϒ ϒ ϒ

"So, Tatius was correct when he said you had returned."

Amarantha smiled, a shift of features that reflected little warmth. She turned to face the King's mother, and bowed curtly.

"Alcmene," she murmured in greeting. "I did say that I would be back."

Alcmene nodded, though her expression remained sceptical.

"Yes, you did," she agreed. "But weeks have a way of turning any truth into a lie."

"Where is Iolaus?"

"Studying," the former Queen replied. "He could barely be contained when Tatius said you had been seen in the marketplace."

"I wish to see him before I leave."

Alcmene's blue eyes flashed with irritation.

"You're leaving again?" She was not pleased. "You assured Iphicles that you would be here, to insure the safety of his child. Is your professed love for my son so changeable that you can dismiss the word you gave as bond?"

Amarantha controlled the rage that exploded in her veins, and drew in several calming breaths before she trusted herself to speak to the queen with a modicum of civility.

"It is my intention to see that Iolaus is safe before I go," she began quietly. "My word to Iphicles is one I would honor with my life, were it possible to do so. There are things of which you know nothing, Alcmene. Things Iphicles will understand too well."

"Make me understand, Amarantha," she asked. "I know what your presence means to my son. He loves you."

Amarantha shook her head, denying the words.

"No," she whispered, the soft utterance a plea. "Whatever Iphicles feels, it is not love. He mourns the death of his queen, and fears for the life of his son. I am a convenience, nothing more. He knows I will guard Iolaus with my own life."

"You're wrong about his love for you, Amarantha," Alcmene stated firmly. "But, for reasons of your own, you prefer to remain blind. Where are you going?"

"I cannot tell you that, my Queen," she said, head bowed. "Please have someone find me when the Prince is free. I have preparations to make."

Alcmene watched her leave the palace again, and a tremor of dread caressed her spine as she considered her son's reaction when he returned to find Amarantha was no longer in Corinth.

ϓ ϓ ϓ

"You are leaving."

The silence of the war chamber was broken, and Amarantha whirled at the unexpected voice. Her heartbeat thundered in her ears with deafening intensity as she faced the cold stare of the young Prince. Iolaus was angry, and like his father, his face reflected every shift in the tide of emotion he was controlling. He was too old to be a child, and too young to be anything else.

"Yes, my Prince," she said with a small bow of courtesy and deference.

Tatius discreetly left them without a word.

"You promised my father!"

Amarantha contained her smile and relaxed again. *That* was the voice of the boy.

"Yes, Highness," she agreed. "But there are things which demand that I honor another bond, a vow made long before our meeting."

"Then why did you tell him you'd stay?" Iolaus demanded sharply. "He wants you to stay here."

Amarantha's smile grew softer, sad. She left the maps she was studying, and went to kneel before the prince. She touched his hair and he flinched away, his blue eyes sparkling with ire, and tears.

"Iolaus," she murmured softly. "This is a thing that I must do. If I could choose otherwise, I would not leave you, nor would I ever leave your father."

Iolaus stared at her, uncannily measuring the truth in her colorless eyes.

"Will you ever return to us?" he questioned, accepting what he instinctively knew was unavoidable.

Amarantha had wondered that very thing herself. She reached up to unknot the cord around her neck. For several moments she looked at the pendant that nestled in the palm of her hand, then she smiled and tied the talisman around the child's neck.

"If you *ever* have need of me, my Prince," she vowed quietly, "give this to Heracles, and he will find me. On my life, Iolaus, I will come to you, and offer whatever service you require of me. My blood oath to you, Prince Iolaus."

Releasing the pendant was near-physical pain for Amarantha, and for that reason she knew she had chosen well in giving the amulet to Iphicles' son. Iolaus paid little attention to the priceless rubies that now hung around his neck. He watched the warrior woman that he knew his father loved, very differently than he had his Queen. Wordlessly, Iolaus took the final step that would place him in her arms, and he hugged her fiercely.

As he had once before, Iolaus ran from her, and did not look back.

The tears that fell were Amarantha's.

The remainder of the day was spent in consultations with the palace guards, and specific instructions to Tatius, who would now be the personal guard of the prince and his grandmother.

ϓ ϓ ϓ

"Travel by night is not generally a good idea."

Amarantha drew in the reins and waited for him to step into the dark road. When he was in front of her, she slid from the horse's back and led Furey to their Master.

"I doubt I would encounter anything that your training would not make inconsequential," she muttered. "What do you want of me?"

"What I've always wanted," Ares replied with a mocking grin.

"And that would be?" she countered coldly.

"You tell me," the War God challenged.

She considered, then nodded.

"I will offer a bargain, Master," she stated evenly. "Fealty, freely given. It will cost you a single gift, my lord Ares," she added, her gaze speculative, and hopeful.

Amused, he folded his arms across his chest, head cocked to one side as he made a show of contemplating her proposal.

"Continue," he directed.

"I will serve you in any and all ways you command," she said, forcing the words past the reactive lump in her throat. "If you will insure Iphicles' safe return to Corinth. Promise me his life, Ares, and I am yours."

"You're already mine," he pointed out.

She laughed, cool irony in the sound.

"Yes," she agreed. "But you are not generally known for abusing women in any fashion. You may be the God of War, but you are also a seducer. Would you rather a woman serving you willingly, or one who despised you?"

"You're a fool, little one," he assured her seriously. "I would have you, willing or not, any time I wanted you. You're not in a position to make demands."

"I want your word, Ares," she responded after a long pause.

"Do you believe I'll keep it?"

This time her smile was genuine.

"Yes," she said after a few seconds quiet. "Because there is within you an honor that is seldom seen. I trust you to keep the bond we make."

He was surprised.

For several minutes they stood, the God facing the slave, an impasse that would determine fate.

Ares acquiesced with a bow.

"Your word, Master," she repeated.

"Iphicles will return to Corinth," he swore, knowing already what she could not. The promise would gain him his prize, and cost him nothing; for that reason he made it easily.

CHAPTER SIX

"You're troubled, Iolaus," Heracles made the observation quietly as he joined the young prince in the vast gardens of the Palace of Corinth. The boy had grown into a man almost overnight, though much of the child could still be glimpsed if one knew him well. His uncle knew him that well. "Why?"

The blond head didn't turn. Iolaus merely waited for his uncle to reach his side, and continued his vigilant watch of the palace doors.

"He should not have married again," the prince said in a voice that was little more than a rustle of sound sighed between them. "Not when he loves someone else."

Heracles considered the observation, and the depth of knowledge it conveyed.

"There was little choice in the matter, Iolaus," he ventured carefully, knowing it would not appease the boy's confused anger at his father's actions.

"Everyone speaks of choices they cannot explain. My father has done it for years. Amarantha swore she was bound by obligations she would never explain. Why?!" he finished in a tone gone soft with lethal anger.

"I can't explain either of them, nephew," Heracles evaded.

"I want you to find her, Heracles," Iolaus stated firmly. "I want to see her again."

Heracles began to object, and swallowed his words when the young prince turned finally to meet his gaze. He held out his hand and waited until the demi-god did the same, then he dropped a pendant into the large, calloused palm and waited again. Heracles examined the rubies and knew the necklace had been Amarantha's, Iphicles' gift to her when they were children in Tiryns. She'd entrusted the precious talisman to Iolaus, and he suspected a promise was attached to its giving.

"She'll understand it's important," Iolaus added.

"We don't even know if she's still alive, Iolaus," Heracles cautioned.

"Yes." Iolaus smiled with bitter irony. "We do. Because my father's heart isn't broken, merely heavy with loneliness." He paused, then touched Heracles' arm in question. "Will you find her for me?"

Heracles hesitated for a long time, then when no wavering in the prince's resolve surfaced, he relented. He was deeply unconvinced of the wisdom in his nephew's chosen course.

ϓ ϓ ϓ

"Why Thrace, Ares?" she asked as they stood side by side and looked over the vast wilderness. The War God's temple was on a mountainside, and spread out before them was a scenic tapestry of forest and rivers. The distant pulse of life reverberated in the rocks and growth that surrounded them, and Amarantha felt an answering throb deep within her. She had learned to recognize it as her body's attunement to the God next to her; in his company, her awareness of all life intensified.

"I would have thought Thebes a more apt choice for your home," she concluded as she turned to look at him.

"Thebes is not distant enough," he murmured without real consideration of what the observation might reveal to her.

Amarantha smiled slightly and nodded.

"Tiryns is too close, and the memories it contains." She peered intently at him for several moments. "What is it you fear, Ares?"

"Fear?"

The word sounded a mocking parody when he spoke it, but she remained serious nonetheless.

"You may be a God, Master," she whispered. "But I have discovered within you the soul of a man. You have fears and hopes, as any other living being. And you fear Iphicles. I would know why."

"I fear no man, little one," he replied after a moment's pause to control the lethal rage that her words had awakened inside him. He kept his tone even, with the effort of will that he reserved for those things which were of great importance to him. "Iphicles is nothing to me."

"He is a great deal to me," she inserted, still watching him closely for reaction. "Is that why you dislike him so intensely?"

Ares laughed.

"You flatter yourself, Amarantha," he chided, tone heavy with irony and sarcasm. "He's Heracles' brother, and an unimportant king of Corinth." In truth, it was no longer Iphicles who wore the crown in the glittering port city. The God didn't share that knowledge with her.

Once she would have been angered by his casual dismissal of Iphicles, and her ties to him. Now, she felt she understood him better, and wasn't quite so infuriated by his sarcasm.

"You haven't mentioned the gift I gave you," he pointed out with quiet speculation. He had added still more beauty and peace to her garden sanctuary within his Temple, though she had yet to mention it.

She turned and impulsively leaned up to kiss his cheek.

"It has become an even more incredible place, Ares," she breathed, her pleasure and enthusiasm echoing in each word. "Thank you."

His eyebrow rose at the unexpected affection of her gesture. He kept his smile hidden and nodded, pleased that she was happier.

"We'll engage a complement from the city today," he informed her. "Are you prepared?"

She repressed a small shudder, then nodded, thoughtful.

"These battles," she began carefully. "Must they be real?"

"Each man who volunteers knows he may die," Ares stated indifferently. "They believe it an honor to die in my service, and more so when it is my hand, or yours, that delivers the final strike."

"Mine?" she repeated, scepticism coloring the word with distinct chill.

"You are my student," he shrugged. "My hand."

She refrained from further comment, unwilling to spoil the easygoing mood that had been between them for much of the day.

"I have no desire to kill men in any way," she murmured as they walked into his temple.

As always, the temple made her shiver inwardly. It was, ostensibly, a place of worship. But, in keeping with the God it served, it bore more resemblance to an armed fortress than a place of spiritual retreat. Shadows threw its inherent darkness into greater murkiness, and the distinct tang of blood sacrifice hung perpetually in the air. The inner chambers of the temple were vastly different, and it was there that Ares had created her garden paradise; using God-power to forge the atmosphere of tranquility and peace. He had added new chambers to it recently, so that she might escape the atmosphere that pervaded other areas of the temple complex.

"Killing is part of living," Ares observed, pulling her wandering thoughts back to their exchange.

"I have never believed that taking life is necessary to continue an existence," she answered quietly.

"You haven't lived as long as I have," he smiled.

She recognized the subtle underlay of steel in his tone and chose to drop the familiar conversation that inevitably left them at odds for extended periods of time.

Amarantha had been in Thrace for a number of years, and each month made her old life less real. Ares, when his mood was congenial, was a challenging and enjoyable companion. She had learned the limits of his patience, and rarely pushed him beyond those explicitly constructed boundaries.

She missed Iphicles from her very soul. *That* was something that would always stand between her and the War God she served. She suspected on some level that she was learning to love Ares deep within her, yet it was such different emotion to the one that had forever been linked to Iphicles. There were times when she nestled into Ares' arms as naturally as she breathed, warmed by his presence, content to bask in his unique and powerful mystery. That closeness was a rare and treasured thing. It had become even more so when she'd slumbered and awakened reaching for him, and called him Iphicles. Caught up in his wrath, Ares had almost destroyed her. He'd seldom permitted her to sleep next to him since then.

"Are you ready?"

His curtness warned her that her thoughts had been obvious to him. She refocused her attention, acutely conscious of the reignited rage that burned within him again. This session would prove bloody and wearing; the only way to now appease his roused fury.

ϓ ϓ ϓ

Ares watched from a distance, his appreciation growing as Amarantha faced several opponents and dispatched them with precision and grace. She had little stomach for bloodshed, but her instinct for survival was uncannily like his own; when she was attacked, she fought back with fury and virulent determination.

A trio of seasoned soldiers were closing behind her, using the weaker men to distract her. For an instant, the God considered stepping into the fray. He smiled smugly seconds later when she whirled and laughed at the surprise on the faces of the men who had planned to take her by surprise with their attack. She raised her sword and stepped toward them, using her small advantage. She had sliced through the nearest man's leg before he realized what she meant to do. He went down, blood flowing freely from between his fingers as he clutched the ruined limb. One of the other men finished him off and launched at the white-haired wraith who moved among them like the shimmering specter she appeared.

Ares winced when she was struck from behind and almost fell. Pain contorted her pretty features for a moment, then resolution took the place of discomfort. She rolled, let the momentum carry her free of immediate danger before she vaulted to her feet again.

Blood slid along the length of one slender arm, and she impatiently wiped it away before it could cause her grip to loosen on the hilt of her weapon. She reached behind her and Ares nodded his approval when the dagger that was hidden in her belt suddenly flew with well-practiced accuracy; the full length of the blade was buried in the exposed throat of a soldier. The man staggered, dropped his weapon, then died falling into a crumpled heap. The remaining man, at his back, stumbled when his comrade fell against him on his way to the ground. Amarantha moved, a sliver of silver darting into the darkness.

"Concede," she murmured breathlessly. "It is the only way to ensure your life."

He shook his head.

"A soldier in Ares' army does not surrender," he decreed.

"This is not a war," she growled furiously. "Merely an entertainment for the God you worship!"

"Then I will die with honor at the blade of his hand."

"You will die a fool!" she snarled, and drove her sword into the man's chest with unnecessary vehemence.

It was always like this, she brooded angrily. As the contest neared its end, and she knew she had survived another test, the horror of what she did would close over her heart. Triumph and victory was not the sweet nectar Ares claimed it to be.

Amarantha pulled her weapon free and held it high in tribute as she bowed her head to Ares.

ϓ ϓ ϓ

"She's quite beautiful."

Ares spun, annoyance clouding his features as he faced his father. He decided to ignore the ancient, powerful God, and turned back to the woman he watched. This garden was his gift to her, a reward for the skill and diligence she had shown recently. The waterfall tumbled over a rock shelf, and the silvery pool at its base was a bathing basin.

Amarantha came here often, and always after one of the grueling battles Ares forced upon her. Sylph-like and gleaming in the mystical radiance he'd created, she was unknowingly stirring another kind of lust in the God who owned her.

"Heracles is searching for her, Ares," Zeus told his son.

Ares' eyebrows rose and he glanced at his father. Contempt came into his mood as he read the desire in the older God's eyes. Zeus would take what belonged to his son, without hesitation.

"She's mine, old man," he warned.

Zeus laughed at the very real threat in Ares' tone and eyes.

"Is she?" he taunted. "If any man truly owns her, it's Heracles' brother, Iphicles."

"She's mine," the War God repeated smoothly. "And I don't intend to permit anyone, including my bastard half-brother, or his mortal twin, to take her from me. Amarantha's destiny has been with me from the day of her creation."

"A creation you insured for ends that may mean your own destruction," Zeus reminded him.

"She will never be my destruction, Father!" Ares declared with absolute certainty. "The Fates have shown what will be."

"Not until her mortal destiny has been fulfilled," Zeus stated, his gaze again on the woman they discussed. "She could still destroy us, Ares. If you hold too tightly, the Fates will intervene."

"She's staying here."

Zeus shook his head.

"Not yet, Ares," he intoned. "Deny her her life, and she will never be what you want her to be."

Before his son could object, Zeus laughed and disappeared.

Following Zeus to Olympus would only enrage Ares further. Swallowing the bitter bile of acquiescence, he left the garden paradise of his protégé and went to observe the offerings left at his temple altars.

ϒ ϒ ϒ

It had taken nearly a year of searching, but Heracles had finally found her again. Shock had been the most dominant response he'd felt at his father's sudden appearance a few months earlier; a shock that had deepened to dread and foreboding when he'd been told where Amarantha was, and whom she served.

Thrace was as wild and beautiful as he remembered, and the temple stood proudly overlooking the richest valley of the country. Uncertain, but determined to keep his word to his nephew, the demi-god began the climb that would lead him into Ares' domain.

Heracles found her several hours later, outside the temple, walking on the sunlit grounds that stretched beyond the rear entrances of the place of worship.

"So it's true, you serve Ares."

Startled more than she should have been, Amarantha spun around and faced him. Heracles was a study in golden hues, from his tawny hair to the shades of earth that he wore. He was, as he had always been, magnificent and imposing.

"Heracles!"

"It's taken a long time to find you."

Her pleasure at seeing him vanished. She stiffened in response to the disapproval in his tone and the anger that burned in his clear hazel eyes.

"I was not aware that you would have reason for finding me," she countered softly.

He smiled, expression grim.

"Not by choice," he agreed.

"You have nerve," she stated, her gaze skimming over him with combined love and hate.

He peered more intently at her, expectation in his eyes.

"Have you come to tell me that you have destroyed your brother?" When his eyes sparked with ire she laughed, a harsh bark of sound that conveyed more emotions than she could clearly define. "Yes, Heracles, even here I know of your madness. How many lives have you taken from him? His children slaughtered by the brother he loves; your own dead with them. Yet Iphicles would not turn his back on you, would he?"

"You know nothing—"

"Does Iphicles remain in service to Eurystheus while you wander freely?" she retorted bitterly, deliberately not permitting him to speak of why he had found her.

"Iphicles is a free man again," he growled furiously. "I didn't ask him to become a slave for my sake!"

"Iolaus adored you," she spat contemptuously. "You cost his father a family and his crown. Having almost killed him in your rage, does he remain faithful to his uncle?"

"Yes," Heracles hissed. "That's why I'm here." He reached into a pouch at his belt and pulled from it the ruby pendant.

Amarantha's stomach lurched wildly. She forced composure and calm with great effort, but made no attempt to close the distance between them when he held out the necklace. For timeless seconds she was standing before the boy prince, and swearing her allegiance to him, and his father, promising to come if ever they needed her. She knew that vow was about to strip of her of any peace she'd gained in recent years.

"Why did he send you, Heracles?" She tried to keep her voice steady, but the success was only partial as she stared at the heart dangling from his fingers. She was afraid to take the talisman from him, and instead tightened her grip on the hilt of the sword sheathed at her belt.

"I was simply asked to bring this to you."

Amarantha spun away, her heartbeat a roar in her head that threatened to deafen her. She dragged in a deep breath, shuddered as it filled her with anxiety, not harmony.

"Iphicles!" It was a sob of denial, and desperate fear.

"Iolaus," Heracles corrected softly.

Amarantha fell to her knees, hugged herself as she fought for control. There was only one reason for the summons. Iolaus might make the request, but it would mean his father was in grave danger. And she knew she'd offer her life to save Iphicles from any real threat to his own.

"He said you'd understand," Heracles noted diffidently.

"I do," she nodded, then glanced upward when he came to stand in front of her. Her eyes pleaded for mercy neither of them could grant.

"What's wrong in Corinth?"

"Iphicles plans to go to war." Heracles gave her the news with such reluctance that she visibly recalculated his presence.

"With you," she surmised. "He plans to go into another war, because you choose to fight, and he will not turn away from you."

He nodded slowly.

"May the Gods deny you peace for an eternity," she cursed him.

"I fully expect that, Amarantha," he assured her icily.

"What does Iolaus think I can do?"

Heracles shrugged.

"Keep his father from making a mistake."

"Will it be a mistake for him to follow you?" she asked. "He survived Troy, and Caledon. Why not this?"

Heracles' eyes clouded and he looked heavenward.

"I fear for his life, Am," he whispered.

Terror froze the rage that had been smouldering in her since his unwanted appearance on the temple grounds. She stared, saw the reflection of her own fright in the even lines of his face.

ϒ ϒ ϒ

"Where is she?" Ares demanded, striding through the labyrinth of chambers that made the temple a maze to those not accustomed to its layout.

Maidens who served him darted out of his path, all of them afraid to tell him what had occurred in his absence.

Ares grabbed the nearest girl and hauled her toward him.

"Tell me!" he shouted, and ignored the cry of pain and panic that crossed her face.

"Heracles came," she stammered hoarsely. "She went with him shortly after."

Ares flung the girl away from him, his roar of fury reverberating through the depths of the temple.

CHAPTER SEVEN

"Amarantha!?"

She smiled as she approached the gates to what had once been Iphicles' palace. Tatius was shocked and pleased in equal measure. She bowed her head and paused at the entrance.

"It is good to see you, also, Tatius," she said quietly. "I would have been happier had it been for different reasons."

He nodded, dark eyes troubled.

"Then you know that the Kin ... that Lord Iphicles is to leave again." He winced, uneasy and decidedly unhappy at the change in the former monarch's status.

"Iolaus sent for me," she answered.

"He fears for his father's life," Tatius confided. "And dislikes what has befallen them."

She nodded seriously. Shrugging, she formally requested passage into the palace courtyard. Gossiping with the guards, even one as trusted as Tatius, was not going to make this confrontation any easier for those involved. Heracles had left her the previous day, requesting that she tell Iphicles he would be in Corinth before week's end.

At the palace doors, she waited again, as she had a lifetime ago. It did not take long for her to gain admittance this time.

"Am?"

She turned just inside the throne room, a shiver of dread caressing the back of her neck as she faced him. The years had taken their toll on Iphicles, the inflicted pain and suffering etched deeply into the lines that crept from the corners of his eyes. His dark brown eyes, too, were testimony to the trials he had endured. He stood tall, and unbroken before her. His quiet composure was a façade, and she knew it.

"My lord—"

"Don't, Amarantha!" he snapped, unexpectedly furious.

Amarantha shuddered, battered by the rage that arced across the small space that separated them; sharp and lethal, this was the violent anger she had hoped would be long vanished. Their last minutes together, years past, suddenly hung between them as though they'd been shared only yesterday.

"Iphicles?"

The new voice was feminine, and the warrior swallowed her desire to lash out when an exceptionally beautiful young woman came to his side and placed her hand on his arm.

"Iolaus requested that I meet with him," Amarantha said after a perfunctory nod at the stranger.

"Iolaus?!" the woman repeated, surprised.

"This is my wife, Am," Iphicles stated, "Tisiphania." When she made no comment, nor gesture of obeisance, he resisted a smile. "Amarantha is an old friend of our family."

"Where is he, Iphicles?" Amarantha asked. "I have no wish to remain longer than is necessary."

The hint of humor left Iphicles' dark eyes and his mouth set in a hard line of displeasure.

"I'm sorry you feel that way," he said quietly. "Tell Iolaus his guest has arrived," he asked when Tisiphania's grip on his arm grew tighter.

The young princess, for it was obvious to Amarantha that this was Creon's daughter, cast a look of open hostility at the white-haired warrior. A look that held far more venom than it should have. Whispers had reached the ears of Iphicles' new wife, telling her things that she should never have known.

"She is a lovely woman, my lord king," Amarantha noted when they were alone in the throne room.

"Yes," he agreed. He came to stand in front of her. His hand rose, brushed over the fine silk of silver hair as he stared into her pale eyes. "Not as lovely as you, Am. None could be as beautiful as you."

"Iphicles," she stepped back, too aware of the rush of heat in her veins. Since childhood his touch had affected her this way; would it never fade?

"I am here because of your son, not to dishonor this wife, as I did Automedusa."

Iphicles laughter was bitter, and it was twinned within Amarantha. They had spent a lifetime in love, and apart.

"If anyone dishonored Iolaus' mother, Am, it was me," he murmured. "The day I married her, instead of you."

"These are things we should leave behind us, Iphicles," she replied. "The past is gone, and we are bound by choices that were made long ago."

"Is that why you serve Ares?"

She shuddered. Heracles had told him after all.

"Yes," she nodded, reluctantly. "I serve him with my life. As I am bound to do."

"You were right, then," he spat. "I should have taken you with me when I chased Melaneus halfway across Greece to avenge the attacks on my kingdoms. Ares' protégé would have been a suitable opponent for those bloodthirsty savages!"

She winced at the loathing in his emotion roughened voice. His love, had it ever been there, was rapidly changing to hatred now that they faced each other again.

"When I was with you, Iphicles, I did not know it was the War God I served," she said softly. In spite of the knowledge that it would change nothing, she wanted him to understand what her life had become. Why she had been forced to leave him.

He didn't believe her, and it was evident in the scorn that contorted his handsome features into a mask of distaste.

"When you finally came to my bed," he snarled, "was it Ares you made love with in your heart, Am?"

"No!" Her composure crumbled instantly, and she lashed out at him in her anger. "I was honest with you, my king. About everything. Ares is my master, but he has never been my lover!"

"Even now?"

"Yes!" she retorted. "Though it is no more your right to ask now than it was then."

"It's been my right since that day when you were five years old and a frightened girl with no one to defend her. I loved you then for the spirit that serves your mentor in spite of me."

"Why does Iolaus want to see me, Iphicles?" she asked, hoping he would accept the change of conversation. "Heracles said you were going to war again. Is it that?"

Iphicles' expression was brooding, introspective. He nodded eventually.

"He's afraid."

"Who are you—" She held up her hands, palms facing outward, and shook her head. "No," she whispered. "This is not my war."

"Heracles will battle Eleius, and I have sworn to be with him when he does so."

"You intend to fight the son of a God?" she gasped. "Iphicles, no! Please?"

He smiled, and again there was no warmth in the change of emotion on his face.

"Amarantha!"

She continued to hold Iphicles' dark eyes for another second, then turned to the excited voice. Her eyes widened in surprise when Iolaus finished the short run that would bring him to them; he embraced her, and she was forced to concede that the child she'd left was very nearly a man now. She held him at arm's length and stared. Like his father, he was a strikingly attractive man, but in a way very unlike Iphicles. Where the former king was dark eyed and dark haired, Iolaus was sun-bleached blond, and his large blue eyes were filled with laughter and joy.

"You have grown, my Prince," she said around a huge grin. He hugged her again, and kissed her temple. It was easy, he was almost her height.

"I'll leave you to entertain your guest, Iolaus."

"Thank you, Father," he answered, seemingly unaware of the irony in Iphicles' rich voice. "Let's go into the gardens," he said, leading her in the opposite direction to his father's exit from the room.

"You're wearing it again," Iolaus pointed at the pendant when they were seated at the farthest end of the grounds. "I've often wondered why it was so special to you."

"Your father gave it to me before they left Tiryns," she told him. "I was heartbroken. Iphicles told me that as long as I wore it, it would mean we would find each other again."

Iolaus accepted the words in his thoughtful way.

"It must have been hard for you to give it to me."

"No," she smiled and held his hand in hers. "Your father is the bond that joins us, Iolaus."

"You shouldn't have left him, Amarantha," Iolaus said quietly. "He needed you." He laughed a little, sadness in the sound. "He still does."

"Iphicles has never needed me, Iolaus," she denied.

The boy's eyes were those of age and wisdom when he held her gaze, and anger had crept in to cool the warmth of seeing her again.

"I don't remember you being blind, nor stupid," he remarked with deceptive casualness.

"Then your memory serves you well, my prince," she answered with acerbic sweetness.

"He'll die if he goes to war again," Iolaus snapped, rising fury suffusing his features. "Doesn't that bother you!?"

Amarantha sought for patience, understanding why he spoke so rashly. Her fear was as great as the dread that tormented Iphicles' son; another bond that went beyond their love for each other.

"Your father is more precious to me than my own life, Iolaus," she said with forced calm. "But there are things which he accepts that you cannot know."

"Why?" he demanded harshly, tears and anger roughening his child's voice to a distant echo of his father's. "I asked you to come here because I believed you when you said you would grant any service I required of you. Was that a lie, too, Amarantha? Like the one you gave my father when you promised you would stay here while he was gone all those years ago?"

"I stayed until I could do nothing but honor the man who bought me as a slave when you were a child," she retorted. "Does that make my apparent betrayals easier for you to accept, young prince? Is my shame the balm your heart needs?"

"You offered my father your oath, knowing you would be forced to betray it for someone else?"

His tone was one of ridicule, derisive and enraged in equal measure. Amarantha flinched inwardly against the backlash of his revulsion.

"Will you die for him, Amarantha? Did you make this master of yours that promise, as well?"

"Do not push me, Iolaus," she whispered, shocked by how deeply sincere her thinly veiled threat truly was.

"Leave, Amarantha," he ordered coldly. "You don't belong here. You never really did."

Before she could speak further, Iolaus walked away from her. He didn't look back.

ϓ ϓ ϓ

"You're still here."

Iphicles' voice held surprise, and she turned to watch him complete the walk to where she sat. The sun was riding low in the evening sky, painting the sweeping vista in vivid, glorious hues of fire and gold. Blue was receding, inexorably smothered by the deeper shades of encroaching nightfall.

"He ordered me to leave," she smiled a little, and forced her gaze from the tapestry of the sky, turning to face Corinth's former king when he sat next to her. "To not come back."

"He's angry," Iphicles shrugged mildly, unconcerned. "Once he has time to think, he'll know you have never betrayed us, Am."

"He was right about one thing, my king," she murmured whimsically. "I should never have come to Corinth."

There was a hint of anger glittering in Iphicles' eyes for an instant, then it vanished, replaced by weariness.

"Why did you come back, Am?" he questioned, looking outward at the panorama of fiery streaks that slashed the sky and crept over the expanse of the Gulf. "Really?" he added, again turning to meet her intent, pale eyes. She was a ghost-like silhouette in the blaze of the sunset, silver and white amid the flames; frost in the midst of an inferno of color.

"You have always known the answers to those questions, Iphicles," she smiled, expression self-deprecating. "Why humiliate me further by making me speak of things that it has never been possible for me to hope for?"

"Why would you think that?" he wondered, dark eyes fathomless in the emerging twilight. "How can you believe that I never shared your love?" He paused, then smiled with ironic whimsy. "How can you not remember the words we spoke the last night we were together?"

Amarantha's heartbeat quickened, and with determined will she forced its pace to slow. She looked at the plum-colored sky, watched the thickening gray shadows that would soon give way to blackness.

"You married again," she observed, keeping her voice carefully neutral. "Iolaus is angry about that. Angry with me."

Iphicles nodded.

"He doesn't understand the politics of court. He's a boy who wants a mother he can love. The mother he has wanted from his childhood."

"And what of his father? What does he want?"

"What he cannot have it would seem."

She heard the subtle resonance of his tone as he revealed a part of his spirit that she had never glimpsed before.

"What *do* you want, Iphicles?" she asked, and reached to touch his face, to make him meet her gaze as she waited for a reply that might cost her her soul, as well as her heart.

"I want you to be with me," he smiled. "I want you in my bed tonight, because I won't be returning to Corinth again."

Cold horror froze her and she stared at him, her eyes
memorizing beloved features as she accepted his truth.
Somewhere inside her, Amarantha knew he had seen his
death, and had accepted it. She could not. Would not.

"Let me go with you, Iphicles?" she requested, knowing
even as she spoke that he would deny her request, and she
had no true freedom to make it.

He shook his head.

"This isn't your fight, Am," he whispered. "And I don't
think it's your destiny to die with me."

In spite of the turmoil his words stirred, she heard a well-
known voice inside her head, taunting, reminding her that
this, too, was truth; *I'm your Fate...*

"Your wife—"

It was an afterthought. Again.

Iphicles laughed, the sound self-mocking and bitter. He
looked closely at her for a moment, then drew her near.
His hands raked the pale, silvery-white fall of her hair and
Amarantha's arms wrapped around him as his mouth
closed over hers with a passion unlike anything she'd ever
felt in him.

A short distance away, hidden in the growing thickness
of gloom, Ares raged as she succumbed to the mortal King's
desire. Her voice haunted him as he vanished, the words
of love for another cutting more deeply than the God would
have believed possible.

ϒ ϒ ϒ

Against her sincere intention to leave, Amarantha stayed
in Corinth. Iolaus had avoided her for the first weeks, then,
slowly, he began to seek her company. Heracles had not
returned, and the boy missed him greatly. He'd been traveling with his uncle, when Iphicles and Heracles had felt
it reasonably safe for him to do so. This had been a difficult
parting for the young man and his father; as if both sensed
it would be the last time they saw each other. Amarantha
had hovered uncertainly in the background, fully aware
of Tisiphania's anger at her presence in the city; in the palace

that had been a home-like place for Amarantha long before Iphicles had married Creon's youngest daughter.

Now, months after the army had departed, Amarantha walked the palace parapets, anxiety and fear choking her. She caught sight of the messenger long before the guard at the gate. Dread kept her silent as she sought composure.

Amarantha was in the throne room when King Creon accepted the herald.

Iolaus noted her tense stance the moment he entered, and came to her side.

"You know already what he'll say."

She shook her head.

"Look at me, Am?" he asked.

Iolaus had rarely used the diminution of her name, it had been his father's way of address; that he used it now made her heart thud wildly within her. She reached for his hand, clutched it tightly and closed her eyes.

The herald began to deliver his news.

The room faded, and blackness swept her into an abyss of terror...

ϓ ϓ ϓ

"Amarantha!"

Iolaus' voice finally penetrated the wall of nothingness that held her captive. Amarantha unwillingly opened her eyes and stared in confusion.

"Thank the Gods!" Iolaus breathed in relief.

"What happened?" she asked, making her tone even and steady with decided effort of will.

"You fainted when the message was presented," he replied uneasily.

"Message?"

"Father's been injured," Iolaus told her. "Heracles sent word."

"Where is he?"

"Moving on to—"

"Iphicles!" she interrupted curtly.

"Pheneüs."

She nodded.

"I will leave now," she asserted softly.

"It's nearly dark," the young man objected. "Wait until morning. I want to go with you."

"Where is his wife?"

"With her mother," he answered with obvious disdain.

"You cannot go with me, Iolaus," she said reluctantly. "If there is danger in Pheneüs, Iphicles would never forgive me for bringing you there."

"This is not your decision to make, Amarantha," he stated intractably. "Nor is it my father's. I *will* go, with you, or not."

"No!" she insisted sharply.

"Why?!"

"I will not permit this, Iolaus," she said, her quiet voice strengthened by the determination she felt. "Iphicles entrusted me with your life. I am not going to betray that oath. To ensure your safety for him, you are staying in Corinth. I will send word to you, as soon as I know he is alive and can return here." When it looked as though he'd argue further, Amarantha drew him close to her in the wide bed, hugging him tightly. "I will bring him back to you, Iolaus," she vowed. "If there is any way, I will bring him home to you."

"But you won't stay with us."

She heard the lack of hope in his tone, and tears faded the room into a haze of wispy clouds. Within the wash of distortion, Ares glared back at her.

"If I could choose..."

"Never mind, Am," Iolaus whispered, pulling out of the embrace. "Do what you have to do."

She shuddered, heart racing despite the weight of trepidation that settled over her limbs. He left the room without looking back, and she knew it would be many years before they would look upon each other again.

ϒ ϒ ϒ

"You will *do* nothing, Amarantha."

She dismounted and walked to meet him.

"I thought you would be waiting," she remarked dryly. "You seem to enjoy standing between me and the promises that bind me."

"Your only obligation is to me!"

He was enraged, and a tremor of honest fear began to snake along the curve of her spine. An insidious, serpentine cold that would quickly mutate into submission if she allowed him to frighten her completely.

"You know that is not so."

Ares' handsome features contorted with wrath and he strode toward her, stopping only when they were nose to nose.

"You left my temple with Heracles!" he charged viciously. "Spent weeks returning to Corinth. For a mortal king who—"

She stepped back, heartbeat roaring in her ears.

"What are you not telling me, Ares?" she implored, no longer concerned about provoking him further. "What do you know of Iphicles?"

He laughed.

"You're not in a position to demand answers from me, little one," he said with subtle insinuation.

Amarantha's hand rose, closed over the hilt of her sword and drew it from the scabbard at her back. She faced him, both hands gripping the weapon as she poised for a battle that would, without doubt, end in her death.

"I do demand an answer this time, War God," she spat in fury. "And you will give it, or destroy me utterly. It matters not."

"You'd die for him?" Ares mocked. "How absurd. I doubt he'd make the sacrifice so willingly for you."

"I do not ask him to," she snarled, then lunged at him.

Laughing, Ares' great sword appeared in his hand and he easily deflected her wild swing.

"If you're going to insist on dying, Amarantha," he taunted. "Do it with some of the style I taught you."

The battle went on for nearly an hour; during that time Ares might have killed her several times. Instead, he enjoyed the exchange, reveled in the skill that she exhibited,

as much as the passion with which she fought. That passion
would one day be given to his desires; and that knowledge kept his hand from dispensing the fatal strike that
would have ended their impasse.

When she was on her knees, gasping and beaten, Ares
knelt in front of her. He touched her chin, forced her eyes
to meet his.

"It means so much, to know he lives?"

Amid the amusement, she heard the puzzlement.

She nodded.

"Yes," she finally managed in a whisper.

Ares measured her with thoughtful eyes for several
indeterminate minutes, then he shrugged.

"Go to Pheneüs, Amarantha," he decreed. "Finish this,
and return to Thrace."

The words had barely been voiced when he vanished.

ϒ ϒ ϒ

The spires of the Royal House of Pheneüs loomed in
the distance long days after her duel with Ares on the
outskirts of Corinth. Amarantha felt the weight on her heart
grow more oppressive, and for several minutes she was
paralyzed with grief. Somewhere inside her soul, she knew
she'd arrived too late.

Furey pranced impatiently beneath her, whinnying
softly in response to the tension in her rider. Amarantha
stroked the soft white mane and cooed soothing sounds.

"Ares, you knew what I would find here," she whispered to the unnatural stillness that surrounded her on the
road. Nothing moved, despite the relatively early hour.
No laughter, nor voice reached her ears. Even the wild-
life was quiet; as though an entire city mourned.

Pushing her mind away from that unthinkable thought,
she forced the mare back into motion. It took only a few
minutes for Furey to pick up speed, and they raced toward
the city; on a course that would lead her into the palace.

The castle gates were open when she flew through them
and reined in the horse, stirring a cloud of dust in the center
of the courtyard. Amarantha slid from Furey's back and

ran for the guards at the entrance. They watched her, wary and hesitant. The last time she'd been in Pheneüs the city had branded her a madwoman. The two who blocked her passage now had apparently heard those stories.

"I want to see Zetes," she demanded.

"Who—?"

"Tell him it is Amarantha!" she snapped angrily.

The delay was stretching her already overwrought nerves to the breaking point. An eternity of minutes later, the Captain himself opened the palace doors and beckoned her in.

"Where is Iphicles?" she asked without preamble.

Zetes flinched, and she grabbed his arms and repeated the query, her voice rising to a shrillness that it never held.

"The King died two nights past, Lady," he answered, his eyes kind and his voice low with compassion.

"No..." Amarantha backed away and turned, eyes tightly shut as she tried to accept the news. The blackness stopped the wild spin of the room, but the crushing waves of confused grief increased in speed and force.

"How?" She whirled around again, unsurprised to see that Zetes had not moved. "Heracles said he was wounded. He did not say that Iphicles was near death."

The Captain looked more miserable than she felt, if that were possible.

"Zetes, what has happened here?" She resisted the need to scream, and kept her tone even.

"King Iphicles died at the hand of an assassin, Lady Amarantha," he finally told her.

Madness was creeping into her mind, rapidly. Her body was detached from the process, barely shaking against the assault that was threatening to destroy her heart and spirit.

"Assassin," she murmured stupidly, her sluggish mental processes having trouble with the idea even as her hand reached for the comfortable presence of her sword.

"Have you found him?"

Zetes nodded.

"He escaped the dungeons less than an hour ago," the Captain supplied reluctantly.

"Escaped?" she echoed. "How could he escape? Why was he not executed immediately?!" This time her voice was a shout, a blistering snarl of rage and condemnation.

"The king said you would come," Zetes replied, nonplussed by her fury. "When he was killed, it seemed logical to await your arrival."

"Logical?" She laughed, unable to stop the bitter spurt of sound. "You have witnessed how logical my justice is when Iphicles is threatened, Zetes. Why did you not simply destroy this man?"

"It was not my place to judge and execute him," the Captain stated quietly. "That task falls to the God of War's justice. To you."

Startled by his words, and ill at ease with their unwanted responsibility, Amarantha walked a few steps away from him. She sought Ares' discipline and control, forced it into her mind, determined to face this loss with some small measure of dignity.

"Where is my king, Zetes?" she asked a long while later, finally able to look him squarely in the eyes again.

"It would be my honor to take you to his tomb, Lady." The Captain bowed and gestured for her to follow him.

She took a few steps, then shook her head.

"I want to see his chambers first," she said quietly.

Again, the captain bowed, and led her to the wing that had been Iphicles' private quarters when in Pheneüs.

Alone in the rooms, Amarantha walked the stone floors, her fingers brushing over each object she encountered as she relived the short time they had truly been together. Her entire life had been devoted to Iphicles, long before either of them knew what it would cost them. As children they'd been friends, as adults, lovers doomed to be apart.

She leaned on the edge of the window and looked outward, seeing nothing. It would be dark soon; the shadows of encroaching night were already gathering in the distance. She sighed heavily and looked around again. She went to the heavy wooden chest that contained the king's wardrobe. She opened it and gazed, startled to spot a familiar shade of palest gray amid the earthy colors he had always worn. She reached into the chest and withdrew the silken length of the dress given to her by Automedusa so many years ago. Tears blurred her vision and she clutched the dress for a long time before she rose and stripped off the leather and armor she wore. When she was bathed and changed, she left the king's bedroom and went in search of his Captain.

It was a brief meeting she held, and her orders were simple: find the assassin, at all costs, and bring him to the palace to face her.

No one questioned her authority, nor her intent.

A short while later she stood outside the tomb. Zetes left her, ordering the Honor Guards to give her solitude. They were dismissed by her before she entered.

Standing inside the shadowy, silent crypt, Amarantha dared not give her resurging tears release. If she permitted that outpouring, it might never end. Clenching her teeth, and making her body obey her will, she walked to the altar.

Candles had been lit, hundreds of them. Each person who visited had expanded the flame of warmth by one light; she lit the taper that had been placed near the king's head.

"Iphicles..."

She touched his hair, bent to kiss his chill forehead. He was even more handsome in death than he had been in life; smooth, even features at peace for the first time in much too long.

"There are so many things I would have told you, my king," she murmured, eyes awash with tears, vision blurred to watery haze. "I promised Iolaus I would bring you home to him, Iphicles."

"So do it!"

The voice was that of a stranger, and Amarantha wasn't truly certain she'd heard it.

"Drag your precious king's body back to his wife! If you live long enough!"

She was slow, her reflexes blunted by the agony of her loss. Amarantha cried out when the sword bit into her flesh, carving a wound that ran across her unprotected midriff as she turned to face the intruder.

She fell to her knees, then rolled away, gasping as she fought past pain to regain her wits and agility. She rose, leapt for the altar to grab Iphicles' sword where it lay on his chest, grasped lightly in lifeless hands. Her hand closed on the hilt and she stumbled again, almost losing consciousness as pain tore a path through her body. She could feel blood flowing, but from a distance.

"Who are you?"

The man before her was young, barely into his twenties; but there was a hatred in his face that spoke of long nurturing. He was a stranger.

"Pendarus," he mocked. "Slayer of a god's brother it would seem."

The maddened rage erupted inside her, pushed her beyond pain and, perhaps, sanity. She attacked.

The clash of swords echoed eerily in the stillness of the shrine to the monarch of Pheneüs. Pendarus had waited and trained for this confrontation, his skill fueled by his fostered rage. Amarantha was dulled by grief, and her body slowed by the steady loss of blood that streamed from her side.

"Why?!" she shrieked. "Iphicles was your king."

"And you loved him," the man spat with contempt. "That's why he died. Because *you* loved him."

She dodged a parry and placed the altar between them.

"I do not understand."

"You killed my father," Pendarus accused. "I watched you."

"Who was your father?"

"Lyaeus," he shouted. "Iphicles' advisor. Your cherished king left him in charge of this petty little kingdom, and you killed him."

"He betrayed Iphicles!"

"You murdered him," Pendarus ran around the altar and they engaged again. He laughed when she slipped and fell, feet tripping in the gray silk that swirled around her legs. Her sword clattered across the stone floor, and she collapsed suddenly, defeat evident in every aspect of her being.

"Your own death wouldn't have been as painful as knowing you killed the king you adored," Pendarus stated as he stood over her. He raised his weapon and prepared to deliver the fatal strike.

Amarantha closed her eyes and waited.

A scream of agony ripped the air of the mausoleum, and it took a second for her to realize it was not her voice that cried out. She looked, stunned and sickened when she saw Pendarus. He'd been hurled into a wall, his skull split open by the impact.

She raised her eyes and a shaken smile came unbidden to her lips. Ares came and knelt beside her, his expression reflecting more tenderness than he could have possibly known. Amarantha reached up to touch his face.

"Your timing is a little off, my Master," she murmured, tone filled with irony and shudders that revealed a complex multitude of pain and torment.

"On the contrary," he whispered, "it's perfect. I have a proposition for you, Amarantha. And a gift."

She shook her head, and coughed as a spasm of anguish wracked her body with fire.

"Let me die, Ares," she begged, voice rough with the depth of her suffering. "Without him..."

"I once told you that I was your Fate," he reminded her, deliberately ignoring the loss in her pale eyes. "That Fate is tied to all the Gods, Amarantha; not only me. You're to become our Champion."

"That is absurd," she gasped, eyes wide with shock. "The Gods need no one. Especially a mortal woman who is nothing to anyone. A slave!" she spat with contempt.

"I made you a slave because it was the only way I knew to bind you to me," he explained with forced patience. "Now," he continued and offered her his hand, "that bond is going to become what it is meant to be."

She watched, gaze animated with trepidation and fascination as his hand filled with the glowing red-gold substance she recognized from myth and legend — the Ambrosia of the Gods. When he placed it carefully in her palm and closed her fingers around it, she stared in undisguised disbelief.

"Why?"

"To serve you must live," he stated softly. "And live for as long as need be."

"You will grant me immortality?"

He nodded, and waited, prepared to force his will onto her if she continued to deny him. The decision took an eternity as she weighed the scope of this destiny against the torture of living without Iphicles. Ares allowed her the priceless minutes, his shrewd eyes closely measuring the span of life left to her. He had planned this too carefully to let her heart destroy her Fate; but he would grant her the illusion of choice. To a point, only.

When she lifted the god-fired Ambrosia to her lips, he nodded approval.

"Ares..."

The shimmer of fire began to burn within her, growing brighter and hotter with each altered beat of her heart. She cried out as the power of the Ambrosia exploded throughout her, changing the very structure of her being. She spasmed violently, choking on the razor-edged slashes of flame that blistered her from the inside outward.

"No-o-o-o..."

Ares held her as she convulsed, wincing at the intensity of her tortured cries. Mortals were not meant to consume the food of the Gods; but this was the only way to grant her the means to achieve her Fate.

"Amarantha," he whispered her name as she lost consciousness for several seconds. When her eyes snapped open and her back arched against the final assault of the power, he drew her close to his chest.

It took several minutes, but her breaths slowed, and her arms gradually slipped around him, clinging in grief and shock; and renewed life.

The Oracle's prophecy was now fulfilled.

PART TWO

Part Two

CHAPTER EIGHT

The utter stillness that dominated the room was as unnatural as the worldwide scenes of destruction that presently filled the vast wall of monitors. Graphic and eerily silent, each new catastrophe was being dutifully recorded by the single, tireless technician who moved among the myriad electronic equipment in the large, otherwise empty room.

Behind a mirrored wall, the mastermind behind the devastation watched, well pleased with the progress of his devoted subjects. It had taken much less time than he'd anticipated to organize everything. His pupils were zealous in their enthusiasm; the very reason many of them had been chosen for service in his personal legion.

He leaned forward, unable to entirely control his excitement as the signals from Athens began to explode with glorious, cataclysmic beauty. Of the many targets he'd personally selected for this initial demonstration of power, the shrines of Greece were the ones he despised the most. The places he most wanted to see in crumbled ruin and ashes. Obliterated entirely from the landscape and, in time, the collective memories of all those who cherished them.

The Parthenon trembled in the backlash of the charges that had been set close to its back wall. The damage would be devastating. But, the ancient building would not fall yet. He wanted to be in Athens when the final strike was dealt. Then, all the holy places would be eradicated; and the pantheon of archaic Olympian Gods would finally fade as they should have many centuries past. As the greatness of his ancestors had declined throughout the ensuing centuries.

The second assault in Greece came onto the screen and he smiled, satisfaction making him want to laugh as the Areopagus was scarred by fire and countless barrages of automatic weapon fire tearing up the grounds of the sacred hill. He truly hated this place, this site that honored their mighty God of War, and his all too human fall from grace.

He despised them all for their frailties; their less than God-like weaknesses. Ares was among the select group he hated most. Ares, who might have been the greatest of the Olympic consortium. *Might have been*, he mused darkly; if he'd not been possessed of the mindset of a capricious, spoiled child. These spots had been carefully chosen; Athena's Parthenon was a tribute to her logic and beauty, and being a warrior, he was determined to humiliate her as he did her brother.

The end of the millennium was nearing, and all his patience would soon pay off. A new age for a new way of thinking, he intoned silently. Time for the old ways to vanish. He'd spent many years building his base of power, and the time was right at long last.

Pleased, he called the technician to him.

ϒ ϒ ϒ

"Nic, this has to stop!" Alexandra all but shrieked as she paced the small, cramped office in the little shop/museum of antiquities. The shrill of a phone ringing forestalled his response, and she strode to the FAX machine and grabbed the page as it finished printing. She scanned the contents on the sheet and her fury rose further.

"The Areopagus has been desecrated now," she informed her fiance and thrust the page into his hands when he reached for it. "What is going on?" she snarled. "The Vatican's been hit, the Mayan temples, the Inca shrines. All over the world, and all religious targets. They were stopped in Tibet before they could do major damage there," she added, tone unconsciously accusatory. "I don't even want to think what the Valley of the Gods may look like by this time," she muttered furiously.

"We're doing our best to contain this madness, Alex," he snarled, his glare easily as dark and enraged as hers when she stared back at him. "So far we've picked up a dozen or more of the people responsible, but not one of them is willing to tell us what this is all about."

"It's about the Gods," she snapped. "Our history!"

"It's not only our history that is being threatened," he reminded her. His cell phone rang, and he turned his back to her as he listened. Sighing heavily moments later, he went to her side and kissed her quickly. "I have to go to the station," he told her. "They've picked up a large group, all armed to the teeth."

She nodded, distracted.

"I'm going to see Andrei," she told him as she grabbed her coat from the back of a chair.

"I'll drop you off," he offered, inwardly annoyed that she was heading to the Temple of Zeus in the midst of this terrorist lunacy, instead of home to their apartment. He also knew it would be futile to argue with her on this point; she was as dedicated to her work as he was to his, and this was violating everything she deemed sacred.

ϓ ϓ ϓ

"Andrei," she went to the old man and embraced him, kissing his weathered cheek before leading him to a seat within the Temple. He was growing frail, and his hair, always thick, snowy white, was becoming dull and fading, a visible reminder that his life was slowly drawing to a close, as well. That was something she was not prepared to consider, the loss would be too great. "I came as soon as I was able," she said, voice shaken and hoarse.

"I know, Alexa," he smiled warmly, his entire manner reassuring despite the gravity of the situation. "The destruction has begun, hasn't it?"

She nodded, visibly worried. She looked around her, drinking in the high stone walls, the ancient tapestries with their vivid depictions of the Olympian Gods and their exploits. Despite the age of this temple, it held a kind of warmth that could never be diminished by time. As if Zeus himself remained present in the very stones that held the temple strong and untouchable. Fires burned in sconces, flickering tongues of flame drawing dancing images on the vaulted ceilings and walls. A hush enshrouded the main area of worship, and she felt the peace of the shrine slowly work its way into her trembling body.

"How long before they come here?" she murmured softly, hating the thought that anyone with such hatred inside them would ever cross the threshold of the glorious temple.

"Soon," he replied, his voice low, but containing surprisingly little fear. "We have been making supplications to the Gods for many months, Alexandra," he continued after a few moments pause. "This is not without warning, though few were willing to heed the signs. The Champion should have been among us by now."

Alex shivered, unable to prevent the icy dread that cringed within her soul each time Andrei mentioned the mysterious defender of Olympus. The terror was without logic, and she resented the depth of fear with which it filled her. She'd heard the stories from her childhood, and it had always been this way; a myth that made her shake with apprehension.

"Perhaps the Champion has never been real, Andrei," she suggested, ignoring the derisive laughter that whispered in her head when she spoke the words. "We certainly can't depend on a legend to help us."

The old man smiled, kindness and gentle mockery in his fading eyes.

"A legend will be all that *can* save our past, child," he assured. "The Gods have long been silent, but they still see and hear all that we do. The Champion will return."

"It's only a matter of time before they come here, Andrei," she said, abject misery in her expression and her voice. "What threat is the past to whoever is doing this?" she added, musing more to herself than asking for any wisdom her father's friend might have to offer.

"Fear is the motive," Andrei said, smiling when her startled gaze met his again. "Many people fear what they cannot understand, and therefore it must be destroyed. Alexandra, this Temple *will* be targeted, you do know that?"

"Yes," she murmured. "But will they find what you have guarded for so long?"

Andrei shook his head.

"Few people even suspect our secret, Alexa," he said softly. "Your father knew, and he believed as we do, that this service is our sacred trust. But, they will come. And, if they are armed with ancient knowledge, they will want the secret of Zeus' temple."

"That's what I fear," she answered reluctantly. "I don't know myself what the secret is, but my father often said it was a charge that would exact an honorable death from any who died in service to the Gods."

Andrei nodded.

"I'll ask Nic to see that a unit is always close, Andrei," she told the old man. "I think he knows, too, that it's only a matter of time before they strike here."

"Thank you," Andrei rose and tugged her gently to her feet. They walked toward the exit and the old man kissed her cheek. "Rest easy, my Alexa," he whispered close to her ear. "All will be as it is meant to be. Trust in the Gods as I do, and they will be with us."

She looked into his aged face and felt a sudden, deep rush of affection for him. Andrei was one of the few people who had truly understood her father's devotion to the Old Ones, as they often called them. Since Jason Christophi's death, Andrei had been a solid and firm anchor in the young woman's life, and her staunchest supporter as she did all she could to keep their history alive and an active part of school curriculums.

She said good-night to the old priest and drove home to her apartment in thoughtful distraction.

ϒ ϒ ϒ

"Have the police discovered who's behind the destruction, Nic?" she asked when he finally made it home late into the night. The two bedroom apartment was in near darkness, with only the streetlights of downtown Athens filtering through the sheer curtains to bathe the living room in silvery shades. Books lined one wall, carefully arranged by their owner, Alexandra. Nic's prized photographic art adorned the walls, at odds with ancient prints of Gods and myths, yet complementary at the same time. The furniture was dark, rich wood, well worn and comfortable. They'd spent over five years together, and the past three had been shared in this apartment. It reflected two distinctive personalities, and suited both. Nic walked through the room and into their bedroom. Alex followed him a moment later.

Once he'd gone through the ritual of storing his gun, he tossed his lightweight sweater into a chair and sat on the edge of the bed to look at her. She was beautiful, he thought absently. Alexandra had long, dark hair, and eyes that stole a man's soul the moment she held his gaze with hers. She was sensual and exotic, curvaceous and as brilliant in mind as she was lovely of body. Nickolas Stefanos had adored her since they were children, and he had pursued her into adulthood with a passion that often amused her, and never failed to inspire a totally reciprocated love. The look in her eyes now was not adoration, but sadness and very real confusion.

"We're working on it, Alex," he admitted with a weary sigh. "I've been questioning the men we picked up in various parts of the city, but it's going to take time to coordinate this. There's more than a single division involved in the investigation. We're setting up a task force unit to work with INTERPOL, since this is obviously an international threat."

In spite of her urge to shout at him, Alexandra remained calm and nodded.

"I'm afraid, Nickolas," she said quietly. "Andrei, and people like him, will be in danger once these lunatics have finished destroying the temples and monuments."

"There's been no indication that..." He stopped speaking when her eyes flared with annoyance. She was right, and inside, he knew it. First the old places, then the people who preserved them and revered all they stood for. Athens was an ancient city, with a long memory; there'd be many among the populace who would stand against whatever this terrorist group wanted. Including his beautiful and cherished fianceé.

"I'm going to Delphi in the morning, Nic," she decided. "I'll be gone a day or two. I want to do some research, and to see how bad the damage to the Shrine is."

"I can't talk you out of this, can I?" he asked, knowing it was useless, needing to at least make an attempt to stop her.

She smiled and reached across the bed to touch his cheek.

"No, you can't," she breathed softly. "But you can get into bed and make love to me."

He pulled her close, hugging her tightly.

"I love you, Alex," he murmured next to her ear.

ϓ ϓ ϓ

Alexandra's first stop was the modern village of Delphi. She'd been here often, but never with the sense of urgency and dread that had driven her on the journey this time. The mountains loomed distant and majestic, and the rich green landscape was a jewel as breathtaking as any the Gods had ever created. She left a note for an old friend, Adara, when she discovered the other woman's small home was empty, then she decided it was time to walk the Sacred Way.

The Museum was the first building she chose to enter on the trail that would eventually take her to the Sanctuary of Apollo. She lingered in the late autumn sunshine, only dimly aware of the many people who had come to view the damage. Like those around her, she was there to look, to reluctantly see the new scars on the ancient stone of the building. Slowly, she went inside. As always, the treasures lifted her heart, and she walked peacefully, virtually alone in the place despite the crowds of people milling outside. She stood for a long time, eyes caressing the ageless copy of the Sacred Stone, reaching on some level for answers that she knew would never be given. A short while later she visited the Sphinx of the Naxians, the statue of Antinoüs, the statue of Agias, and the many other wonders within the timeless museum. Each step in the archaic atmosphere filled her with familiar hope, and the serenity that she had only ever found in the vast and rich history of her country.

She strolled to the Anteroom at the top of the stairs and gazed upon the Delphic Omphalos, (the center of the world). She let her fingers brush the relief decoration on it, and a tremor of ice kissed her spine. She pulled her hand back abruptly and stared, filled suddenly with uncertainty and profound fear. Still shaking inwardly, she left the Anteroom and walked the short corridor which led to a room behind the stairs. Here, the central showcases exhibited the splendid Bronzes of different periods from the eighth to the fourth centuries BC. Here also were the mythical Sirens, and she looked at them as though seeing them for the first time.

She'd been to Delphi on more occasions than she could remember, yet something *was* different this time. Alexandra left the Museum, and stared at the expansive vista, appreciating anew the dazzling beauty before her. The city of Delphi and the Sanctuary were built on the southern slopes of Parnassus, in a landscape of indescribable beauty. She had often thought this the single most spectacular tableau in Greece, and that reflection again came into her mind and stayed there.

She shook off the distracting thoughts and emotions that were plaguing her today, and moved onward. The theater, containing five thousand seats, was northwest of the temple, and she chose that direction. It was here that she found more devastation. Standing within the center stage, looking upward on the rows of stone seating, she could see where the guardians of Delphi's treasures had fought to put out fires and conceal the abrasions left by modern weaponry. White stone was now blackened by fire and gouged with random destruction.

Sickened, she decided to move onward to the Castilian Spring, then complete her visit with a stop at Apollo's Temple. As with the Theater, the Spring showed the signs of recent abuse. She knelt beside the trickle of water and bathed her face, aware that she was being watched by an invisible presence, one that had been with her since she'd begun her journey into the past. Memory reminded her that this was the place where Pythia washed before speaking her prophecies.

Unsettled still, Alexandra's look wandered idly as she walked into what yet stood of the Sanctuary. Tall, symmetrical columns in the center of the circular place of worship rose before her, their charred surfaces mute testimony to all that had occurred. Slipping past the police lines that had been placed, she went to kneel at the remains of the altar. Without realizing what was happening, she discovered with some surprise that she'd begun crying, and the tears continued to rain tracks along her cheeks as she asked for knowledge — for some hope that they could defeat the derangement that threatened everything she cherished so dearly.

The Champion will return...

Alexandra's head snapped up abruptly as the whisper caressed her mind. She didn't know the voice, despite the words being those Andrei had spoken the previous night. Her eyes rose to the towering heights of the columns that had survived the ravages of time and change wrought by the passing centuries.

"Apollo?"

She winced at the sound of her own voice, at the absurdity of her involuntary supplication. She shivered, chilled to the bone. Seconds later she distinctly heard a soft, barely perceptible trill of laughter deep in her mind and soul.

Then the sunlit day was swallowed by blackness...

Light returned gradually, as though she fought her way through a dense fog. When she was able to clearly discern her surroundings, Alexandra shrieked in silent terror. Before her, the splendor of Delphi was laid out in exquisite wholeness. Walking among the ruins were two figures, and as they passed, she felt herself drawn after them, as if a cord had been tossed around her waist and now compelled her to follow where they would lead. She tried to call out, but she had no voice, only the sense of what was granted to her in this reflected world.

"Ares, Beloved, why are we here?"

Alexandra shuddered at the soft, feminine voice, at the hint of uncertainty that was so evident in it. She allowed herself to drink in the vision the couple presented, awed in spite of her fright. Ares, God of War... He was as handsome and fierce as the legends said, and the woman at his side was a stark contrast to his darkness. Pale, white haired, and fair-skinned, she looked almost fragile walking next to his imposing stature.

"Apollo seldom wants to see me, Little One," Ares replied, his voice a sensuous rumble of sound that caressed Alexandra as much as it obviously affected his companion. "It must be important. He asked me to bring you."

"Apollo likes me even less than he does you, my Master," she murmured, turning suddenly and peering directly at Alexandra. The young anthropologist and historian froze, her breath caught in her throat. She was stunned in the next heartbeat to realize she was not visible to the couple. She could not be seen by a God and his companion. As her mind accepted the impossible knowledge, they moved on, with her trailing them against her will.

"He was insistent that you attend, Amarantha," Ares made the statement with real amusement as he considered her annoyance at the surprising announcement. "He tells me Pythia has seen an event which will affect us both."

Amarantha was no longer listening, and Alexandra's heart seemed to be exploding within her as the other woman walked away from the War God and strode toward her. Fear rose in Alexandra's throat, a tangible element that would choke the life from her at any second, she knew. Mere inches from her, the tall, graceful woman stopped and peered intently at her. Their eyes were locked, and Alexandra shuddered at the silver tongues of flame that rose in the pale greyness of the stare that bored into her. Yet, miraculously, nothing occurred.

"Amarantha!"

Ares' sharp voice demanded compliance, and with a final, puzzled look, the white-haired wraith turned and walked away from her...

Alexandra heard voices around her and fought back the irrational desire to scream her terror. It faded moments later when a cool, firm hand touched her forehead and a smooth, lightly accented voice urged her to open her eyes.

Her body obeyed, despite her mind's lethargy in understanding. She blinked rapidly, blinded by the radiance
of sunlight pouring down on her. The sun was blocked
in the next instant and she saw the face of the man who
had touched her.

"I'm Doctor Len Callagher," he smiled and assisted
her to her feet. "You fainted, I'm afraid," he went on
consolingly. "It must be the heat."

"Yes," she agreed, and tried to summon a smile for the
man's well-intentioned help. "I don't remember ever
fainting before," she added shakily. Her rescuer was a
middle-aged man, with gray-streaked sand colored hair,
his blue eyes were friendly and compassionate, with a
detailed network of fine lines radiating outward from their
corners. He was tanned, trim, and wearing light-weight
clothes. She would have pegged him as English even if
he hadn't spoken.

"Perhaps lunch and a cool drink would restore your
strength, Miss...?"

"Christophi," she supplied. "Alexandra Christophi.
Thank you for your concern, Doctor Callagher, but I think
I'll be fine. Please, go on with your visit to the site," she
suggested, spotting the group of tourists who watched
and waited a short distance from their position near the
altar.

"Are you certain?" he asked, his worry genuine.

"Yes, very certain," she smiled, feeling slightly more
able to walk. "I have been here many times, and it is a
place you shouldn't miss, truly. Again, my thanks for your
assistance, Doctor."

He nodded, and went to rejoin his group.

When they had moved on, Alex looked upward to the
columns of the Sanctuary.

"Have you spoken to me this day?" she asked of the
phantom Gods of Olympus.

Her knees knocked together again when laughter
answered her query; deep, sensual, mocking laughter,
a ripple of sensation that vibrated with macabre amusement.

She fled the Sanctuary, and headed for Adara's home in the city/village of modern Delphi. She'd had enough of the past for one day.

CHAPTER NINE

Alexandra had been back in Athens less than two hours when she headed for the Temple of Zeus. Andrei dismissed the young men and women he instructed each afternoon, and invited her to join him for afternoon tea in his private quarters within the temple. Safely within the old and comfortable rooms, Alexandra relaxed slightly. She loved this place, and felt safe with the old man and his beliefs. Her father had spent many hours here, and she sometimes felt his presence as acutely as Andrei's when they would sit before the fire and talk well into the night.

"You have news," the priest observed with a smile, once she'd curled into a chair and was watching him go through the ritual of making her favorite herbal tea.

She laughed gently.

"You know me very well, Andrei," she chided. "Much better than Nic does sometimes," she concluded wistfully.

"Nic is young, Alexa," Andrei chuckled. "He is a man in love, and can rarely see past that emotion to the soul he cherishes so."

She looked doubtful, but chose to remain quiet on the point.

"I've been to Delphi," she told the old man when he had brought the tea and they were both seated, Andrei across from her in a second worn armchair. He nodded and she went on quickly. "While I was in the Sanctuary, I asked for help, Andrei, and..." She dragged in a deep breath, calmed the tempest of conflict within her, and met his suddenly shrewd eyes. "I heard something," she whispered, afraid even now to give the words voice. "And I felt someone with me during the entire walk."

The old man nodded slowly.

"And this has not happened before," he mused, knowing the answer, but seeking her response anyway. When she swallowed hard and clasped her hands together around her teacup, he reached across to place his aged fingers over hers. "That is a very good omen, Alexandra," he assured her. "Do not fear it."

"I've always been frightened of anything related to Ares' Champion, Andrei," she confessed in a hushed tone. "Each time I encountered references to what must have been her presence, it's terrified me. I can't help it," she finished with a shudder.

"Ares is not remembered for his wisdom," Andrei noted with a wry irony that made her smile return just a little. "But in choosing to listen to the Oracle, He insured that we would always have hope of retaining our heritage and historical richness. Few even know of His foresight."

"He's a War God," she murmured. "His Champion must also be as cruel and single-minded as the God she's served throughout the centuries. If she comes among us, Andrei," Alexandra lifted her uneasy gaze to his, and took a deep, steadying breath. "If she comes, she may be no better than those we fight." She trembled as her voice trailed off, emotions warring within her as she tried to soothe fear and accept what she felt innately was a betrayal of her personal beliefs. She didn't tell him that she thought she might have actually seen both the God and his servant that afternoon.

"We need her," Andrei finally spoke after a lengthy hesitation. "There is no one else, Alexa," he whispered, sharing some of her doubts, in spite of a lifetime of belief. "We must trust the Gods, and the One they chose so long ago."

Alexandra's smile was bitter, and she shook her head.

"It would have been much easier to have faith in some-one chosen by Athena, old friend. Ares has always been given to us as a God men fear, and I can't help but believe there is good reason for that fear."

"And that is not for us to judge, is it?" There was mild reproach in his age-roughened voice, and Alexandra's eyes darted from his, her shoulders rigid with tension.

"What are you not speaking, my Alexa?" Andrei prodded gently when the silence lengthened.

She trembled violently and he put aside his cup, rose, and stood in front of her, forcing her eyes up when she would have looked anywhere but directly at him.

Alexandra remembered the terror and the pain of that afternoon, and her eyes filled with tears, despite her efforts to stop it. She opened her mouth, sought the simple words that would explain, and felt them stick there. She swallowed hard, and tried again, this time determined to control her body and mind.

"I think I saw them, Andrei," she made the words audible, though barely so. "Ares, and his Champion. He spoke her name. They were going to see Apollo and Pythia." Panic eclipsed reason for several eternal moments, then she turned her eyes away, and in a gasped sob, concluded, "She knew I was there, Andrei. She looked at me, but did not see me!"

When the old priest drew her up into his arms, she clung to him and cried for what felt like days, pouring out her fears and doubts, having them soothed by the man who had taken on the role of a father in recent years. He understood, and she knew, in her soul, that Nic would not even believe her had she the nerve to tell him what had happened in Delphi.

"Will you attend the lecture I'm giving later this week, Andrei?" she eventually asked, once she'd recovered her composure and they could once again talk reasonably about what was happening.

"Yes," he smiled and patted her hand. "Of course, I will."

There was a chirping ring from the depths of her shoulder bag and Andrei rose.

"I will leave you to talk with Nickolas," he said. "I have students waiting."

She nodded, and stood to kiss his cheek.

"I'll call you tomorrow, Andrei," she promised, then flipped open the persistently ringing phone.

ϒ ϒ ϒ

The ancient, hallowed halls of the Temple of Zeus were quiet again, the only sound the low brush of slippered feet moving steadily toward the rear of the old place. Andrei sighed, tired and worried in equal measure. He'd been growing more agitated as the night settled, and knew that he was anticipating the approach of the final minutes of his life, and what might yet unfold within that precious and short span of time.

He didn't have long to wait, which was both blessing and curse.

The first indication of something wrong came in the form of small noises that should not have been heard in the Temple. They were circling, some inner voice told Andrei. Once they'd surveyed the grounds and the temple walls, they began to close on the place, preparing to enter the sacred building.

Muffled voices reached the old man's alert ears, and seconds later the boom of the heavy doors being thrown forcefully open echoed ominously in the quiet. He turned, his body miraculously free of the aches and stiffness of age as he awaited his fate. In the center of the large, golden-lit main chamber of the vast temple, Andrei sat, and watched their advance while he prayed to mighty Zeus that his strength and fortitude would be enough.

They fanned out in military precision, checking corners and columns, speaking softly to each other through head-sets. They were heavily armed, their faces hidden by camouflage and cowls. When they had assured themselves that Andrei was alone in the Temple, another figure entered and approached the waiting priest. His steps were slow and deliberate, designed to invoke fear. This one, Andrei thought, would never understand that the priest was beyond intimidation.

"You've got courage, old man," a low, seductive voice intoned long minutes later.

Andrei remained impassive. Earlier in the evening, obeying instinct, Andrei had sent all the others from the temple, on tasks that were both real and created for the purpose of placing them elsewhere.

"What do you want?" Andrei asked, holding the shadowy gaze of the man before him. Heavily cloaked, his features were veiled in mystery. His voice completed the illusion.

"I think you know what we've come for," the leader purred softly. "It is only a question of time and how much pain you will suffer before you tell me."

"Time is meaningless to me," Andrei stated calmly. "And pain is something with which I have long been acquainted."

"We'll see," noted the absurdly comforting voice. He turned to the waiting team of disciples who'd accompanied him to the Temple. "Take him. Quietly. We can't risk being found."

"Cowards rarely risk discovery," Andrei noted blandly.

His impudence was rewarded immediately when one of the guards slammed a solid blow into the priest's back. He crumpled, moaning softly, and two others stepped forward to lift him and take him from the temple.

ϓ ϓ ϓ

Alexandra glanced at her watch and grimaced. Nic was almost an hour late. She was on the verge of giving up when he walked into the restaurant, his smile apologetic even before he reached the table. He bent to kiss her, then sat across from her.

"Sorry, Alex," he said. "This business with the shrines and temples has everyone up in arms, one way or another."

"Have you found out who's behind it, Nic?" Her tone was even and calm. She laughed a moment later when he stared at her, faint suspicion in his dark eyes. "I'm trying to be reasonable. Isn't that what you want?"

"Yes," he stated. "It's just not what I expected. And, to answer your other question, no, we haven't found a clue as to who is responsible, though we've put people on the streets to see if we can pick up anything that way."

"I hope you can put a stop to this before it gets too far out of control," she mused, her mind still preoccupied with

Andrei's assertion that Ares' Champion would be among
them soon if things were not set right.

"What are you afraid of, Alexandra?"

Startled, she stared at him for a second. He spoke again
before she could form an answer, a denial. He knew her
so well, always had, she realized in that moment. Her
darling Nickolas, the man she'd adored from childhood.
He was, as he had always been, handsome, intelligent, and
so compassionate. His sensitivity to her personal presence
both amazed and humbled her on a regular basis.

"I can see it in your eyes, honey," he told her quietly,
pulling her from the momentary distraction of her whimsy.
"And I think it's more than simply an attack on our history that has you frightened."

"I'm afraid for Andrei," she evaded. "I have a terrible
feeling he's going to die before this is over."

"Are you sure it's not more than that?" he wondered,
still perceiving something she wasn't telling him.

"No," she shook her head, "of course not." She forced
a cheerful smile and reached across the surface of the table
to curl her fingers around his. "Now, why don't we have
a lovely dinner and try to forget this for a few hours?"

Nic thought it a wonderful suggestion, though he
doubted sincerely that it would be off her mind for even
an instant.

ᚷ ᚷ ᚷ

"We can do this in many ways," the leader intoned
quietly. "All of them excruciatingly painful, Priest. You
could make it easier to bear by simply telling me what I
need to know."

Andrei's baleful glare was all the answer he supplied,
and he bit back a scream when yet another blistering blade
seared the flesh of his back. The stench of charred skin and
muscle brought bile into his throat, and he closed his eyes,
his heart imploring the Gods for mercy.

"Since you are such a believer in the old ways, we'll do
what we can to accommodate your faith in ancient practices.

The Gods could be crude, but always effective, don't you think?"

The mockery was lost on the old man, he was battling within himself to stay strong and remain silent in the face of their cruelty. It was not going to be easy. In a distant part of his mind, he was also battling memory, because he was certain that at some point in his lengthy life, he had met this particular tormentor before. The thought fled in the next heartbeat and he cringed inwardly, fighting escalating terror when he spotted the archaic instruments of torture that were being laid out before his objecting eyes like a surgical tray, and he knew that each item would be wielded with the precision and skill of a surgeon.

His head bowed and he offered what seemed the latest in a steady stream of prayers to the mighty Zeus. Deep inside him, Andrei doubted, for perhaps the first time.

ϓ ϓ ϓ

Worlds away, in another time and place, a tremor rippled the placid surface of the heavens. High in the clouds above Greece, in the palace of Olympus, the King of the Gods listened. At his side, his queen, Hera, watched him closely.

"It's begun again?"

He nodded.

A perverse pleasure twisted the composed contours of her features and she laughed.

"Ares will not be happy," Zeus remarked absently.

Hera's amusement grew and he had pause to wonder at the underlying hatred within the stranger he had married in the dawn of time.

ϓ ϓ ϓ

Nickolas Stefanos was dreading the coming meeting, and he hesitated outside the small shop of antiquities, gathering both fortitude and resolve. He climbed from his car, told his partner, Philos Arvanitidhis, to wait, and went inside. Katina Panopoulos, Alexandra's assistant and friend, watched him with wary eyes as he headed directly for the office at the back of the small building.

"Alex?"

She looked up from the computer, measured his mood, and slowly rose. He wasn't encouraged when she went behind her desk, distancing herself from him.

"What's happened?"

He paused, wondered for a few brief seconds if he could postpone this until she was safely at home, and he had time to be with her. That faint hope was eradicated an instant later when she sank into her father's worn chair and put her head down onto her arms.

"Andrei," she said very softly.

He didn't confirm or deny her assumption, there seemed little need. Eventually, she lifted her head and looked at him again.

"We found his body about an hour ago," he said gently. "The students at his temple called to tell us he hadn't been seen since last night. The unit that was in the area didn't see him leave. I really don't know how it happened, Alex." He waited, unsure of her reaction.

She nodded, holding onto her composure with considerable effort as she accepted the news her heart had known for most of the day. Finally, she trusted her voice to speak evenly again.

"He knew, Nic," she stated. "I think I knew too, the last time I saw him."

There was more, though he hesitated to tell her. And, as often was the case, Alexandra knew his mind.

"Tell me all of it, darling," she asked.

"He was tortured," Nic said, and this time he ran to catch her when she stood, swayed with shock, then tried to push him away. He refused to be pushed aside, or locked from her grief.

"I'm sorry, Alex," he offered, hugging her close as she shook with inaudible sobs. After only a few seconds she clung to him, and he relaxed as she allowed her heart to mourn a loss almost as great as the one she'd suffered at her father's death a year earlier. It was a long time before she eased back enough to look at him.

"I'm really afraid, Nic," she whispered, confiding something that she'd never given voice to before now. "This feels so wrong, and not simply because it's what I study and cherish. It's been growing for a long time, years, and I think it's going to cost me everything. Andrei is just the beginning."

"You're talking foolishness, Alex," he chided softly. Looking into her beautiful dark eyes, he was given pause to wonder if the reassurance was for her benefit, or a balm to his escalating sense of dread. He kissed her forehead and held her face between his hands, smiling his love into her eyes. "We're going to find whoever killed Andrei, I promise you that, Alex. At this point, there's nothing to link his death to—"

"They've desecrated the shrines, Nic!" she snarled, her quick-silver temper rising to strike. "He was tortured! They wanted the secret inside the Temple."

"What secret?" he demanded, gripping her arms in a painful hold when she would have jerked free of him. "Alexandra, I need to know what you've been hiding from me."

"I'm hiding nothing," she snapped, suddenly furious at him, not certain why she felt the emotion so vehemently. "In fact, it's all going to be out in the open after the lecture tomorrow night."

"You are *not* going to be standing before a crowd of people tomorrow night, Alex," he shouted. "You'll be an easy target if you're right about this."

"You know I'm right," she charged, her voice a low whisper of rage between them. "And you also know there's no way in hell that you're going to stop me. This was scheduled months ago, Nic, and I intend to use it to remind people of our past, and what it means to us."

"I can shut you down before you get started, Alex," he warned, meaning it with shocking sincerity.

"Not at the Herodes Atticus," she stated triumphantly. "The Acropolis is the perfect site to make people see what's at risk if these lunatics aren't stopped."

They'd reached an impasse.

Nic relented, for the moment, and left her in the small office. He tried not to feel guilty about the loss

and disappointment in her eyes when he dared to
glance back before slamming the door behind him.

ϒ ϒ ϒ

Anxiety and excitement were churning in the pit of her
stomach as she looked into the crowd that had gathered
at the foot of the ancient Acropolis. There was an edginess
to the mood of the people gathered, and she knew there
would be an inordinate number of police patrols cover-
ing the entire area. Pulling herself together, mentally and
emotionally, Alexandra stepped onto the stage and waited
for the crowd to acknowledge her presence.

Once there was quiet, she began to speak from the
prepared lecture she'd worked on for several weeks. The
tone had changed somewhat during the past forty-eight
hours, but much remained as it had been from the time
she'd agreed to speak on behalf of her University's History
department. She spoke for half an hour to an audience that
listened with genuine interest to her belief that they
possessed a unique and rich culture that needed to be
preserved and passed on to the generations that would
come. It was only when she asked for questions from the
assembly that she was forced to defend her beliefs.

"There's a growing faction who believe that the Gods
never existed," a young man posed. "That everything
written about them is fiction, passed down through time
as the basis of our religion and history. Can you prove
otherwise, Doctor Christophi, or are you asking us to
believe in myth and accept it as fact?"

She smiled at the rumble of the crowd, not able to gauge
if the murmur was agreement with the man, or dissatis-
faction.

"The existence of the old Gods is like the existence of
Christ, it requires faith to believe. If faith isn't enough, you
need only look around you to see the evidence that remains
with us thousands of years after the Gods themselves have
chosen to live apart from us. There are wars being fought
all over this planet; doesn't that suggest that Ares is still
well-represented? Love and passion are still a major part

of the human condition. Aphrodite and Eros appear to be doing what they have always done. Monarchs rule as Zeus ruled Olympus, Hades tends to the dead, Dionysus indulges our tastes for entertainment. Can you really believe we are not watched over by those who have always been? The very basis of modern literature and culture finds its roots in the ancient Gods."

"There is only One True God," the young man stated, unswayed as the rest of the crowd had been by her words. "None of your fables can change that!"

ɤ ɤ ɤ

A short distance away, discreetly concealed, Nic took special care to photograph the boy who argued so heatedly with Alexandra's views. The rest of his team was spread out in the crowd, and there'd be countless photos to sort through by this time the next day.

ɤ ɤ ɤ

Thrace was glorious this afternoon, Amarantha thought in a separate part of her mind, a part that wasn't fully occupied with evading Ares' sword. The sun shone brilliantly, and the air was sultry and invigorating, as was their current exercise. She wore little beyond a short wrap that would not interfere with her movement, and her silver-white hair was tied in a severe warrior's knot. Ares was clad in less, and she tried not to be distracted by his magnificent body. It wasn't easy.

"You aren't paying attention, Little One," Ares mocked as he struck yet another blow to his student's back. "Concentrate!" he ordered.

"Do you never tire of taunting me, Ares?" Amarantha hissed back, enraged more by her slip than his censure.

"I tire of nothing about you, Amarantha," he decreed with fierce intensity. He deflected a thrust of her sword that would have sliced open his middle if he'd been a heartbeat slower with his defense. He nodded, smiling with approval. "You still surprise me," a pause and the flicker of a smile, then he added with a nodding bow of his head, "from time to time."

"I have to," she retorted. "Otherwise you'd lose your passion for teaching me."

"It's not merely teaching you that inspires my passion," he reminded her, gravelly voice rich with sensual insinuation.

"Then perhaps you should try a little harder to win your prize, my Master," she said, and slipped past him to whirl and strike. Blood flowed momentarily from a wound in his upper arm. Her victory was short-lived when he caught her by the waist and tossed her onto the ground. His sword was poised at her throat before she could move again. He laughed with pleasure and quickly withdrew, pulling her to her feet with the motion. They again faced each other and engaged in yet another variation of their deadly dances. Before long, Amarantha's enjoyment dimmed; he was more intent than usual and that determination usually meant he'd demand a total victory before relenting.

Seconds later she was a breath too slow in deflecting his sword and it slid deep into her side. Pain seared her, blotting out everything but the red haze of an inferno lit behind her eyes. She reacted instinctively and stepped forward, toward him, seeking. As her vision cleared, she saw the amazement in his dark eyes, and they eased away from each other. Blood poured from the wound in her side, but the real source of his surprise was the dagger that was buried hilt-deep in his stomach.

Amarantha dropped to her knees, gasping. She knew she was in no danger of dying, but until Ares healed the injury, the pain would be horrendous. She watched as he pulled her knife free of his body and the spurt of his blood was quickly stemmed. He went down on one knee before her, returned the dagger to her, then placed his hand over the tear in her flesh. Her back arched in reflexive pain and pleasure as the flood of God-fire burned into her body, healing all of the injuries their training session had inflicted this time. Each time he did this, she felt dizzy and disoriented. It was a shade of the Ambrosia's transformation energy, but always it made her shudder with awareness of the scope of his tremendous power. When he took his hand away a few minutes later and sat back, she slumped down, sitting on her heels, her breathing ragged.

Finally, the tremors passed and silver eyes rose to stare at him, startled, but amused, too.

"I thought I knew all your moves," she murmured. "It appears there are still a few to learn."

"Let me show you later," he grinned. "Right now I want to bathe, and make love."

ϒ ϒ ϒ

The meeting had gone on and on, only breaking up when Nic and his police team finally broke into the arguments being thrown from stage to crowd as several more young people goaded Alexandra into defending her beliefs, only to be derided for them by the troublemakers. She was furious and Nic was worried about a potential riot.

"You didn't have to scare away the people who came here tonight!" she all but shouted as they prepared to leave the theater.

"Alex," he said with false calm. "This is my job. I don't intend to discuss it with you before I do what needs to be done."

"This was a public meeting, Nic."

"Yeah," he agreed sarcastically. "One that was promising to get very nasty."

"You're over-reacting."

"Then let me," he snapped. He took her arm and was all but dragging her to his car when the shot rended the relative quiet of the late evening air.

Alexandra went down, and didn't move.

ϒ ϒ ϒ

Amarantha held out her hand and he pulled her to her feet. They walked into the temple and continued through to her garden, the one Ares had built so many centuries past it seemed to have been there forever. She turned to see him watching her, and despite the long years, she still trembled when he stared at her with such profound hunger. His smile grew seductive as she began to shed her flimsy garments, tossing them aside without concern. She dove into the deepest part of the pool, and swam, rolling repeatedly in the shimmering, crystalline waters.

Minutes later, Ares caught her.

"I wish we could be this way always," she whispered as they stood, arms wrapped tightly around each other.

He turned her back to face him and began to undo the confinement of her flowing white hair. Once it was free, he ran his fingers through the long, silken tresses, and then he turned her again to look at him. He bent his head to kiss her, focused only on his lust. She shifted in the buoyant waters of the pool, her arms sliding around his neck as her legs locked around his waist, then she screamed...

CHAPTER TEN

The Champion of the Gods felt the tingle of life force transference and braced herself for an overwhelming and terrifying surge of awareness. This had occurred more times than she could remember over the centuries, yet it never ceased to take her by surprise. Particularly when Zeus took her from Ares' arms with no warning whatsoever; something else that had occurred often throughout the centuries. She knew that the other Olympian Gods took perverse pleasure in her fear, and Ares' rage, when they were separated so unceremoniously.

Her body ached, and she knew it was a combination of the loss of her lover's touch, and the mortal pain of a stranger's hurt. The sounds around her were mildly disturbing, and in the first minutes of adjustment, she became conscious of a hand clutching hers. Inwardly offering a prayer to Athena for wisdom and calm, Amarantha opened her new eyes.

"Alex! Thank God!"

Alex? Was she male in this guise? If so, she was decidedly uneasy with the concern and anguish in the face of this handsome man who hovered so close to her side.

"Detective Stefanos, you'll have to leave and give us room to work," another voice, female, intoned. She sounded impatient and anxious, but firm nonetheless.

Amarantha attempted a small smile in an effort to make the man do as requested. She needed time to get her bearings, a jittery presence was too distracting to that process. She could feel the body she inhabited healing itself of whatever injury had caused *Alex*'s death; that miracle would take place only once, at this critical point of life transfer. If Amarantha died prematurely in this body, it would be permanent for her, as well as the mortal she would become for the duration of this decree of the Fates.

"Is she going to make it?"

Amarantha watched his features flood with fear and felt a distant pang of empathy for him; his *Alex* was already lost to him, though he would not know it for some time.

"We'll do everything possible, Detective," the feminine voice reassured. "But, you will have to leave."

"I'll be right outside, Alex," he whispered, and Amarantha attempted a weak nod when he kissed her forehead and released her hand with obvious reluctance.

For a moment, the only thing Amarantha was able to discern were white-clad bodies, and the tinny sounds of machinery at work. She'd been in this century before she realized quickly; some of the noises were faintly familiar.

"Wh..." She swallowed hard, then made her eyes focus on the woman who stood next to the uncomfortable bed she was lying on; the stranger's look was sharp and intent. "Where am...?"

"You're in hospital, Doctor Christophi," was the reply, and Amarantha stared. Doctor Christophi? Was she expected to replace a Healer in this life? She had no skill with that type of art; her master and trainer had been the God of War, not Apollo.

"Do you remember anything about the attack?"

Amarantha chose silence as her answer, and the woman nodded. As she watched, the Champion saw that she was at the center of much attention. Beeping equipment flanked her on either side, and there seemed a constant stream of people in and out of the small room she occupied. It smelled too clean, the air sharp with chemicals that made her want to sneeze. She could hear the muted sounds of pain and crying around her. Terror seized her insides and began to squeeze, making her close her eyes again as tears formed behind the lids. She resisted the urge to shriek to the heavens; this was always the most difficult part of the life transfer, the first minutes when her aloneness threatened tenuous sanity.

"The O.R.'s ready, Doctor," a new voice announced.

"We're going to administer the anesthetic now," the woman told Amarantha.

"Why?"

"Doctor?"

Amarantha and the other woman, obviously the doctor being addressed, both glanced at the man who'd just entered the room and now stood on the opposite side of the bed.

Pulling aside the sheet that had been placed over the patient, he said, "This doesn't require surgery."

"She's been shot, Stavros! We know the bullet has grazed the heart."

"Really?" He sounded thoroughly disgusted. "Then will you explain why this scratch is the only visible injury on her body?"

Amarantha remained motionless and expressionless as the woman paled and shrank back. Dark eyes met hers, and there was a genuine glimmer of fear in the gaze.

The man called Stavros snorted derisively and began issuing orders to have the room cleared. He stopped long enough to glower at the doctor who'd been attending Amarantha.

"Tell the detective to take his fianceé home, she's fine. And the next time you send for me in the middle of the night, Penny, be certain I am needed!"

Amarantha was left alone moments later as the doctors went to find Detective Stefanos. The minutes gave her time to observe covertly the technology that was present in the room. There was a coldness about the place, something truly alien to her. The people who came in and out worked in silence, glancing nervously at her, then looking away if she caught them.

They were afraid of her.

Their fear was no greater than hers.

She strained to hear what was being said just beyond the doors. Voices were raised, and their cadence revealed tension and anger—and fear. They were discussing her.

"Ares..." She whispered the name unconsciously, wished fervently that he could answer her. During their timeless relationship, Amarantha had learned to cherish his strength as much as she'd always respected it; separated from him, she inevitably called upon the discipline of his teachings to soothe her anxiety. As she did now. Before she could fully regain her composure, the attractive young man who called her *Alex* returned to her side.

"Doctor Stanford tells me you can go home," he informed her, puzzlement and worry in his eyes. When she made no reply, he frowned. "Do you know me, Alex?"

Amarantha smiled, and shook her head. Once she'd been taken from Olympus, the Champion recalled all of her own vast history, but the past of her mortal host was gone, the soul sent into Hades' keeping.

"She said the trauma may have caused..." He sighed heavily. "Never mind, we have time."

He eased her into a sitting position, and Amarantha caught his shoulders to steady herself as the room spun wildly for a second, fading to a dim gray before coming back into focus by virtue of her determination not to faint. The idea was absurdly appealing, and for that reason alone she rejected it.

"Your name?" She was intrigued by the seductive throatiness of this new voice, and wondered what Ares would think of it.

"Nic," he whispered, his tone filled with regret. "Nickolas Stefanos, your fiancé." He paused a moment, peered closely at her. "Do you remember your name?"

Again, the Champion shook her head.

"Alexandra Christophi," he supplied. "You were shot tonight, Alex. You should be dead," he added, and she saw the near disbelief in his soft brown eyes when he continued to stare at her.

She nodded, kept her features schooled to bland acceptance. She was quite immune to the pain her lack of response sparked in his eyes, and waited expectantly.

"Let's go home," he said quietly. "Maybe things will be clear in the morning." He sounded hopeful, and she wondered how badly hurt he would be when he realized that his Alexandra was truly gone.

ϓ ϓ ϓ

Home was a comfortable, moderately sized apartment in downtown Athens. Amarantha would know Athena's city in any time, and she was pleased to note that even in this era, it retained its beauty and charm. The Goddess would be pleased to hear it, if Amarantha was able to survive this test and return to her proper place in time.

Nic held open the door and motioned for her to go inside. Amarantha smiled and stepped onto rich, plush carpeting. Her smile deepened when she saw the soft tones of earthy green and brown that dominated the room. The furniture was highly burnished dark wood, obviously antiquated and cared for with meticulous attention. Books filled the shelves that covered one wall, and she couldn't wait to peruse them thoroughly when she was alone.

"Do you want to shower?"

She spun around, startled when he turned the lock on the door then hung his dark jacket in the closet next to it. She had a few moments to discreetly observe him. He was a pleasantly attractive man, handsome even; she estimated his age to be roughly thirty; he was tall, almost as tall as Ares, had the same dark hair as the War God, but it was short, the neatly shorn waves barely touching the back of his collar. His features were a striking blend of angles and planes; and warm brown eyes were large and expressive. His mouth was generous, well suited to the smile that seemed his most natural aspect. He was broad-shouldered, but slender; she sensed a quietly contained strength in him. He could have been appealing to almost any woman. And, beneath her uneasiness and annoyance, Amarantha sensed something dangerous in his presence, though she was not ready to analyze what it might be.

"Perhaps you should lie down?" Nic suggested when he came into the room and stopped a short distance from her.

"Yes," she agreed, and looked around, uncertain. She was wary when he came to her side, took her elbow in a light grasp, and led her down the corridor. They went into the larger of the two bedrooms in the apartment, and he released her, then went directly into a smaller room that adjoined it.

Amarantha sat gingerly on the edge of the bed and tried to relax. The sound of running water told her that she would be alone for a short time, and she needed the reprieve to find her emotional equilibrium. The bedroom was as one would expect, she derided herself. Intimate, for lovers. The bed was large and comfortable, the softly scented sheets smooth and inviting. The thought of sharing the cozy chamber with a stranger made her nerves jangle. The last time she had been thrust into mortal existence, this particular arrangement hadn't been one she'd needed to be concerned with; at that time, it was highly frowned upon for a couple to behave as though married when they were not. She had laughed at the hypocrisy of the high-handed morality, but had been relieved, also.

Amarantha rose and did a quick search of the bedroom and its contents. Alexandra Christophi was a woman with very good taste, the Champion decided. She passed before a mirror and halted abruptly when she caught her first sight of the exotic yet alien presence who housed her. Alex was lovely, she decided. Taller than Amarantha, with inky black hair and equally dark eyes. Her skin was deeply tanned, and she glowed with health. She was also curvaceous and sensual.

Glancing away, Amarantha became aware of the sudden silence. Nickolas would be coming back into the room at any moment. She darted to the tall chest of drawers and selected a long sleeping gown, then rapidly changed from the stained hospital clothes. The undergarments were a nightmare for several moments, and she finally peeled them off without real notice; she'd examine their mysteries when she was alone. A minute later she was tucked into bed and had her back turned to the bathroom door.

He didn't turn on a light, and she felt the whoosh of steamy air that flooded from the other room when he stepped over the threshold and came into the bedroom. Tension began to bleed into her muscles and she forced her breaths to even and lengthen, giving the illusion of sleep.

Her resolve almost shattered when she felt him slip into bed beside her. Warm, damp skin was too close, and she prayed that he would not force her to reject an advance. She felt a light kiss on her shoulder, then he withdrew.

For a long time, Amarantha listened, and finally knew he slept. She rolled onto her back and stared upward into the darkness. She'd been in this life hours, and, as always, had no clue why. She had made her choice so many eons ago that it no longer felt real, until the terrible moments when she would be torn from her master's side and tossed into the sea of mortal life that the Gods so often disdained. Yet, despite their arrogance, they would tolerate no slight, nor any threat to their place in history.

She had defended against many forms of sacrilege over the millennia, and never knew until she felt success what it was she truly fought for. They waited for her to fail — some more than others. They hated Ares for her creation, but she had learned to see past their contempt to a deeper truth; they envied him, too. Together, the God of War, and his chosen Champion, had discovered a tranquility that made them mates in unexpected ways. Amarantha would never call it love in the romantic sense that Aphrodite embodied, but she knew it to be sacred; a gift worthy of the fight they mounted each time the Fates called upon her.

She let her memory drift to the moment of this separation and shuddered with frustration and loneliness. Ares had taught her passion with the same intensity and ruthlessness that he'd used to instruct her in the arts of survival. As she lay alone in a distant world, she longed for him, for his possession. The man beside her stirred and she deflected his instinctive reach for her. He mumbled, and she slid from the bed to retreat to the living room.

Amarantha curled into a stuffed, comfortable chair and stared out a window. She had endured many assaults, some the most intimate kind. She would not accept any man's touch, however loving in intent. The hands that had calmed her horrors and overcome her loathing belonged to a God; and none but Ares would possess her willingly.

Time shifted again in her mind, took her back to the life that was real to her...

She had spent a long time in Ares' company before they'd become what he assured her they were meant to be. She'd mourned the death of Iphicles for years, and during that time, Ares had often raged at the mortal king who would eternally be her truest love. Amarantha had never really understood his hatred of Iphicles, and perhaps never would. She had grown into the warrior and woman Ares wanted her to be, and she had long since reconciled herself to the loss of her King. She had even made her peace with Heracles and Iolaus, in time. But, it was Ares who had long been the center of her world, her purpose and master of her fate in ways that the other Gods resented deeply.

She smiled, recalled the fierce battle that had led to their first joining. A minor war in a distant part of the country, and they had fought side by side. Until Amarantha had fallen to the sword of a nobleman who worshipped Athena, not the War God. Ares had destroyed him on the spot, and taken his Champion back to Thrace. She woke, healed and whole again, and had gone to her bathing pool, shaken and afraid.

The waters were as they always were, cool, soothing, the spectacular falls a shower of diamond-sharp lights of all colors. She stripped off her gown and waded in, her heart swollen within her chest as she accepted the torrents of shifting emotions that roiled inside her; grief, shame, and a loneliness so deeply profound that it made her weak with agony. Her body ached for the peace she'd once known in King Iphicles' arms, and her soul reached outward, seeking. The answer that breathed into her troubled spirit brought little comfort, and greater trepidation. Ares was her Master, certainly, but could he truly be more to her? The questions, so complicated, and so simple, plagued her. She adored him in a very different manner than the complete faith she'd given Iphicles without reservation. Ares' only true love was Aphrodite, he had countless children with Goddesses and mortals both. Yet, he repeatedly returned to Thrace, to the home he'd given Amarantha. They shared it in all ways, except this one.

"Your thoughts are as wild as your fighting was."

She flinched, but didn't turn to face him. His voice caressed her naked skin in a way quite apart from its usual stroking softness. She shivered, and immediately the gardens warmed a few degrees.

"It is not the air that chills me, my Master," she confessed, her voice a small quiver of sound in the stillness.

Ares' smile was one of incredible satisfaction when she permitted herself to turn and look at him. He held out his hand and waited, refusing to take a step toward her.

"This is your sanctuary, Amarantha," he explained, his tone rough with erotic seduction. Beneath the obvious hunger, she heard the unmistakable, exultant triumph, a thing reflected in the dark pools of his wondrous eyes. "I will not intrude without invitation."

She trembled violently, torn between undeniable desire and the safety of their decades old impasse. He stood before her, proud, savage, more breathtakingly handsome than any mortal man could possibly be, and she knew his patience would not be tested much further by her denials. In this one area, he had shown her lenience that was not present in any other part of their complex relationship. The choice would be hers, and she knew well why. Zeus took what he wanted, who he wanted, and Ares refused to be like his father in things that were important to him.

"If I ask you to join me here?" she queried, eyes drinking in his presence, thrilling to the aura of beauty and God-fire that emanated from him.

"I will not be a replacement for a dead mortal, Am," he warned darkly.

Shaking with a violence that made her very bones rattle, Amarantha nodded and knelt, her hands offered to him, palms upward, in supplication. Tears streamed from her eyes as she finally freed her heart from the bondage of grief and accepted yet another destiny woven by a God and the Fates.

Ares had shown her ways of pleasure unlike anything she had ever known. And in their intimacy, he had forged a bond with her soul that would transcend the barriers of time on more than one occasion.

Amarantha wrenched her thoughts back into the twentieth century, and dragged air into suddenly starved lungs as she fought for composure, and freedom from the enormity of her past and the God who owned her, even across countless centuries. As had often happened, she was still wavering between two worlds and times, heart locked in one, head seeking for purpose in another. Her equilibrium would reassert itself, soon. As the thought solidified, so did her resolve.

"Tomorrow," she whispered into the silence of her imposed solitude. "This time I will know quickly why they have taken me from you, Ares."

She heard the low chime of a clock on the wall, and curiosity made her rise. She went to the desk that sat beneath the clock, and picked up the book that had been placed on one corner. A book organized as a calendar. The date on the top of the page made her stomach knot with dread: November 1, 1999. The end of the millennium was approaching, and such times were always dangerously powerful.

She sighed heavily, listened to the deepest intuition of her heart — she'd found her first clue, and it filled her with grave apprehension.

CHAPTER ELEVEN

The news was filled with reports of the attempt on Doctor Alexandra Christophi's life the previous night. The old theater, a shrine in its own right, had been the scene of much controversy in the span of a few hours. What angered the man watching the reports more than anything else was the scope of coverage for the failed assassination. Because of the strikes he'd so carefully arranged, an attempt to silence the renowned Anthropologist and Greek Historian was of consequence to many people who would not otherwise have been even slightly interested. The purpose of her meeting at the Herodes Atticus had been well publicized. The ill-conceived execution attempt had drawn unwanted attention to her defense of the old Gods, and brought many of the neutral minds over to her side. The last thing he wanted to happen at this juncture.

He was furious.

Leaving the room full of monitors and news broadcasts, he went to face the assembled followers of his new religious order. They were restless and as he passed through their number, he heard snatches of hushed conversation; they were abuzz with speculation about the shooting.

As he stepped onto the dais, the room grew quiet.

"I assume you have heard of the effort to kill our enemy, Alexandra Christophi?" He posed the question to the entire gathering. The rumble of acknowledgment drifted back to him and he nodded. "This was not part of our plan," he reminded them, eyes scanning the uneasy faces before him, seeking to find the one that would reveal guilt. None gave the appearance of guilt, merely confusion and apprehension.

"The True God will soon be among us," he intoned, pitching his voice to the low, hypnotic cadence that had served him so well during the years of preparation for the impending revelation of his sect. "We have not yet paved the way for his arrival. This could turn many against us before we have had the chance to reveal our God and his plan."

Again there was the shifting of feet and the whisper of uncertainty.

He watched them for long minutes, and eventually turned to leave the room. Their relief was almost tangible in the aftermath.

ϒ ϒ ϒ

The shadows were cool, soothing, as he sat in contemplation of what lay ahead of him. The room, his private chamber, was deliberately spartan, impersonal. He liked to come here, to think. There was nothing of modern distraction to interrupt, only the occasional intrusion of his aide, Timothy. He felt more than heard the stealthy arrival of his oldest friend and follower, but chose not to notice just yet.

Renata he called himself now, the Reborn. It suited him. It suited his dreams. He was the builder of a new faith that would, ultimately, unite the religious world. He'd spent years in study, becoming fluent with every Holy Book known to mankind, as well as any legend that so much as hinted at religion. He could quote the Bible forward and back; recite from the Qur'an. He knew the Vedas, as well as the Brahmanas and the Upanishads; the Jataka and Buddha-charita; the Tao Te Ching; the Talmud; and the Book Of Mormon. He could decipher hieroglyphs in countless dead languages; and recount any variation of the legendary Gods of his homeland, Greece. He had taken the best from all he had learned, and rewoven the tenets and doctrine into a canon that would honor the One, True Faith; that of his Order, The True God.

It meant widespread destruction of anything that kept alive old beliefs, things that were a sacrilege to The True

God who would soon show himself to the waiting world. He would save their pitiful planet, as Christ had been unable to do; as all others before and after Him had been unable to do.

And, Renata would be His voice.

His High Priest.

Timothy stirred slightly, and Renata finally gave the other man his attention.

"What is it?"

"We have to move ahead more quickly than planned," Timothy said slowly. "This thing with Doctor Christophi has upset the momentum. If we don't move now, they'll start to unite against us. The papers are filled with phrases such as 'religious fanatics' and the like," he hesitated, then added very softly, "those that aren't calling us a new order of terrorists."

"Claim responsibility, but nothing more. Do it quietly, not in the media. Let the police find our name, and let them draw attention to us," he ordered after careful thought. "Let the fools speculate about what they're up against." He laughed then, a short bark of mirthless sound, and turned his baleful gaze to Timothy. "See that the message is given to Detective Nickolas Stefanos."

Timothy looked unsure, and decidedly ill at ease.

"While you're at it, see that Endre Spaneas is disposed of, quietly."

"Endre?"

"He was responsible for the fiasco involving Alexandra Christophi. He's a danger to us now."

"He would never betray you."

"I don't intend to permit him the opportunity."

The challenge hung between them in the silent room, but it was Timothy who relented with a curt bow, then he was gone.

Renata brooded darkly.

He still hadn't found the key to his plan. If things had gone differently, once, he wouldn't have had to decipher the clues alone. He might have had the help of the very people with whom he was now at war. Even as the possibility took shape, it was disintegrating to vapor inside his head. No, that would never have been a reality, a voice deep within him taunted, she'd hated him too much, even then.

And, Andrei Adonidas had never broken his vow to protect the secret of the Temple of Zeus.

ϒ ϒ ϒ

The first light of dawn had long since faded when Amarantha woke. Disoriented and uncomfortable, she opened one eye and listened closely. Memory flooded in and she gritted her teeth to contain the curse of fury that wanted to spew from her. The muffled sounds of another person close by reminded her that she was now sharing the life of a stranger, a man who clearly knew her host in the most intimate of ways. She quelled a shudder when she considered the emotional battle ahead of her when this man, Nickolas Stefanos, reached for her in the nights to come and she would turn him away.

There had been a time many centuries past when the Champion of Olympus had almost succumbed to the passion of someone other than Ares, and she still felt the pain of his fury when she allowed herself to remember his wrath. During the Crusades of the tenth and eleventh centuries, she had met a young king, a monarch who had the eyes of another king. Temptation had been strong, for he'd had Iphicles' spirit and heart, as well as his handsome countenance. All of the few men who'd tempted her had possessed some aspect of the King she still loved, even with centuries between that life and this one.

"Alex?"

The whisper jerked her awareness back to the present and she feigned sleep, seeking a delay in facing Nic's questions and concern. She felt a fleeting pang of remorse when she rejected him in this subtle way, but she was not prepared to face him until she was more at ease in her present guise. He moved about the room, quietly. He was dressing, and glancing repeatedly at her. When he bent to kiss her, she knew he was almost ready to leave her alone.

She mentally followed his footsteps through the apartment, heard him go away, and return. A short while later, the door closed firmly and silence settled over the flat.

Heaving a sigh of relief, she climbed out of bed and decided to explore Alexandra's home more thoroughly. She found Nic's note, placed carefully on the top of a chest of drawers, and opened it. He wished her a good day, and said he loved her. Amarantha wished it stirred something other than irritation within her.

Feeling a small sense of freedom, she relaxed and went into the bathroom. It had been a number of decades since she'd last been in modern civilization, but she was fairly certain she knew how to run the shower. She peeled off the silken nightgown she'd grabbed the night before, and stood before the full-length mirror that adorned one wall. She bit her lip and smiled a little as she considered the very pleasing beauty of Alexandra Christophi's face and body. Ares would undoubtedly like this form more than some of the others she'd inhabited during the long ages of her existence.

Smiling whimsically, she twisted the knob in the spacious shower stall and adjusted the temperature to a moderate warmth. She stepped in, closed the door and shut her eyes as the satiny caress of water washed over her.

The skin she wore was smooth and unblemished, as her own was, despite years of injuries. Ares healed any wound he inflicted, sometimes in the most pleasurable of ways; his talented hands were as skilled at seduction as they were at war-making. The garden he'd created for her had become a haven to them both.

Memory expanded and she braced her hands against the tiled wall of the shower as her mind filled with her true life...

The garden was a glorious creation of colors and scents, gilded by eternal sunshine. The blue waters were the shade of summer skies and the sand beneath her feet fine, white powder. She shuddered when the well-known hands of her master slid around her waist, then moved upward, shaping her breasts with sensuous pressure before continuing their gliding exploration of her lithe curves.

"*I was beginning to think you'd never return,*" Ares *grumbled, his rich, gravel-textured voice a growl near her ear.*

"*I had feared the same thing, Ares,*" Amarantha *returned in a shaky whisper.* "*I have missed you, Master,*" *she told him, trembling violently as his hand slipped between her thighs and probed delicately.* "*Hypnos gave me a dream that was as much torment as comfort.*"

"*He built the bridge to be permanent, Am,*" Ares *murmured, turning her to face him. He bent his head to take a ripe nipple into his mouth. She arched against him, her sobbing moan testimony to how much she wanted his touch now. It had not always been that way.*

"*They'll know, Ares,*" *she managed to gasp.*

He left his erotic play at her breast and took her face between his large hands. He shook his head to answer her remark, then silenced her with a long, evocative kiss...

Amarantha groaned in frustration when she pulled herself away from the past with near bodily pain. She ached for Ares, for his domination and his profoundly exquisite lovemaking. She might have given herself physical release in Alex's body, Nic was obviously her lover, but it would not be enough to assuage the need of Amarantha's soul; that completion required Ares, and no one else.

Angered by her lapse, despite it being among the most common of the emotions that assailed her in any new form, Amarantha finished showering and dressed. A short while later, she found coffee in the kitchen, still warm. The modern kitchen was a marvel she needed to explore, but it would have to wait until more pressing concerns were seen to.

Sipping experimentally at the aromatic brew, she walked through the apartment and learned every inch of the place that would be her home until she'd accomplished her task here. When she entered the second bedroom, she found it had been converted into a small library. It wasn't long before she felt her prayers had been answered. Alexandra was a meticulous researcher, and she wrote everything down, Amarantha was soon to discover.

Hours were passed in reading the many journals kept by the pretty professor. Amarantha dared to hope that this time the separation from Ares would not be one of years, or decades, but merely months. She was more comfortable with Alexandra Christophi than she often was with those she inhabited. Alex was fluent in history, the Gods, and many other things that were personal reality to Amarantha.

When she finished exploring the library, she returned to the living room and went to the desk. Amid the books on the shining surface was a volume she'd learned to recognize already; leaning forward she picked up the current journal being kept by the Historian/Anthropologist. Skimming over the most recent entries, Amarantha was saddened for a few moments. Alexandra wrote eloquently and emotionally about the loss of the Priest of Zeus' temple, and the pain it caused her. She also spoke of her fear that his belief in the Champion of Olympus would be proven truth. Amarantha's thoughts were darkly amused. Alexandra had good reason for her fear, though she'd never know it. Her death signified Amarantha's return. On some level, she must have known the Champion's arrival would only be made possible by the loss of her life.

Annoyed by the melancholy that had crept into her mood, Amarantha tossed aside the journal and picked up the photograph that was on the corner of the desk. Alex, and an older man, her father from the way they looked at each other. Behind them was a small museum and antiquities shop.

A sudden ringing made Amarantha whirl around in fright, then she realized that it would be the telephone. She'd seen the communications instruments the last time she'd walked the earth in mortal form, though she'd never actually used the thing. Her eyes zeroed in on the white device placed a short distance from the photograph. Hesitantly, she lifted the top and put it to her ear. There was nothing, and she was about to drop it when she heard a faint voice. She lifted it to her ear again and listened.

"Alex? Doctor Christophi? Are you there?"

"Yes, this is Alexandra Christophi," Amarantha answered carefully.

"Alex! Thank God you're there. I was worried after everything that was on the news. Are you all right?"

Amarantha stared at the phone for a moment, confused. "The news?" she stalled.

"You haven't seen it?" came the incredulous reply. "Alex, it's all over the television, the papers, everywhere! The phone's been ringing ever since I got in."

"Got in?" Amarantha repeated, "where are you?"

"I'm at your father's place, where else would I be at this time of the day?" A pause. "Are you planning to come in today?" The tone had moved swiftly from mild irritation to concern. "You are all right, aren't you, Alex?"

"Yes, I am fine," Amarantha said, smiling inwardly. "I'll join you shortly."

"Don't walk, Alex," was the advice from the other end of the line. "I'll send a taxi for you. The last thing you need is for some other nut to take a shot at you. Nic'd kill me."

"Thank you."

Amarantha put the receiver down and walked back into the bedroom.

Less than twenty minutes later she was standing on the sidewalk outside the building in which she lived. Minutes after that a car approached, and she waited, watching. The driver looked at her, but when she made no move toward him, he leaned out the window and spoke.

"Hey, Alex! You going to stand there all day? I've got other people to pick up, honey."

Amarantha's eyebrows rose as she considered the casual familiarity of his manner. Alex obviously knew a great number of people, and was, apparently, well liked by them. She walked to the car and he swung open the rear door for her to get in.

"Kat said you were going to the museum," he told her cheerily. "Anyplace else first?"

"No," she smiled cautiously. "Just the museum, thank you."

They pulled up to a small, dignified building twenty minutes later. It wasn't the distance that held them up, it was the congestion of traffic that jammed the streets of downtown Athens. Amarantha marvelled at the number of people who moved within the city, and her gaze never stopped moving over the multitude of tourists and natives who roamed amid seeming chaos. When the car slowed, then halted, Amarantha took a moment to peer intently at the place before her, recognizing it from the photograph on Alexandra's desk. She remember that this world worked primarily on the exchange of money and she dug into the purse she'd picked up. Moments later she reached across the back of the seat to hand him several of the paper sheets she'd found in a smaller purse.

"What's this?" he asked, startled.

"Payment," she answered with a faint frown. "Isn't that the correct procedure?"

He twisted in his seat and looked closer at her.

"You okay, honey?" he asked. "You have an account, remember? You pay me once a month."

She nodded, and put the money back into the purse.

"I'm sorry," she apologized wanly, her confusion totally genuine. "I must be a bit more shaken up than I realized," she added, winning a huge smile from him, and a nod of sincere understanding.

"It's okay, Alex," he assured. "Maybe you should spend the day at home?"

"No," she disagreed instantly, and climbed out of the car. "I'll be fine now. Thank you again." She paused, and he realized she'd forgotten his name.

"Angel," he grinned.

"Thank you, Angel," she repeated, answering his grin with laughter.

He waved to her and was gone before she reached the door to the museum.

Inside, the tranquility was a balm to her spirit, and she took a few minutes to walk around the subdued and soothing interior. The display cases held semi-precious treasures, nothing of real value in the antiquities world, but things of real interest to the everyday historian. Jason Christophi clearly loved the past, and Amarantha felt a sense of admiration and affection for the man she had never met. When she reached the rear of the main room, she saw the pretty, dark-haired woman she assumed was 'Kat'. A quick glance at the name plate on the counter gave her a full name, Katina Panopoulos. She'd read that name in the journals, the girl was Alexandra's assistant, and, if she read correctly, her friend, as well.

"Hi!" Katina gave her a friendly wave from where she was standing at a small counter, with a coffee maker before her. She held up her own steaming mug, asking without words. Amarantha shook her head. She'd already consumed two cups of the stuff at home, and it was not sitting well on her stomach. Nor, she admitted, did she much like the taste of it. Katina looked surprised, though, so she knew immediately that Alexandra must consume large quantities of the beverage.

"You sure you're okay, Alex?" Katina questioned.

"Fine," she assured her. "Where are my father's research journals kept?"

"Your office," Katina answered, tone soft with uncertainty. "In your desk. Alex, are you sure you should be here today?"

"Yes," Amarantha stated firmly. "But I don't want to be disturbed, by anyone, including Nic."

Katina nodded, and Amarantha felt her curious stare following her until she shut the office door solidly behind her.

Sighing wearily, Amarantha went to the desk and began rummaging through the contents of the drawers. She found what she was looking for, acquainted herself with the Christophi specialities and studies, then she started on the current history that was contained in a file that Alexandra had been compiling.

Katina knocked at the door and entered with a paper bag in one hand, and a tray in the other.

"I thought you might like to break for lunch," she smiled. "It's been slow, and I didn't want to disturb you so I closed long enough to go for this."

Amarantha smiled warmly and went to take the tray from her hand.

"Thank you," she said. "I had forgotten about eating, and I think I'm past due for something."

They laid out the lunch and Katina gave her a cold juice drink.

"What have you been doing in here all morning?"

"Trying to discover who or what might be behind the defamation of the old shrines and temples," Amarantha chose to answer honestly.

"Why aren't you using the computer, it's much faster," Katina said, noting the blank screen on the machine.

"I'm not comfortable with machines," Amarantha again gave her a truthful reply.

"I know you hate the damn thing, Alex," Katina laughed. "But, if you want to get any really current news, it's still the best way to do it. Want me to help?" she offered cheerfully.

"Please," Amarantha was delighted. If this computer/machine was all the girl said it was, the speed would be invaluable to her.

Katina went to the system and turned it on. Amarantha's eyes widened as the thing came to life amid beeps and colorful images.

"Finish your lunch, boss," Katina laughed. "I'll get us onto the news database."

Concealing her confusion, Amarantha ate the delicious bread and salad that Katina had brought for her, and sipped at the fruity beverage.

ϒ ϒ ϒ

Nickolas Stefanos rubbed his tired eyes and released a heavy sigh as he leaned back in his chair and stretched weary muscles. He'd been poring over reports all day, and staring at photographs that had been taken at Alexandra's lecture the previous evening. The scant information he'd gleaned from a day's research was bordering on pitiful, and he was suffering a major headache for his trouble.

He rolled his office chair close to his littered desk again and sorted out the last file that had landed on the others a short while ago. He flipped it open half-heartedly, expecting more non-information. The face that looked back from the picture clipped to the upper corner made him straighten in his chair and give the file his complete attention for several minutes. He glanced at the desk across from his and wondered when Philos Arvanitidhis had left the Squad Room. The thought had no sooner formed than his partner's face poked around the partially open door.

"Nic," he said quietly, "we need to go to the morgue."

"Philos," Nic ignored the statement for a moment, holding up the folder. "I found him. The kid in the pictures I took. His name is Endre Spaneas."

"The morgue, Nic," Philos repeated, this time with steel in his voice. As he'd expected, the tone captured Nic's attention fully. The young detective grabbed a lightweight jacket off the back of his chair and headed for the door, stopping long enough to grab the file again.

Less than thirty minutes later they were entering the non-descript building in downtown Athens.

"Is this really necessary?" Nic snapped as he was led into the morgue. He had said, several times, that the name he'd finally uncovered was more important than an un-identified body on a slab. Philos had been suspiciously silent during the short trip from Police Headquarters.

"I think you'll find it educational, partner," Philos replied without any of the edginess that was so evident in Nic's manner.

They waited and the coroner checked his records and went to select one of the storage drawers that lined the wall. He pulled it, nodded and walked back to his office, located a short distance away. The two detectives went to the gurney and Philos flipped back the sheet.

Nic resisted the urge to groan his annoyance and frustration when he saw the young man's face.

"How long has he been dead?"

"Almost as long as we've been looking for him, kid," the older man said with real kindness. "Is this the one who was giving Alex such a hard time?"

Nic nodded and walked away. He knew his partner would follow. As he passed the wastepaper basket, he dumped the file. Behind him, Philos retrieved it without comment.

"So what did you find out about this kid, Spaneas?" Philos asked a short while later. He placed a mug of coffee at Nic's elbow and perched on the edge of his desk, sipping his own strong Espresso.

Nic bit back a retort and forced his mind to think rationally, not emotionally. Philos was reminding him, without actually saying anything, that there was probably something in the file that they could use to at least begin a search.

"He's a runaway, but one with a lengthy past," Nic answered after an appreciative sip of coffee. He nodded his thanks to Philos, who smiled wryly, and then continued; "From what I've been able to get out of his case workers, he's been involved in several cult groups. Most recently, he's turned to religion. A few weeks ago, he disappeared from his home, and wasn't seen again until he surfaced at the lecture."

"Alex may be right," Philos suggested, thoughtful. "All of the destruction has been linked to religious shrines and temples. Not just here, but all over the world." He went to his desk and sorted through some of his own files, then reached for the phone. "I'm going to arrange a meeting with a friend of mine, someone who specializes in this kind of thing. He might have some idea what groups are likely to be active on this large a scale."

While Philos talked, Nic spotted a messenger coming toward him, envelope in hand. He accepted the thick manila packet and the young man walked away, quickly.

ϒ ϒ ϒ

Amarantha eased back in her chair, tired and restless at the same time. The past few days had become a blur of uneasy confrontations with Nickolas Stefanos, and endless reams of paper filled with more facts than she could recall, but told her nothing. She'd been poring over printouts and reading off the computer screen for hours on end again today. Katina had long ago been sent home, and the Champion of Olympus was chafing at the confinement and endless inactivity of her present state. She needed to get some rest, yet she was also anxious to pour her physical energy into something tangible.

She rose from the desk she'd been seated at for most of the evening and proceeded to pace the relative restriction of the office. She wondered if she should return to the apartment Alexandra Christophi shared with Nickolas Stefanos. She hadn't actually seen the young detective for over two days. She'd been sleeping, albeit uncomfortably, on the battered and worn sofa in the corner of the office.

She went to the coffee pot, poured the last of yet another pot into a mug and strolled to the window, sipping at the bitter brew as she contemplated the lack of progress she was making. Part of her brain reminded her that she'd been in this time less than a month, but deeper in her heart, she felt time was running out much too rapidly. Sighing heavily, she went back to the desk and sat, staring balefully at the electronic monster in front of her. She would rather have faced one of Hera's hydras at that moment, at least that type of monster could be slain and forgotten. This machine before her seemed to both complicate and simplify her research in maddening ways.

Late into the night, she finally conceded that she'd fought with the world wide web long enough for one day. She shut down the machine, turned off the lights, and went to the couch again. She settled on the sagging cushions and stared into the darkness, her mind sifting through the multitude of facts and fictions she'd unearthed during the past few days...

The serene silence was interrupted a short time later by the sound of footsteps moving stealthily in the corridor outside her room. There was something disturbingly familiar about the footfalls, the paces were even, careful, and clearly knew well the ground they tread.

She listened, straining to hear past the thunder of her heartbeat. Cursing inaudibly, she rose and went to the door, cracking it just enough to see into the hallway. There were two people there, a short distance away. She drew back instantly when one of the men lifted his hand in an age-old gesture for quiet, then he turned to stare in her direction. It took precious seconds for her to realize he wasn't actually looking at her, but past her. It hardly mattered, his face was clear in the low light that illuminated the corridor, and rage all but blotted out reason as she fought the urge to kill him where he stood.

Lyaeus!

It made no sense, a voice inside her mind shrieked. Lyaeus was dead. She'd killed him herself. Hadn't she? Confusion made her thoughts a sluggish quagmire of conflicting emotions. Only one thing held firm in her head, if she was wrong, Iphicles was in terrible danger. She tore open the door and ran, determined to gain the room at the end of the hall. As she neared, her voice rose in a shout of warning and terror...

"Iphicles!"

"Alex! My God! Wake up, darling."

"Iph..." She bolted into a sitting position and stared around wildly, searching frantically for the strangers.

"Alex?"

The concern in his voice finally reached through her panic and she turned to look into the gentle brown eyes of Nickolas Stefanos. For a moment, she saw Iphicles staring at her, then the world spun away in a cloud of gray mist as she fainted.

$$\Upsilon \; \Upsilon \; \Upsilon$$

The world swam back into focus on a twinge of real pain, and Amarantha winced as she sat up and opened her eyes. The source of her discomfort was a headache that pounded like a fist behind her eyes. She was still trying to orient herself when full awareness flooded in. She looked around in near panic, then gritted her teeth when she saw that she was in bed at the apartment Alexandra and Nickolas shared. She was also clad in a filmy nightgown of silk. Nic had to have put her to bed after she'd lost consciousness in the office.

That thought led her back to the moment she'd awakened, and all the rampant emotions that had rocked her senses then came rushing back. Lyaeus. Why dreams about a man who had been dead for millennia? And why now?

A sound at the door made her start and her look swung in that direction. Nic stood watching her, his expression one of loving warmth. For a moment, staring into the darkness of his eyes, seeing the love and the kindness there, she again felt Iphicles close to her.

"What happened?" It was a breathless whisper of sound fanned across the space that separated them, and Amarantha tried vainly to turn her gaze to anything other than Nickolas Stefanos and his suddenly intense presence.

"You fainted," he said and came into the room to sit next to her on the bed. "I think you were dreaming, Alex," he added, again with such warmth that she shivered almost imperceptibly in response to the stroke of his voice.

"Yes," she murmured, distracted by the longing that was seeping into her body. *How had she not seen into this man's eyes immediately?* Some inner voice questioned, though the logic that was forming such thoughts was remote. She looked at Nic, for perhaps the first time since she'd taken the form of his beloved Alexandra. *He is **not** Iphicles!* She tried to hold the assertion firm, but it was melting away beneath the growing heat of his stare.

"Were you dreaming of me?" he asked; his head tilted to one side and a glint of teasing sparkled in his dark eyes.

"Yes," she repeated, unaware of the whisper as he leaned closer and his lips covered hers in a kiss that ached with sensuality. For several minutes, Amarantha absorbed the unexpected thrill of a love so ancient she'd believed it truly gone. His touch was so like Iphicles', she wanted him with a passion that she'd thought long dead within her heart. The part of her mind that was still apart from her body's wanting tried to whisper a warning, to remind her that thousands of years had passed, and Iphicles was nothing more than myth. Nickolas Stefanos was not the Corinthian King she'd loved more than life in that ancient world.

Nic's hands weren't idle as she accepted his touch in a way that he'd begun to fear was gone forever. He caressed well-known curves and she arched beneath him when he lowered her back onto the bed and covered her body with his.

Amarantha's mind splintered from her body for moments that were heartbeats of time, and eternal in the same brief seconds. She was drawn back to Delphi, to a place in time when Apollo had summoned her to his favored Temple, along with the God of War.

"Nice of you to come, brother," Apollo taunted when Ares and his Champion stood before his altar.

"Why have you asked me to attend, Apollo?" Amarantha questioned, deliberately averting a confrontation between the two Olympians. They enjoyed their squabbling too much, and she was genuinely afraid of Apollo's reasons for their presence.

"Because Ares is so much more pleasant when he has his favorite pet with him, Champion!" the golden-haired God noted with patently false warmth. They all scorned her, even as they sometimes feared her. She understood neither reaction, and had less patience for it than they would ever know.

"You said Pythia had a message," Ares challenged, his tone dark and dangerous with subtle warning.

"She does, brother," Apollo assured him, smiling. "She wanted me to inform you that your creation will betray you. And," he paused for dramatic effect, then concluded with near tangible triumph, "when it happens, you will no longer have the means to guide her when she is not at your side." He watched them closely for response to the message, fully aware that it would be taken seriously. Neither warrior looked the least bit perturbed by the warning.

"You don't seem inclined to take me seriously," he noted to Ares.

"Amarantha would die rather than betray me," Ares decreed, with so much certainly that it was Apollo who experienced visible doubt.

"Is that it?" the War God demanded after a lengthy silence.

"Isn't that enough?" Apollo retorted. He smiled, and bowed. "You might want to remember my caution, regardless, brother," he stated softly, then vanished in a spray of glittering diamonds in the sunlit afternoon...

The memory came too late to be undone. *Your creation will betray you... when it happens, you will no longer have the means to guide her when she is not at your side...*

"No!"

It was a weak, half-hearted protest, given much too late into their intimacy. Amarantha felt Nic's body poised above her, and she shuddered, her heart and mind at war. The near explosive pleasure that seared a path along her veins intensified, and he was inside her, his hips moving in an ageless, erotic dance that her limbs knew well. He pulled back enough to look into her eyes, and she saw Iphicles smiling down on her. Ignoring the guilt that taunted her soul, the Champion of Olympus closed her eyes and let her heart soar as it hadn't since she'd knowingly and willingly gone to Iphicles' bed, and helped him to betray the vows another woman had made to the King she loved.

♈ ♈ ♈

The corridors of time itself trembled with the force of the rage that rocketed along their endless, labyrinthine passages. Ares knew the instant she succumbed to another man's passion, he'd felt her body melting in the other's arms, heard her feeble protest, and then reeled as she slipped away from him. The silence in his mind was unnerving after so long a time, and he quickly filled the emptiness with a fury unlike any he'd felt in several millennia.

"No..."

The faint, fragile denial offered him a distant kind of hope. She hadn't betrayed him completely, he rationalized. She'd attempted to reject the lover who held her, even if that attempt had been more reflexive than from the heart.

A rejection, however weak, was still a denial of deliberate intent.

Laughter echoed wildly in his head, and he recognized the voices as those of his parents and family.

Fury rose again, and struck outward...

CHAPTER TWELVE

Amarantha cringed, frozen with agony and terror. Nic's body, again positioned intimately over hers, felt the flinch of fear and he pulled back instantly. She rolled away, shaking violently as hatred and rage cloaked her, searing her from the inside out. She knew the source of that ferocious and savage fury, knew it so well it was part of her.

"No," she put her hands to her mouth, and ran for the bathroom, retching and crying as the magnitude of her actions began to crystallize in her mind. "Ares," she moaned in a low wail of misery. "What have I done?"

"Alex?"

Nic's voice was filled with concern, and he went to her side.

"What's wrong?"

He felt chilled to the core of his being, though the reason wasn't readily definable.

She cried. Pain screamed at him as she cringed and writhed in her anguish. There were no words between them; no anger; only tears that seemed endless poured from her as she mourned a loss so excruciating her pain was an entity that shared the small space with them. Nic's eyes grew bleak, and eventually he left her to her grief. He'd found Alexandra again for a few precious and passionate hours, yet, in the light of day, he knew he'd also lost her completely. She'd never be part of him again. And he'd never be whole again because of it.

♈ ♈ ♈

"Alex?"

Amarantha looked up from her desk and smiled shakily. Katina, encouraged by the response, entered the office. She walked over to stand next to Amarantha and glanced down at the files that were scattered across the desktop.

"The University just called," she told her boss. "They want to know if you're still going to do the lecture on Ancient Rituals."

Amarantha's heart sank. Another area of Alexandra's life that was a complete mystery.

"When is the lecture scheduled?" she asked warily.

"About two hours from now," Katina replied, her expression somewhat sheepish. "I was supposed to finalize things, but I forgot about it after the incident at the Acropolis. I'm sorry, Alex," she added, sincerely regretful.

"I'll do it," Amarantha assured her, certain she could easily speak on the subject without difficulty. "Where would my notes be?" she asked, tone distinctly ironic as she lifted papers and peered at labels, hopeful she'd find something that resembled a lecture guideline.

"Usually they're in your briefcase," Katina said with a smile and went to get the case from beside the door, where it had been for several days. She opened the case and rummaged for a few moments, then grinned triumphantly when she produced yet another file folder to add to the pile that were threatening to make the desk collapse.

"Just what you needed," she observed smartly and dropped the bright green folder, then made a quick escape. "Do you want me to call Angel?"

"Sure," Amarantha murmured absently, scanning the contents of the file and seeing the carefully plotted course of the lecture. Alexandra Christophi was meticulous in her work, and that attention to detail had already proven to be a tremendous help to the Champion on more than one occasion.

"Is there anything you need me to do while you're at the University?" Katina called from her office a few minutes later. "Angel will be here in an hour and a half," she added.

Amarantha rose and went to the office door that separated them. She leaned against the frame and smiled.

"Thank you," she answered, addressing the information about her ride to the University, then shook her head in reply to the first part of the query. "You might as well take the rest of the day off, if you have things that you'd like to get done, Kat. I may not even come back here once I've done the lecture. I was thinking about a trip to Delphi."

Katina was startled but made no comment on the information.

"Thanks, Alex," she grinned. "I think I can find something to do with a few hours free time."

"I thought you might," Amarantha remarked with dry humor.

ϒ ϒ ϒ

"What have you got there?" Philos asked, gesturing to indicate the file folder his partner had been engrossed in for almost a full hour.

Nic glanced up, dark eyes confused for an instant before his brain caught up with the question.

"The kid who came in with this, is he one of our usual couriers?"

"Didn't see him, Nic," Philos replied quietly. "Why?"

"Someone's claimed responsibility for the desecrations," Nic said with real trepidation in his deep voice. "If this is legit, we may have a lot more on our hands than a bunch of fanatics, Philos."

Philos extended his hand in wordless request and Nic gave him the file, watching his partner's face as he scanned the basics of the information contained on the few pages of paper.

"The One True Faith?" Philos said, tone incredulous.

"Read further, it gets better," Nic said sharply. "These lunatics swear they'll destroy all other faiths to bring their order to prominence." He closed his eyes and sighed heavily, leaning back in his chair. "Once Alexandra hears this, there's going to be no stopping her."

"How are things between you and Alex, kid?" Philos asked, once he'd tossed the file back onto the cluttered surface of Nic's desktop.

Nic opened his mouth to make an automatic kind of reply, then he saw the slight shake of Philos' head and knew he'd be wasting his time. The older man knew him far too well to be put off with platitudes.

"I don't know," he finally forced the words into the open and recognized despair in his own voice. "She's been so different since the night we thought she was shot. Like a stranger who wears Alexandra's face, but isn't remotely like her. We have moments," he admitted, "sometimes she's reachable. Then she pulls back and I don't know her anymore."

"Maybe it's this mess with the Gods and the shrines," Philos suggested. "You know what all this means to her, Nic. Maybe you just need to let her work it out alone, and she'll reach out when she needs you."

"What if she doesn't?" Nic dared to speak another crippling fear to this man who'd been like a father to him over the past few years, and he felt his chest tighten in response to simply hearing the thought spoken aloud.

"She loves you, Nic," Philos smiled his reassurance and nodded at the paperwork. "Trust it. Now let's get on with some work, kid. My wife's starting to forget what I look like it's been so long since I was home for an evening meal."

ϓ ϓ ϓ

The University of Athens, Theology Division. Amarantha walked the halls in appreciative quiet, taking in the peace of the atmosphere. She was only twenty minutes early for the lecture, and the serenity of the University was a much needed balm to her troubled spirit. She'd been ignoring the hollowness inside her all morning, pretending it wasn't there because she was completely unable to accept it. She knew very well what she'd done to her Master, and the price he would exact if they were ever reunited. She couldn't face it. Not yet. Not until she knew this life would not be her last.

That thought had been worming into her brain for days. Her life, her mortal life so long past, was emerging to meet her in this modern incarnation. And she dreaded the knowledge of why it was that the Fates were tormenting her with Iphicles, and his death, and her own pathetic weakness when faced with his spirit in another man. She'd encountered this test before, and it had never tempted her so deeply. Yet, this time, in this body, she had betrayed Ares.

"Professor Christophi?"

She turned, saw a young woman smiling at her.

"Your lecture room is over here," the girl explained quietly. "I'm looking forward to your talk."

"Thank you," Amarantha answered, and tried to smile. It was a weak effort, at best.

Two hours later, she was once more alone in the corridors. Classes had resumed, students were in scattered groups, and she was free to wander. She came to the administration wing and saw rows of framed photographs on the walls. Curious, she went to look at them, and was quickly absorbed in the study of faces.

Halfway down the wall, she spotted Alexandra, and Nickolas. They were happy, and their love genuine, it showed in both glowing, smiling faces. Further along, her blood turned to ice in her veins and she reached out, gasping inaudibly. Her palms were flat to the glass of the large frame, and she was fighting to retain her hold on consciousness when a distant voice pierced the fog that had very nearly overwhelmed her.

"Doctor Christophi, are you all right?"

The voice was gruff, older. She shook her head, unable to speak, equally unable to tear herself from the face she was staring into.

"Who is that?" she finally sputtered, pointing to the face that laughed at her from the wall. "Please," she whispered, near tears of frustration. "Who is he?"

Puzzled, the man glanced at the wall, then back at her.

"Leksi Mylonas," he supplied the name slowly, as though worried by her lack of knowledge. "He was your fiancé's closest friend when you all attended classes here."

Amarantha felt sick again, and the fog was enshrouding her mind in thicker mist. She would never recall how she came to leave the University and return to the haven of Alexandra's antiquities shop.

ᚋ ᚋ ᚋ

"I thought we were having dinner tonight, Alex."

She looked up from the papers she'd been poring over, vaguely disoriented for a few seconds. It had been almost a week since the night she'd dreamed about Lyaeus. She had been going home to Nic most nights, and had been enjoying his company. She had allowed no further intimacy, and he was hurt by the withdrawal. His pain bothered her, though she was again determined not to look too closely at the reasons. He was still affecting her senses in much the same way she suspected he'd affected his beloved Alexandra, and that alone was reason to avoid prolonged contact with him.

Knowing it didn't make it more appealing, and thus far, she'd ignored the continual warnings that were roiling deep in her consciousness.

In a weak attempt to escape her increasingly intense attraction to him, she'd spent most of the past two days in the small museum. She'd closed it entirely to the public and had again been sleeping on the office couch. Katina had only left her a few hours earlier. Nic had called numerous times. He now looked angry and worried.

"I'm sorry," she apologized, distracted by the reading that was still engaging most of her attention. "I must have forgotten. Perhaps we could go out another night."

She meant it as a dismissal, and he knew it.

Amarantha had to resist the urge to strike him when he grabbed the sheaf of paper from her hand and threw it aside.

"What in hell is wrong with you, Alex?" he demanded furiously. "We haven't spent a full evening together since the night you were shot! Since the night I *thought* you were shot," he corrected with distinct sarcasm. It was easier to approach the shooting from the safety of annoyance, rather than face that he had almost lost her, but by some miracle, she'd walked away from a potentially fatal wound without a scratch to show for the ordeal. He softened slightly, adding, "The other night..."

"I've been busy looking into what's been happening all over this world," she interjected, before he could remind her of the passion they'd shared that night. It was safer for the moment to pretend that hadn't been real. She chose to attack, at least verbally. "Have you found this cult leader who wants to destroy all organized religion in this world?"

"This is not a worldwide conspiracy against religious order." Even as he said it, he heard his doubt. Alex clearly read it in his voice.

"Then what would you call it?" she charged angrily. "And, more importantly, what have you done about stopping it? This is your heritage at stake, too, in case you may have chosen to forget that fact!"

"We're doing our best, Alex," he snapped.

She nodded, and her scorn was plain when she spoke again.

"Your best is unacceptable." She glared at him. "Do you even know who is behind this? Have you at least discovered his name?" She had begun to trace a thread that was based more on suspicion and intuition than actual fact, and while it enraged her to the core, she wasn't yet ready to share the potential lead with anyone. Not until she was certain her hunch was correct.

"No," he admitted, swallowing the bitterness with difficulty. She was deliberately goading him, but despite the knowledge, he couldn't ignore it and leave her quietly. He also couldn't escape the sensation that he'd lost her, totally, and would never be close to her again.

"I have work to do, Nickolas," she said, and retrieved the pages he'd scattered on the office floor. "Would you mind locking the door behind you?"

"Yes, I would. You're coming home with me."

"No, I am not," she stated, her tone one that left no room for argument or discussion. "I have spent a good many hours learning all that has been going on in this world. The weapons and madness are such that even Ares would be appalled by the inhumanity. Organized law cannot stop the profaning of the Gods, in all their guises, so I intend to do what I must to end it."

As she spoke, she knew Alexandra Christophi was no longer even a shadow within her; the Champion of Olympus had just revealed herself to a mortal who didn't know who or what he gazed upon.

Nic shuddered imperceptibly as Alex's dark eyes flared with silvery light. She was alien to him for those heartbeats of time, and he was afraid of her. Then, just as quickly, the illusion was no more. But there was no warmth or love in her eyes when she looked at him, only a tinge of sorrow.

"I need to work, Nickolas," she repeated, softer now. "We will talk later."

He knew it was a lie, but it no longer mattered. He went to stand before her, touched her hair and her face with a feather-like caress, then he kissed her. His heart broke within him at the lack of response in her body. The Alexandra who loved and wanted him had been killed leaving the theater, and whoever remained had no further need of him.

"Good-bye, Alexandra," he whispered, and kissed her cheek.

Amarantha went, somewhat unwillingly, to the window and watched him drive away. He had paused just a moment, to look up at her, then he'd climbed into the vehicle and was gone.

"I am sorry, young one," she said to the empty air. For several moments the words filled the room with her, and with them, gradually, came unwanted memories.

Less than fifty years after her transformation, Amarantha had found herself the unlikely liege to a man who declared that his destiny was to serve her. She'd thought him absurd, but he would not be dissuaded. In the end she had accepted his presence, and over time, she'd grown to love him. Ares had very nearly destroyed her when he learned of the man's constant presence. The argument they'd had was one of the most vicious of any they'd ever engaged in, before, or since.

That day returned to her now, as sudden and swift as a bird taking flight...

Amarantha's hair whipped around her face, blinded her for precious seconds as she avoided the sword of her newest would-

be assassin. She hated this body she had been thrust into, its lethargic responses, even after years of awareness of the weakness, were still infuriating, and dangerous. She breathed deeply, searched the core of her spirit for the strength that her God and master had taught her. She shuddered when her attacker's weapon sliced into her right arm, cutting close to the bone.

Canthus yelled a warning, cursing furiously as he tried, vainly, to free himself from the men who held him from his charge to aid her.

Pain lit trails of fire and agony that rippled through her, and she forcibly blocked her awareness of it. She dodged, motion graceful and easy as instinct overrode the restrictions of an alien form. Ares' voice murmured approval and she smiled inwardly. She could only hear him when she was near the end of her mission; and his well-loved tones gave her new strength.

Amarantha continued the pirouette of movement, and as she swung to face her enemy, she focused intently on her purpose. This infidel was the last of a large group who had been defiling and looting the Temples of the Gods. With his death, that desecration would finally end.

And the Champion could return to her own place in time.

"Who are you?"

She smiled, the gleaming blade of her sword poised at his throat.

"I believe you already know," she murmured softly, tone pitched to a lethal purr of anger and contempt.

He shook his head, dark skin suddenly tainted with ash gray as he denied inwardly what his instincts taunted him with as he stared into her eyes.

"You cannot be..."

She laughed, the sound bitter, and layered with irony.

"Amarantha," she supplied.

He closed his eyes and waited, now certain of his demise.

She struck, the pure silvery metal of Hephaestus' God-forged weapon sliding through the sinew and bone of the mortal before her. His blood flowed freely and she screamed inside her head; demanded of the Gods her release.

The whirl of life transference began as the slain soldier completed his journey to Hades' domain. Amarantha clenched her teeth as her own body, held in the stasis between all worlds, began to wake fully. She whispered a prayer of thanks to Zeus, aware as she did so of the incongruity of it. The King of the Gods, like the others on Olympus, would not be overly pleased that she had survived yet again. Only one of the Twelve would welcome her, and she smiled with the knowledge of their reunion.

When the dimensional spirals and spins ceased, she slowly sat up and looked around. She was in his Temple, the surroundings of home a vision that made her heart soar with relief. She rose and glanced at the polished mirror, reassured by the face that looked back at her from the glass. Waist-length white hair, palest gray eyes, and the lithe form that had been her mortal body. She turned to glance at the bed, smiled as she went to lift from it the gossamer, trailing white silk gown; the raiment he always chose for her return to him.

The garden outside the Temple was lush and in full bloom when she stepped into the afternoon sun. She spotted him instantly and ran to his side.

He spun around, caught her to him, and she thrilled at the touch she had craved so often during the years of separation. This time it had been a span of nearly two decades that they'd been apart. His hands cupped her face and she knew he drank her image as deeply as she did his in those first, cherished moments.

"You were reckless," he admonished after several minutes of silence. "Numerous times. It is getting more difficult to sense you as our world drifts from real time to memory."

"I know," she nodded. "I lost your presence many times, Beloved," she whispered. "But when I needed you most, I heard your voice."

"That may not happen again," he said.

"Ares, why do they want me to fail?"

The God of War smiled; a dark, cold shift of strikingly handsome features.

"They know you will live long after we have become myth," he told her, velvety voice rough and textured with countless nuances and subtle emotions. "That I created you to preserve our place in history was an act to which few were happy to concede. They see you outliving Gods and mortals, because you are both, yet neither."

"I am what you made me," she replied quietly, uneasy. "First your slave, then your student. I have served you in all ways,

as I do your family. The Fates decree what my existence means, in whatever life I am needed."

"They've also foreseen our end," the War God imparted, voice hushed, troubled.

"I am bound to you," she began, then hesitated when his dark eyes flared with rage and power. "Ares?"

"You will walk the earth long after us," he stated.

"No," she shook her head, tried to free herself from the suddenly suffocating strength of his arms.

"It is your Destiny," he said simply, then kissed her; a long, intimate caress of sensuality and need. "Consort to the God of War; Champion of Olympus; more eternal than time itself ... That was the Fate I chose for you, Amarantha."

"Yet if I fail—"

"You won't," he interrupted quietly. "Unless you choose to die. I did not train you to die in a mortal form, worlds away from me."

"No," she nodded in agreement. "And I have chosen to be all you have demanded." She leaned into him, and closed her eyes as he held her tightly to him, by trying to ignore the whispers of fear that plagued her. Slowly, she became aware of his anger, and it created a sliver of fear that sliced upward along the curve of her spine. She eased back, stared into his stormy eyes.

"Amarantha..."

She shuddered, weakened to the core of her being when she heard Canthus' scream of agony.

"Ares," she trembled against him. "Please, help him, my master."

The God's smouldering gaze held hers and rage rose from deep inside her.

"You are permitting his death," she charged. "WHY?"

"Because he's lain beside you every night for years," Ares snarled. "Because I want his death."

"No," she shook her head and tore free of him. "Damn you, Ares!"

She ran, spirit searching outside herself for the way back to her last death. She rarely did this, moving through time, it frightened her each time she made the perilous journey.

Her body was assailed by bolts of excruciating pain as she found the path, and continued.

When she was able to see Canthus again, he was bleeding, badly. She knew he was near death. She'd been too late to save him.

"Ares..." She had no strength left to fight, not in those moments, and she knew He was close. His hand on her shoulder seconds later was both comfort and torment.

"He's on his way to Tartarus," the War God growled.

"He deserves better than that!"

Silver eyes met ebony and held in a clashing confrontation of wills. He laughed minutes later when he knew she would not back down.

"You're a fool, Amarantha," he declared softly.

"The Elysian Fields, Ares," she asked. "Please, Beloved?"

He shook his head and she took a step backward when his handsome features contorted with fury. It took several moments to realize that his wrath was not at her, but directed to another God. Amarantha looked, and felt mixed emotions when she saw Aphrodite. The Goddess always created an unreasonable apprehension within the Champion. Perhaps because she was the only one who could tame Ares' rage when it threatened to blossom beyond sanity.

"He'll go to the Fields, Amarantha," Aphrodite said with a smile. "He died protecting the one he loved. Ares simply wants him to suffer because that was you."

"He was a good man," she told the Goddess.

She nodded, ethereal and pure in her beauty and empathy...

"I have never forgotten you, Canthus," Amarantha murmured, voice barely audible in the stillness that had enshrouded her since Nic's departure. Nic, she thought, was much like Canthus had been. And much like her beloved Iphicles, as well, which was perhaps even more dangerous for him. And for that reason more than any other, she had needed for him to leave her. She could not afford another affront to Ares' pride. His jealousy was too dangerous a thing to incite, even after so many centuries. She had committed one offense that might irrevocably separate them from across the span of time, a second lapse of judgement and she would be well and truly lost to the world she loved.

Shrugging off the melancholy and sudden loneliness for a life long gone, Amarantha pushed herself away from the window and went back to the work that was demanding her attention. She was waiting for calls from all over the world, for Alexandra's contacts to supply her with information from their own countries. In spite of the blocks thrown in her path, she *was* beginning to put the picture together into cohesive sequence, and probable cause. It was the latter that stirred unwelcome trepidation deep within her heart.

CHAPTER THIRTEEN

Delphi was as timeless as the Gods themselves, and Amarantha felt a rare moment of peace and familiarity as she began the Sacred Walk to Apollo's Shrine. In any age, this place was both mythical and magical. The narrow streets of the bustling village were filled with tourists from all over the globe, and all wore varying expressions of reverence and excitement. The friendly voices of the local people rang out as greetings were exchanged, and she smiled at the age-old atmosphere that remained constant, despite the passage of many centuries. Apollo's favored city had always been this way, a place of peace and tranquility. With only a few exceptions throughout history, it had also been left free of the destruction of invading forces.

Blocking her inner awareness of the other people present, she strolled, feeling new life seep into her being as her mind translated the remnants of her present reality to the majesty of the past. While she gazed upon ruins and columns, her mind gave her images of the structures as they'd been when she'd first walked this path. With a God.

The Stoa of the Athenians came into view and she stared, seeing the multitude of columns and bracings that had held the layered roof high and proud over the tiered ground. Further down the path she came to Apollo's Temple, and in spite of her temporal happiness, she was saddened to note that only seven of the many columns had survived into this century, and none of the roof and walls had weathered the passage of time. She walked up the ramp and stood in the center of what should have been the temple's main area of worship. The gargantuan columns dwarfed her presence, while inspiring the sense of awe that was a nearly tangible part of any of the temples dedicated to the mighty Olympians. This ruin was both exquisitely beautiful, and heart-wrenchingly painful to witness. Apollo had been one of the most cherished of the Gods, and this place had been both sacred and joyous in its splendor. As the ravages of time filled her vision, she was chilled by the loss that overwhelmed her previous serenity.

"Apollo," she mused softly. "I think I am glad that you cannot see what has become of all you built on these grounds." She laughed at her whimsy, then sighed. "What am I doing here? I have no weapons to fight the madman who is trying to obliterate you from history, my friends." She sighed inaudibly, her mind alive with conflict that was only partly born of her presence in this alien time. So many things had returned to haunt her in this other life, things so long past, they were no longer even history, but myth and legend. Iphicles had not filled her heart and thoughts for many centuries. He was always part of her, but the grief of his death had not been so raw for more years than she cared to contemplate. And there were dreams of Lyaeus. She had never been plagued by dreams of her mortal past before.

Was this the end of her existence then? Had the circles of life finally turned their full course and brought her back to her beginnings in this modern, yet archaic time?

Ice kissed the back of her neck and she felt honest fear. An answer, an unwanted knowledge began to make itself known to her soul. She was going to die this time. Fate had brought her to her end. The Gods were gone in this world, and their Champion would soon follow. She was less myth than they, known only to scholars and poets who understood the old languages and ways. Ares had thought she would outlive mortals and Gods, and she now knew she would be lost to both. Lost to Him.

She tried to silence the whispers of discouragement that nagged her, and decided to go on to the Sanctuary. But, before she went to see the modern day Pythia, she wanted to see other places that were part of Delphi's complex.

Memories of the glorious Pythian Games came into focus and she wondered if she would be able to visit Olympia before her time was done. She'd loved the Games almost

as much as the Gods themselves, and had competed in
several areas on occasion. Ares watched over her, but did
not interfere with her ability to meet the mortal combatants
fairly. She'd thrived during the competitions, learning from
the humans she worked with, and learning to respect their
drive and determination in ways she had never been able
to appreciate as one of them. She had lost as often as she
had won. In victory or defeat, she had enjoyed every minute
of the events.

Moving on, Amarantha almost wept when she came to
the once grand theater. There was no longer any sign of
the impressive stage, only broken remains of the countless rows of stone seats that had been filled by enthusiastic
audiences over the centuries. She closed her eyes, reached
across time for the sense of wonder and euphoria that had
consumed her when Ares himself had brought her to the
theater. The performance had honored the Gods, and when
they returned to the temple in Thrace, she had finally given
herself fully to the Master she'd learned to love in such
a different way than she had Iphicles.

The day was hot and the sun brilliant. She closed her
eyes, let her mind's eye guide her steps to the stage area.
There she stood, wrapped in ancient truth and modern
misery. The heat warmed her skin as the past rimed her
heart in ice. Ares' face swam before her; not the fury of
battle and bloodlust, but the tenderness of affection spilling
from his dark, eternal eyes. Had she ever told him that she
did, in fact, love him? Somehow, it seemed to matter now
that it was impossible to correct the omission of her deepest
truth concerning him.

Turning away, she walked on. The Doric Treasury, what
little still stood of it, eventually came into view, and she
hugged herself tightly, fought away the cold that was now
residing in her very bones. The buildings that had once
housed priceless sculpture were hardly more than piles
of rubble in this century. The Tholos was no more than a
trio of age whitened stone fingers reaching into the dazzling
effulgence of the azure sky. Everywhere she looked she
saw scarred magnificence, and it weighed heavy on her
already burdened spirit.

Amarantha was weary of looking at tumbled stones. She headed for the Sanctuary, and pretended she didn't notice the destruction that surrounded her while she concentrated her mental energy on the Oracle's ancient presence. Anger tweaked her consciousness when she saw the roped off quadrants where the damage was still being assessed. It would be years before any real repairs could restore what remained intact of the precious site. And, if there was any hope of restoration, she would not see it. If there was no other certainty in her mind now, it was that simple assurance of her impending failure and death.

She stepped up to the altar and waited, eyes closed.

Pythia, I need your guidance. The Gods forbid help, but is guidance to be denied me, as well?

Silence pressed down upon her and she bit back a curse of fury, tainted with sincere dolor. It had been a desperate hope, thinking that she might obtain some glimmer of useful knowledge through the lingering spirit of Apollo's adjutant, but the futility of her present lack of direction was feeding a fear she had not felt in many, many years — if she had ever truly been this certain of failure and loss. The year 2000 had begun with worldwide celebrations, and more acts of terrorism, yet she was no closer to discovering who wielded the real power behind the strikes. A religious order called *The True God* had claimed responsibility for all that had been taking place, but no one thus far had been able to learn more than that. The group's leader, the real power, remained out of reach, only an unsubstantiated suspicion murmuring within her soul.

ϒ ϒ ϒ

Throughout the week, Amarantha made visits to the Hill of Muses, stared for hours at the Acropolis, walked repeatedly through the Theater of Dionysus. With each visit to the ancient places, she grew more confused, and more determined to find the people responsible for the continued destruction and desecration. Athens swarmed around her in all its surging life and abandon. She felt claustrophobic in the city, and frequently escaped to the familiar cities of her past life. Nickolas Stefanos was fading to memory, as was her indiscretion with him. She had virtually moved into the small museum, and he had not objected strongly when she'd told him of the decision. That more than anything assured her that he knew his beloved Alexandra was no longer reachable. It saddened her as much as it had relieved her. Today, she had resolved to brave the crowds of the heart of Greece and visit the Athenian Acropolis. When she decided it was time to see the Parthenon up close, she was unprepared for the defilement that awaited her in Athena's beloved monument.

Stumbling against the backlash of her fury and revulsion, Amarantha turned her back on the Parthenon and dragged air into objecting lungs. She took time gathering her composure, then went in search of a phone. The time had come for her to do more than mourn and question her fate in this century. She needed to *do* something. Regardless of the futility of the exercise.

"Katina?"

"Hi, Alex," was the bubbly reply. "Where are you? Nic's been by again."

"I want you to bring something to me," Amarantha said, ignoring the reference to Nickolas Stefanos. "Can you do that?"

"Sure," Katina answered, her tone revealing her uneasiness. "Where are you?"

"There's a case in the museum. A long, slender case. It's in the storage room. Meet me at the Areopagus."

"Alex..."

"Just do this for me, Katina," she breathed softly, voice colored by fatigue that was now a permanent part of her. "I will deal with Nic later."

"I'll see you soon," Katina promised.

ᚷ ᚷ ᚷ

While she waited for Katina in an outdoor café, Amarantha mentally pored over all the research she'd gathered in the long months since her arrival in the new century. The destruction and fear that dominated the people of this era had sickened her once, as such things always had, but in a deeper part of her mind, she recognized several unwelcome truths, also. She was to honor and defend the place of the Ancient Gods in this world, and it had become impossible. This world had no need of Gods to guide them. They ruled themselves in whatever fashion was expedient and profitable. Cynicism was the religion most placed their faith in, never questioning what had brought them into their present.

The Gods of Olympus and their contemporaries had been capricious and carefree, with little compassion for the mortals they toyed with on so many levels. Yet, even their casual disregard for humanity was not so cold or cruel as the disdain that presided over this era of mankind's history. The Gods could not exist here and be Gods. They would be thought deranged mortals. Power and indifference ruled this time, not the hope and charity that she had often found throughout her long lifespan.

One True God, indeed. The ideal was corrupt before it was fully formed, because the one who preached it had already succumbed to the lure of power and omnipotence.

Amarantha finished her coffee, looked at the watch that adorned her wrist, and rose. A final glance at the busy, energetic city of Athens stirred melancholy for a few moments, then she dismissed it and braced herself for the confrontation that instinct assured her was now only days away.

ϒ ϒ ϒ

It was dusk when Katina finally arrived with the case that Amarantha had told her to bring. The Areopagus was shadowy and looming, a presence as awesome and intimidating as the God for which it had been named. Katina stared up, sensing a darkness that had little to do with the encroaching night.

"What's in the case?"

"Nothing you need be concerned with, Katina," Amarantha said softly. "Thank you for bringing it to me."

"We should go home, Alex," Katina suggested hope-fully.

"I have things that I need to do here," Amarantha replied, gazing at the infamous Hill of Ares.

"Do you want me to wait?"

Amarantha smiled at the whisper of anxiety in Katina's voice. She shook her head, and the girl's relief was almost palpable.

"I'll see you soon," Amarantha said, and gave her an impulsive hug. "Be safe," she murmured, and watched the young woman disappear in the thickening shades of twilight. As she waited again, the sky darkened from plum to purple, and finally coalesced into blackness. A crescent moon rose to slash the velvet carpet spread above her, and the crystallized tears of the Gods began to wink into being.

When the last of the tourists finally drifted away, Amarantha climbed the hill, carrying her case with familiar ease. When she reached the top, she knelt, the receptacle placed carefully before her. For a long time she merely breathed in the tangy air, and prepared mentally for the exercises in which she was about to engage. As night cloaked the Areopagus, the Champion opened the case and donned the leather and armor of her true self. She'd pur-chased close replicas of her garments, and she had also purchased a sword; a weapon crafted almost two centuries earlier, and one that was a true weapon of battle. Once she was attired for war, she began the ageless movements and choreography of battle. Her borrowed body, so young and vital, so unlike her last form, quickly attuned to the rhythms, and her spirits lifted as she flowed into the motion.

Her mind, apart from the dance though remaining in harmony with the action, recalled another time...

The air had changed, the cool transformation of season replaced by a breath of summer returning briefly to bless them. She turned her thoughtful gaze eastward and clutched the stone balustrade of the balcony that adjoined a room high in the temple of Thrace. Then she felt Ares' approach.

"Come down to the garden with me," he asked quietly.

She smiled, and followed him, her hand clasped loosely in his. There was no need for conversation as they stood side by side and watched the miracle of daybreak.

The first rays of the emerging sun were thin fingers of gold that curled upward to reach beyond the shelf of the night's horizon and breathe golden splendor over all of Greece. This was a rare moment of peace between the War God and his student, and Amarantha concentrated more intently on the flow of the bond he had created with her in this tranquil sharing. Ares' mental kiss brought a smile to her lips and he drew her into the place that few rarely saw, his soul.

The brilliance of the burning sun was almost painful as the first rounded slip of the fiery star crested the skyline. The blackness had receded, driven back by the powerful enchantress that was the sun. Red-gold glory painted the sky a new shade, fading blood against blossoming blue. The rays strengthened, gradually brightened to even more beautiful yellow.

Amarantha basked in the incredible spectacle that filled her vision. She felt as though she were being reborn, awakened to the hope and possibility of eternal life. She raised her arms, and her head fell back as she bathed in the warmth of the new day. The wash of gentle heat caressed skin that was impossibly flushed, and tears formed behind her closed lids.

Time had become suspended in the minutes that held them enslaved by the sunrise. Amarantha didn't want the beauty she saw to ever fade. Ares kissed her temple and murmured into her ear.

"Now we begin the day's work, little one."

She turned, bowed low before him, and caught the sword he tossed to her as he stepped back and away.

"It seems an affront to mar such beauty with war, my master," she all but purred at him.

Ares' smile didn't reach his eyes, and she cried out when he struck in earnest, and she fell to her knees, blood pouring from her midriff.

"Ares!" It was a gasp of disbelief and anger, and she raised her weapon in automatic defense when he would have struck a second time.

"Why?!"

"Never let yourself be seduced by beauty, little one," he growled. *"It destroys your ability to see an attacker until it's too late to stop him."*

... Scorn-filled laughter jolted her from the memory, and she turned, livid with rage and eager to do battle with whoever dared to mock her.

♈ ♈ ♈

"Your recovery is something of a miracle, Doctor Christophi," he murmured, dark eyes shrewd and fathomless. When she lowered the sword she held and stared at him, silver-shadowed brown eyes glittering with anger, he stepped closer to her. The warrior's stance stiffened, and he noted the grip on her weapon became more alert as well.

"You are the Gods' Champion, aren't you?" he enquired as he drew closer, circled her. His gaze was an inspection, and she ground her teeth in response to the insolent scrutiny. "It would seem Alexandra had good reason to fear your existence."

"Who are you?" Her breath quickened, and every cell in her body screamed for action.

"Your master," he replied with a smile.

Amarantha's expression changed radically, and she laughed as she smoothly sheathed her sword. Real recognition had finally given her vague fears a point of focus. She did not know this man, yet she did. Her heart, the truest voice she had ever known, fed her the knowledge she'd been unable to find elsewhere. And rage blossomed to the brink of insanity for several timeless, eternal seconds. When she was able to control the fury that permeated her entire being and speak past it, she inclined her head curtly, the gesture one of ironic contempt.

"No man is my master," she assured him with quiet sincerity.

"Of course not," he answered, tone condescending, inciting her wrath. She surprised him when she smiled again, met his ridicule with her own arrogant irony.

"You have not named yourself," she pointed out a few moments later as they continued to watch each other in measuring appraisal.

"Renata," he supplied, and bowed.

"The Reborn?" She savored the name, and stepped closer. "Your true name, mortal fool."

"As you give yours," he taunted.

"Amarantha," she whispered.

"The flower that never fades... Champion of the Gods of Olympus—"

"Slave, student, and lover of Ares," she interrupted with a smile.

"The old texts hint at your existence. I thought you as much a myth as those you were said to serve. It does make a kind of sense, who would know but an ancient? You have the location of what I seek," he surmised. "Otherwise, they would not have sent you to me."

"I know nothing of you," she said, voice a low hiss of renewed anger. "But," she smiled, and the threat surfaced to her eyes, "should I find that you are responsible for the destruction I have seen in this century, the Gods themselves could not protect you. Not," she paused, "that they would want to."

"They'll bow to me before long," he remarked. "*If* they exist."

"If they exist?" she repeated thoughtfully, tone sardonic. "The Gods are all around you," she assured him. "They are in each sunrise and sunset; in each changing of the tides; in each season and living thing that graces this pitiful world in which you hope to rule. They *are* life, Renata."

"Spoken like the archaic peasant your heart will always reveal you to be."

She bristled.

"This *archaic peasant* could kill you where you stand," she reminded him with lethal softness.

"Only if you wish to die where your lover once stood trial," Renata replied, and waited as several men joined them, all heavily armed and ready to destroy the woman who faced him.

Darkness was complete for several moments as the silvery-white moon slipped behind cloud cover. In that precious few seconds, Amarantha made her escape. She heard the explosions of automatic weapon fire following her into the night as Renata's men tried to locate her by sheer number of bullets fired. His order to cease fire was a relief. There were people at the base of the Hill of Ares, and she knew the police would be all over the area in minutes. She knew with equal certainty that Renata and his people would vanish as swiftly as she had.

Her heartbeat was roaring wildly in her ears as she ran, anger and fear roiling rampant within her mind. How was she supposed to fight a war in this world when her only real weapons were a sword, and primeval courage? The scope of the task had never truly registered until she'd seen the destruction that could be wrought in less than two minutes. The Areopagus was scarred and defiled, and a madman now knew an ancient Champion walked among modern mortals.

Uncertain, and genuinely worried about her chances of success, Amarantha headed for the Christophi museum. She'd seen Renata's face, now she would have to begin the arduous search for his true identity. Her suspicion would not be all that was needed, however certain the foreboding had become during the brief confrontation on the Areopagus.

She needed knowledge, and if permitted, time.

She was not sure she would be granted either luxury.

♈ ♈ ♈

Hours after fleeing the Areopagus, Amarantha sat in silent fury while she watched the news report about the latest attack on the Temple of Zeus. She had no doubt that Renata and his followers had left the Hill of Ares after her, and gone directly to the Temple. Had they thought she would go there? If that had been the case, then the key to what they were after was hidden somewhere in the Temple. She did know that there was one item of value in the Temple's depths, but it was not something that would be important to anyone other than her. So, what did they expect to find in the ancient building?

Too many questions plagued her, and she had little in the way of answers that would make things clearer. She glanced at the computer system. She'd been watching Katina use the machine, and was fairly confident that she could operate it unaided by her friend. She hoped so, at any rate.

It took time, but she was able to finally locate a piece of what she needed.

In the late hours of the following night, Amarantha keyed in still another in an endless run of random passwords and, minutes later, was miraculously granted access to the heavily protected website that had been created, but not launched to the world. Yet. She quickly discovered that Renata's new order was calling itself The Followers of The One True God, and their gospel was the Doctrine of The True God. She scanned what there was in the way of excerpts of the canon, and her rage grew. He'd taken from every known faith on the planet, pieces from mythology, cultural tenets, and the laws of many Christian faiths. In time, she also found the madman's real name, though it was well buried beneath layers of rewritten life history.

Another dawn was beginning to flush the sky when she decided it was time to go to the Temple herself and retrieve what she had hidden there lifetimes ago.

On her way out the door, she ran directly into Nickolas Stefanos.

"What are you doing here?" she questioned tersely.

Nic's attractive features tightened with anger, but he held his temper in check.

"I want you to come home," he said quietly, with forced patience. "I know you haven't been to the apartment in almost a week. You've barely left this office during the past few days!"

"We've had this discussion before, Nickolas. I've been busy, and you knew I've been staying here most of the time," she replied, annoyed at having to explain anything to him, but knowing that he had a right to his anger and frustration.

"You're going to get yourself killed, Alex," he whispered, allowing his fear to be heard. "Honey, let me help you do whatever it is you're trying to do. I know how important this is to you, but don't you know that you're everything to me? That's why I'm here. To try to make you see reason. I need you, Alex. I love you! I won't give up on us without a fight."

"Nic, this is not the time. Nor is it the appropriate place."

"Then make time," he snapped.

"Once I've stopped this madness," she evaded.

Nic took her arms in a firm grip and made her look at him.

"No," he objected. "We need to talk now, not when this is over. When it's done you'll only make more excuses."

"Then perhaps you should simply let me go," she suggested coldly.

"Alex..." He stopped, uncertain.

"The man behind this, do you know his name?"

He shook his head.

"We found the gun that was used in the attempt on your life. And, probably, the man who used it. He was dead, the prints and ballistics confirmed we had the right weapon."

"Who was it?"

"Endre Spaneas."

She ran the name through recent memory of all those she'd been able to confirm as followers of The True God, and she recalled seeing it in the files she'd put together. She nodded.

"He's one of them," she murmured unconsciously. "Do you have a name for the leader of this new order?"

"Not yet, but we're getting closer."

"Research your old school friend Leksi Mylonas," she told him. "His lineage goes back to ancient times. One of his ancestors, a man called Lyaeus, betrayed and killed a king." Amarantha stopped the wash of rage and hatred as it threatened to overwhelm her. She forced calm into her system, and put the past back where it belonged. Nickolas watched her with narrowed eyes, but said nothing about the emotions he had certainly seen with shocking vividness.

"I lost track of Leksi years ago, you know that. Why do you think he's part of this, Alex?"

She sighed.

"Just do it, Nickolas," she repeated. "He's the one you're looking for."

"Where do I find him?" he asked, not bothering to attempt concealing his sarcasm.

"The Temple of Zeus would be my guess," she retorted sweetly.

She started to sweep past him and he grabbed her. She pushed away from him with a force that made him stumble. He continued to stagger when a gunshot split the morning stillness and he was flung toward her, taking the bullet in the center of his back.

"Alex..."

She caught him and lowered him to the sidewalk, her eyes darting to the rooftop across the street. A figure watched, saw her scrutiny, then ran. She looked back to the man who clutched at her.

"Nickolas," she said gently. "Try not to talk." She rummaged in his jacket pocket for the phone that she knew would be there. She began to dial, but he took it from her hand and threw it aside.

"Who... are... you?" he gasped, his voice filled with pain that was as much emotional as physical. "You look like Alex, but..." he swallowed, hard, went on, "I know... you're not!"

She smiled, touched his face with fingers more gentle than he would have thought possible. He had briefly brought Iphicles back to her heart and her life, for that she would always be fond of him. Nickolas deserved the truth, he was dying because he'd been trying to protect her. Sadly, he was not the first to die in such a way, nor would he be the last if she continued to survive.

"You're very wise for one so young," she murmured. "My name is Amarantha. I was born in the time of the Gods, and I am here to defend their memory. Alexandra Christophi died the night she was shot, Nickolas. Though I wish it were not so, I think you will be joining her very soon." She smiled through unexpectedly real tears. "You are much like my Iphicles, young one," she whispered. "I think you will soon know that." She kissed his forehead, and added in a whisper, "tell him he remains in my heart, Nickolas."

He smiled, heard the distant wail of sirens, then closed his eyes as the world started a steady, irrevocable descent into blackness...

"Go in peace, young one," Amarantha murmured, then closed her eyes for several moments in prayer. "Give him a place with his beloved, Hades, he has died in our service, too." She extricated herself from the awkward position they'd fallen into, reached inside his jacket a second time, and retrieved the weapon holstered under his left arm. Tucking it into her own coat pocket, she left him on the sidewalk.

She hadn't taken more than a single step when the back of her head tingled in warning.

A heartbeat too late.

Pain exploded within her skull, a blinding burst of diamond-bright shards of stark white brilliance that died to pitch black in the space of an instant. Nothingness rose to embrace her and carry her into the abyss of another kind of nightfall.

CHAPTER FOURTEEN

The walls were damp with mildew, and the scent of mould and decay was suffocating. But the absolute darkness was not something Amarantha feared as she crouched in a corner and stared into nothingness. Her clothes were filthy, and her skin crawled with invisible parasites. She no longer knew how much time had passed since she'd been taken outside the Christophi museum/shop. It had not been a pleasant captivity, but she had endured worse in other lives.

That fact was small consolation to her present discomfort.

Sounds from somewhere far above teased at her mind, tortured her with the knowledge that she was being held in this prison, and deliberately ignored. They never told her precisely why they'd taken her; of course, that hadn't really been necessary. They'd denied her food and water for what felt like several days, kept her in shackles that were anchored securely within stone walls. The tiny pin-pointed daggers that were engraved deep into the metal cuffs scraped and scarred her wrists, kept the pain a dull but constant companion.

Yet, no one had spoken. Not even the madman who'd ordered her capture. Renata, she sneered internally, was a monster like many others she'd encountered throughout history. He was twisted with unfulfilled desires and truths so distorted they were no longer truth in any form. She'd spent some time in the University library after seeing his photograph on the wall of the administration wing. She'd learned a lot about his academic background, and in the guise of Alexandra Christophi, she'd been able to contact people who'd known him as a young man. Several of those people had been very forthcoming about his infatuation with Alexandra in those years, and his inability to fit in, despite the presence of his once friend, the very popular Nickolas Stefanos. It was simply one more irony added to many that the body housing the Champion of Olympus belonged to the woman Leksi Mylonas had once desired so intensely. He hadn't dared to touch her. So far.

She smiled inwardly. He was hoping to drive her to the brink of madness with whatever tortures he and his followers could think to inflict. Then, and only then, would he offer her an end to the misery, in exchange for the knowledge he was seeking. She'd begun to suspect what that knowledge might be, and knew she would have to choose death rather than give him the power he so desperately craved.

New pain knifed through her body as she attempted to shift into an easier position, and she stifled the sob that wanted to spurt from her. Amarantha sometimes forgot what mortal pain was, and the reminder was never welcome when it occurred. She bit into her bottom lip until the pungent, metallic taste of blood turned bitter in her mouth. Her hands closed into fists and she felt the weight of hopelessness crush her. She leaned forward, head on crossed arms as she pulled her knees to her chest and began to rock.

"Ares... Help me..."

It was a whisper of sound in the dank cell.

In her mind, it was a shrieking howl of anguish that went spinning into the cosmos.

She despised the weakness that spawned it, and cried softly, almost soundlessly.

ϒ ϒ ϒ

In another place and time, Ares tensed where he sat brooding in his temple. Thrace was not a place he spent much of his time, but whenever Amarantha was taken from him, he retreated to the one place they called home when they were together. It was also where the fountain of time was housed. Forcing reason past the fury that had electrified his very being when he'd sensed her betrayal, the War God rose and went to the murky pool. At the moment, all it reflected was the blackness of his rage, threaded with tendrils of crimson blood. He'd seen this temporal embodiment of his anger only a few times throughout the millennia, and it both disturbed and fascinated in a macabre, detached way. If he couldn't banish the anger this time, he might never know what had befallen her.

The God waved his hand over the lifeless pool, and waited for the darkness to recede. He was not overly surprised when the only shift in the waters was a small rippling pulse that died as quickly as it had been born.

"She's beyond your reach, Ares."

Muscles bunched in the War God's shoulders and his stance stiffened to rigid fury.

"You'd better hope that isn't permanent," he snarled in a low rumble of sound, then added with acidic contempt, "Father."

Zeus' laughter lingered long after the tingle of God-magic faded in the vast temple.

ϒ ϒ ϒ

"This could be much more comfortable if you'd simply tell me what I need to know, Amarantha," Renata crooned smoothly.

She looked up at him, a crooked smile tugging the corners of her mouth.

"As the priest, Andrei, told you?"

"He was a fool, Champion. I am assuming you are not."

"Then tell me what you want?" she countered, her shrewd eyes skimming the tense features of the young men and women he'd brought with him. "Or are you afraid to have them know that the God they await is already—"

He struck her, a severe, sudden blow that made blackness engulf her for precious seconds. When she could see past the haze of agony again, he stood alone in the dungeon. Distant footsteps told her he'd ordered his disciples away before they could hear her words. And possibly turn on him for his planned betrayal of them.

"We'll see how brave you are when my men are through with you," he said softly. "What will the God's consort do in the face of captivity and the whims of mortal lust."

"You presume that is a new and unique caveat," she remarked snidely. "I doubt you could comprehend the number of times I've heard threats of that nature, and then endured their consequences."

He laughed, amused at the bravado.

She joined him in his dark amusement, and his confidence slipped for the briefest of instants.

"Are you certain it is not you who wants to indulge your own lust, Leksi?" she asked, employing the full richness of Alexandra Christophi's beautiful voice. "I know how much you once wanted me, Leksi," she purred sweetly. "Nickolas is not here to stand between us now."

Renata closed the distance a second time and dragged her, moaning, to her feet so he could look into her eyes.

Amarantha smiled, they were so close that she could see the silver flaring within the brown of Alexandra's eyes as they were reflected back at her from Renata's inky-black gaze.

"Don't try to taunt me with Alexandra, Champion," he warned in a lethal tone. "She's as dead as her precious Nickolas!"

"And you never had a chance to say good-bye," Amarantha whispered. "I doubt Hades will allow you the opportunity now."

Renata slammed her hard against the stone wall, watched her fight to stay conscious, and fail. She crumpled at his feet and he backed away a few feet, then waited for her to open her eyes again. It wouldn't take long, he knew. Her strength had been a source of silent amazement to him as he'd watched her rally, over and over, during the long weeks of her captivity.

The darkness began to draw back in her mind, and Amarantha tried desperately to cling to the peace it afforded her, to hold tightly to the shades of her oblivion. And, again, she was denied to the illusory haven of nothingness. Slowly, she was forced into complete awareness of her surroundings. It took only a heartbeat to realize she was not alone when she returned to full consciousness.

"Still here, I see," Amarantha remarked, voice once more a rasp of pain.

"I didn't want you to think I'd forgotten my promise to give you to my men," Renata answered. "They're waiting."

"For what?" she spat. "For me to break? It won't happen, I assure you. Ares still breathes in me, bastard!"

He nodded, and his smile this time was genuinely amused.

"We shall see," he mused thoughtfully, then walked away.

She trembled in his wake, her mind alive with centuries of remembered tortures and abuse—and the remnants that clung to her soul, the fears that had once endangered the more intimate aspects of her devotion to Ares...

The God's hands touched the flesh and form of his cherished student, revelling in the feel of her body so close to his again. When she stiffened reflexively, he turned her to face him, dark eyes alive with barely restrained anger.

"What's happened to you, Amarantha?" he asked after peering intently into her eyes, seeing true fear there for the first time in many centuries.

"I will be fine, my master," she whispered, voice shaken and weak. "I would ask that you be patient."

"Patient?" His lip curled with contempt as he repeated the word, made it an offense with his tone.

"Please, Ares," she shuddered. "I simply need a small amount of time."

"And I need the truth," he reminded her, with uncharacteristic gentleness. "You have been gone from me for over twenty years, little one."

"They..." She stopped, rethought her words, then began again, forcing detachment into her voice as she told him. "The armies of the king of England captured me. I was an enemy because I fought with the Saracens. I was given to the soldiers for their

amusement." She stopped, turned away, and hugged herself tightly. "I know it was not this body they defiled, Master, but my soul is still filled with their abuse."

Ares knew well what men were capable of when the woman of an enemy fell into their hands. He had often given such prizes to his own legions. This time it was his mate who had been raped and tortured, and the rage that ripped through his being was blinding as well as devastating in scope and intensity.

"I will not allow you to be destroyed by men, or Gods, Amarantha," he vowed, and she turned to seek refuge in his embrace when he would have left the Temple, intent on mayhem and bloody, violent vengeance...

Amarantha's stomach churned wildly when she heard the first of Renata's men come into the cell, and she drew on ageless discipline of will to stifle the screech of terror that was teasing the back of her throat.

ϒ ϒ ϒ

Much later, in the silent aftermath of violence, Amarantha felt their eyes on her. She smiled, the expression hidden by the dark curtain of her hair. Every part of her ached with an enormity that threatened to drive her into fits of keening screams. She pushed away the agony with a control that she'd begun to believe broken. Her mind cleared, reached outward.

'*Ares?*'

Instead of the terror-drenched shrieks of the past hours, she forced her thoughts to be cool and direct. Hunger gnawed at her gut, and she crossed her arms tighter to her body. They hadn't allowed her more than the most essential and meager nourishment. It was creating a fogginess in her mind that distorted her thoughts, her ability to hold onto the threads of her sanity.

"Help me..."

The futile plea was spoken aloud and it startled her. She lifted her head and stared with unerring certainty toward the camera that she knew was concealed in one dark corner of the cell.

"I *will* destroy you," she said, voice quiet, certain.

ᚸ ᚸ ᚸ

"She's known all along that we're watching her."

Renata laughed, the sound rich with sincere amusement.

"Of course she has, Timothy. I would have been extremely disappointed if she hadn't spotted the camera at once."

"I... will... destroy... you..."

The soft murmur came from the woman locked in the cell several floors beneath them. Timothy shuddered and turned away, suddenly sick. The words were barely audible, but inside his mind, Timothy flinched at the vastness of her rage and the sound of her voice seemed to surround and crush him, the sheer weight of it making him moan softly as he groped for some kind of solid and tangible support.

Renata laughed again. His humor was shaken momentarily when he realized that the words had been repeated by a second voice, a deep, gravelly echo inside his head, and the image of Ares' Champion, expression serene and smiling, reached out from the screen to kiss his spine with ice.

ᚸ ᚸ ᚸ

Amarantha groaned again as the beauty of a dreamed memory shattered into hated reality. They were opening the barred cage door. Reason drowned beneath the sudden surge of hatred and she leapt without warning.

Her scream of rage and pain tore through the hollow cell as the chains snapped her back into a crumpled heap. She'd forgotten momentarily, and the shackles had been stretched to their limit by her motion. Momentum flung her backward, left her writhing on the stone floor.

"Ares..."

It was a keening screech of rage. She felt the tears begin again, and tried not to allow them to see her weakness. His name, voiced so clearly, had slipped from her before she could suppress it. Once they had started, the flow of misery-induced tears seemed far too vast for her parched body to contain.

ϒ ϒ ϒ

Renata watched her for a long time, naked and chained. He remained unmoved by the horror of her piteous cries. Ares' name was a litany, the lifeline to her sanity. Renata had thought her broken. It annoyed him to realize that her love for an ancient God of War was emerging as her salvation.

He had offered her his mercy, told her all she need do to receive it was talk to him. Yet she refused to speak, except to goad and deride him with her contempt.

He was snatched from his reverie by Timothy's unexpected arrival. He spun away from his monitors and scanned the slightly disheveled appearance of his friend. After a lengthy hesitation, Timothy finally dared to look directly at him.

"The police are searching for you," he said without preamble. "They know your name." He glanced furtively at the monitors. "They know everything. She must have found a way to give them everything she'd discovered, before we took her." Timothy drew in another strained breath, then concluded his report with, "they are also holding you responsible for Nickolas Stefanos' murder."

Renata felt the tide of Timothy's panic, and he smiled. The expression didn't appear to reassure his friend. Renata's smile grew wider. For several more minutes he remained silent and thoughtful, mulled the implications of the news. It wasn't unforeseen, but he hadn't anticipated public discovery quite this soon. Especially when it was proving all but impossible to bend Amarantha to his needs.

"They're going to find us before He comes among us," Timothy said in hushed tones that were textured with fear. "If they see what we've done to Doctor Christophi, we'll never be able to explain. She'll confirm everything they suspect. And if you are labelled a murderer, Leksi, no one will believe we did this for the sake of mankind."

Renata snorted his contempt of the assessment.

"We are talking about a single woman, Timothy, not a Goddess."

Timothy shuddered, chilled with the dread he'd been plagued with in recent days. He wanted to plead with Renata, to make him see the insanity of his present course of action, but something in the oddly gleaming eyes stilled the protests. And, for the first time in the many years they'd known each other, Timothy feared Renata.

"Amarantha is an anachronism, and, therefore, a danger," Renata stated with eerie calm.

"Alexandra Christophi was loved by everyone who knew her," Timothy insisted, in what he knew was a pointless attempt to dissuade the other man.

"Admiration does not translate into loyalty."

"Fear is fear," Timothy hissed in an undertone. "And fear is something we are all familiar with, old friend. The old Gods are not to be underestimated, Renata. This woman is not merely one of Ares' favored children, she is his chosen mate. Somehow, He'll destroy us for taking her from him."

"You assume she means that much to him," Renata laughed harshly.

"Isn't that what you're counting on!" Timothy reminded him with sudden, irrational anger. "Isn't that why we took her captive? To use against their power. You're beginning to sound mad, Leksi. Make up your mind! Is she bait, or amusement for your warped sense of humor?"

Renata's patience ran out and he grabbed his friend with an abruptness that shocked Timothy into silence.

"Be very careful what you say to me, Tim," he advised with a small smile. "Ares' whore holds no appeal for me. I've never been pushed to seek my pleasure in company that low, old friend."

Timothy shivered. The insult was born of pure malice, and not a little envy, he knew. Renata, when he had been Leksi, attracted many women, but none had ever remained with the enigmatic man. Most often, they learned to detest him, and fear him to such an extent that they frequently disappeared altogether from whatever city they resided in. Despite Renata's feigned disdain, Timothy knew that

Amarantha/Alexandra was the type of woman Renata had *always* been drawn to; lovely, intelligent, strong, and extremely passionate.

The thought came to Timothy, unbidden, unexpected: *The Champion of Olympus would rend Renata limb from limb if he attempted to touch her as her lover would. The other assaults she'd endured would pale and seem inconsequential if Leksi touched her, and Timothy knew she'd find the strength to kill him before he could force her into submission.*

Renata read the thought, naked as it was in Timothy's mind, and he laughed with pure delight. He ignored him and strode back to again take up his vigil at the monitors. She'd stopped moving and was curled into a tight ball, all but hidden in the farthest corner of the dank cell. The masses of dark hair that obscured her face were tangled and filthy. Her previously unscarred body was torn and stained with blood. Beneath the ragged exterior, Renata glimpsed the beauty and sensuality that captivated a God, and held him bound. Just as Alexandra Christophi had once held him.

"Don't, Renata!" Timothy pleaded when Renata snapped off the video and headed for the door.

The leader hesitated for an instant, then he gestured toward the blank screen. "By all means, watch, if it will amuse you, Tim?" He knew the cruelty his remark exhibited, and shrugged when the other man's eyes darkened dangerously. As he'd expected, Tim held his retort in check and left the room from the main door.

ϒ ϒ ϒ

"Amarantha?"

She heard the quiet murmur of sound, and a breath of ice tingled along her spine when she recognized the note of power within the lilting voice. Not the intrinsic power that resonated in her master's tones, but a strength that echoed of another kind of power: obsession and madness. Curiosity forced her gaze upward, and the cold deepened inside her.

She drew back, inched away from his approach until the damp wall was a solid resistance to further movement. Loathing rose within her in the seconds that it took him to close the distance between them. He squatted down in front of her and brushed aside her hair. His touch was the ice of death.

"He's left you to die here, Champion," Renata said with a regret so falsely sincere she might have believed him — had she been anyone other than Ares' student.

"I *have* died in service to the Gods before," she replied in a voice rusty with misuse and ravaged by pain.

"Why?" Renata asked, again in the oddly sincere tone. This time, it was truly more genuine, because he was intrigued in spite of himself.

Amarantha smiled, but refused to answer. Some things were not worthy of response.

"Would you like to leave this cell?" Renata enquired softly. He heard the uneasy shuffle of feet behind him. The men who followed him were loyal, but they had all been frightened by her rage. It would require one of them to free her, and Renata knew none would do it willingly.

Again, she simply stared at him. For a long time, he waited for an answer. She used the introspective moments to compose her thoughts, to banish the numbing sense of defeat to a corner of her heart that she could temporarily ignore.

"At what price?" she finally questioned.

Renata smiled, and his fingers traced the curve of her cheek.

"I simply wish to know where the secret of Zeus' Temple is hidden," he replied.

"You *wish* to challenge the Gods by proclaiming yourself one of them, fool," she snarled. "And you are afraid your pitiful children will desert you before you achieve your goal."

"Tell me!" he shouted, angered anew by her disdain.

Amarantha contemplated him with serious, thoughtful eyes, then, after a brief pause, laughed with obvious irony.

"I prefer my own company to your attempts at reasonable persuasion," she hissed with vehement fury. Before he had time to move, her foot shot out and struck a blow that tumbled him to the floor.

Renata's rage boiled to the surface of his mind and he grabbed at her, his hands coiling through her hair as he slammed her into the stone wall. He pulled her up with him as he stood, and then glared down into her recalcitrant, flickering silver-shadowed brown eyes. He bent his head to hers and she spit at him. He rewarded her gesture by slamming her skull against the wall, the strike savage and meant to inflict pain. She shuddered and tried to squirm free of his grasp, her fists pushed vainly at his chest.

He was so embroiled in her torment that he barely heard the exclamation of panic that Timothy uttered as he ran into the cell to join them.

"Stop! You're killing her!"

Renata finally loosened his hold, then lost it entirely when Timothy shook him violently. Slowly, the haze of rage dissipated and he turned huge eyes to her. She had fallen to the floor again and stared up at them, indifference and mild triumph amid the shifting hues of her gaze. Timothy's angry voice penetrated the final shreds of the daze that held Renata, and he glanced at his concerned friend.

"I'm all right, Timothy," he whispered, shaken badly.

Before she could provoke him a second time, he gestured for Timothy to precede him from the cell, and heard the metallic clang of the barred door banging firmly into place. His scattered followers trailed at a discreet distance.

ϒ ϒ ϒ

Several nights passed uninterrupted, and Amarantha barely felt the rough stone beneath her. She no longer had the energy to fight for life. Renata was nearby, the Champion could feel the malevolent presence as a contagion in the very air. He was completely obsessed, and beyond all reason. Pain had become a palpable part of her existence throughout the past days, yet Amarantha smiled inwardly. She was near death, and much of the torture to which Renata and his minions had subjected her seemed apart from her now, unable to touch more than the surface of her mind. She was naked, bleeding what little blood remained within her veins, and she knew if she could care, she'd see that her body was a map of scars and still open wounds. She wasn't able to heal fully, she had that power only once, when she took her new form on the mortal plane. If she died in Alexandra Christophi's body, then her existence would end, for she had been unsuccessful in the task she had been sent to complete.

Her wrists, shackled once again, were burned raw, gouges torn so deeply into her flesh that she was certain if she did survive she'd wear these marks permanently, even in her own form. She had betrayed Ares in a way that had never happened before, and she knew he would exact a price for that, a punishment that would remind her of the act each time she glimpsed it. Visible scars would remind her as little else could after centuries passed. Movement near the door attracted her erratic attention and she turned her head just enough to see who entered. Her eyes met those of a boy she hadn't seen before. He appeared to be barely into his teenage years, but she felt an older spirit very much alive within him. His dark gaze was invidious, and she sensed a twisted, cruel nature within him. He smiled, and she knew he would enjoy her pain. She had thought herself beyond caring what happened to her, but some part of her could still be reached it seemed. The boy stepped closer, and the ornate, long handled dagger now visible in his hand grew huge in Amarantha's vision; and the hands that caressed it evoked fresh horror.

She tried to pull back, away from the approaching figure, but didn't have the strength to do more than shake her head in denial.

He squatted down beside the helpless woman and grinned at the unconcealed terror in Amarantha's huge eyes. He ran a gentle hand the length of the captive's spine, caressed once smooth skin. He laughed softly when her muscles tensed in automatic rejection of the touch.

"No!" It was a weak gasp of air, unwillingly torn from Amarantha's throat. She felt tears well in her eyes when his fingers stroked over her thighs, then parted them. When she tried to get away from the offensive touch, his fist slammed into the curve of her back. Agony swirled into her consciousness, a red fog that cloaked the sensations of an assault her entire being recoiled against. She felt the knife, the razor edge of it slicing open her flesh, the heavy handle forcing its way into her, guided by the boy's skillful, merciless hand.

Ares' face hovered before her mind's eye, then fragmented when she could no longer hold on to the beloved face. As the lifeline of his image grew ever more faint, Amarantha finally accepted defeat.

ϒ ϒ ϒ

"She won't speak at all," the latest tormenter reported to the robed and angry leader of the new order. "It doesn't seem to matter what we do to her."

Renata dismissed him with a curt gesture of his hand, and turned to stare at the monitors that showed him every inch of his secluded fortress sanctuary. The abandoned monasteries were still good for some things, especially the ones that were well and truly hidden in the vast countryside hills.

"She's dying," Timothy said flatly. "She won't tell you where to find it."

"She will," he hissed. "I have no intention of permitting her to die before I have what I need."

Uneasy silence fell between them. When Renata said nothing else, Timothy left him.

ϒ ϒ ϒ

Amarantha shivered in the silent gloom. Recent tortures were pushed into a dark corner of her mind as she sought the peace necessary to create the bridge Hypnos had granted centuries earlier. *If it was still possible to bridge the millennia in this way.* Her heart wavered, unsure, as she considered that her ability to find Ares might be lost for numerous reasons, not the least of which was the fulfillment of the Oracle's prophecy of betrayal. She was now certain she would not survive this challenge, and she needed to see Ares again before she truly died.

Υ Υ Υ

The foundations of the vast temple in Thrace seethed with the torrents of emotion that lived and breathed fire into the stones. Ares stormed the silent halls, his dark countenance vivid with hatred so profoundly intense that his maidens had fled in terror. He walked alone, proud and defiant of his peers, assailed repeatedly by the backlash of her torture.

For months the agony of his slave had been a murmur in the back of his mind. Over the past days, the whispers had become true screams. And he was growing mad with the constant presence of mourning and loss that layered the shrieks of horror and anguish.

She was dying.

Amarantha was dying!

It was not possible.

But it *was* happening.

And Ares, one of the twelve great Gods of Olympus, could not stop the slow, pain-laden extinguishing of her life force.

A ripple of God-fire disturbed the air and he whirled, ready to descend in wrath on whoever dared to approach him. Mighty Zeus stood before him, expression strangely kind.

Ares was in no mood for kindness in any manner it was offered.

"Not a word, old man," he hissed from between tightly clenched teeth.

"She dies, does she not, my son?"

Again, nothing but enquiry and a measure of concern in the quiet words. A perfect foil for the raging inferno of the War God's impotent fury.

"Have you come to celebrate?" Ares shouted, unable to keep the accusation from his voice and eyes as he tried not to care what his father's presence might mean to him. To her.

"I have come to tell you she needs your power to return to us."

Disbelief dominated the handsome features of the warrior God. It was quickly overshadowed by scepticism, and a faint scorn.

"Us?" Ares snarled. "Since when do you care if she survives, Father?"

"She's part of us now," Zeus replied, refusing to be baited into battle with his son. "It's something we should, perhaps, have accepted many centuries ago."

Ares laughed. It was a sound colored by thousands of years of contempt and anger. He walked away, stared outward over the timeless beauty of her garden sanctuary. The scrying glass was utterly blank now, no longer reflecting even his rage. He had truly lost her.

The magnitude of his grief threatened to engulf and eclipse his rage.

Zeus vanished.

The waters of the seer's font glittered and stirred to life...

CHAPTER FIFTEEN

The trance of sleep slipped over Amarantha's pain-wracked body with agonizing slowness, but she eventually established a link with the deepest recesses of her mind. Carefully, she began the descent into the netherworld of her dream center, the one place where she could reach the God she needed. She knew she had achieved the necessary level of detachment when the lullaby voice of the God of Sleep caressed her mind.

"You risk much asking this of me again, Champion," Hypnos intoned solemnly.

"It is necessary, Hypnos," she replied, moving further into the sleep-realm. "I am dying in the mortal world, and have not succeeded in my task to stop your enemies. I wish to speak to Ares a final time."

There was a long hesitation, more than was usual, and fear woke inside her.

"Hypnos, please?" she asked softly. "I know I have betrayed him, but surely he will not deny me this last moment in his presence?" She was truly afraid of the possible answer to her question.

"You ask me to defy Zeus' order, Champion, and then tell me you may fail us. Why should I grant your request, Amarantha?"

She knew then that it was Ares he communicated with in those brief seconds between their exchange of thoughts. It gave her small courage. And hope.

"Ares will know if you do not," she answered his query with false confidence, a weak effort to mask her anger and fear that he would banish her from his realm without permitting the contact she desired. "See me, Hypnos, know why I ask this of you, Lord of Dreams and Sleep."

For eternal, spellbound heartbeats of time, there was
nothing, then very slowly, she became aware of the shifting,
ethereal shape that bathed her in momentary serenity.

The God looked upon her, and she sensed a glimmer
of sorrow within him as he searched her heart as only a
God could. Finally, he nodded, and she waited, alone in
the darkness. This blackness lacked shadowy demons,
though, and a small part of her soul was healed by the
tranquility Hypnos' world contained.

"You are truly near death, little one," a new voice noted,
and she all but collapsed in relief.

"Ares," she gasped. "I am afraid, my Master," she confessed. "There is much left to do, and this body is dying
rapidly."

Ares stepped toward her in the shifting murkiness of
the dreamscape they shared.

"You *must* fight, Am," he said, his richly textured voice
thickened with a note of obvious, desperate fear.

She nodded, and knowing time was short, gathered her
courage. Hypnos, like the other Gods, was capricious and
unpredictable, he could sever their bond without warning.

"Is it possible that the Ambrosia could exist in this time,
Ares?"

He was surprised, and she waited while he considered
the unexpected question.

"Possible," he conceded. "Though it wouldn't be of
much use to any mortal."

"What about one who has studied the old ways, and
is holding me captive? I think he plans to use my blood
to activate the dormant power of the Ambrosia."

"What is the year?"

"The end of the year 2000 is only hours away," she said
after a moment's thought.

"The turn of a millennia can be a channel of mystical
power," he informed her, and there was a gleaming spark
of fury burning in his dark visage. "If this lunatic knows
the proper rituals, and performs the rites on ancient holy
ground, he might achieve what he desires, Amarantha.

Even in human form, your blood carries the essence of your immortality."

"Where would the Ambrosia be hidden?" she asked, sensing an imminent end to their contact.

Ares shook his head, uncertain. He was being distracted by the image of her abused and scarred body. Quelling rage with iron will, he concentrated.

"Does the Temple of Zeus still stand?" he growled, unavailing anger layering his voice.

"Yes."

"Look there."

"Ares, I am a prisoner," she reminded him.

She shrank back, the reaction instinctive when he lunged for her. The War God caught her wrists and pulled. Pain ripped the entire length of Amarantha's body and she screamed her agony, seared inside and out. Stars exploded behind her eyes and their fiery tails struck her flesh and burrowed into her veins, running through her in merciless invasion.

She sobbed, and twisted away...

And woke.

'Find the Ambrosia, then bring them to me...'

The mandate lingered in her mind, echoed with his omnipotent strength. She clung to his voice, the memory of him, and it afforded her a measure of peace, as well as reinforcing her desire to succeed against the daunting challenge the Gods had set for her this time.

With the return of awareness came a dull, aching loss; it took mere moments to recognize its cause. She had not thought to express her repentance for the betrayal of which he undoubtedly knew. She had not told him that it was him she loved, above all others. And now, her chance might well be lost forever.

Before tears could immobilize her again, Amarantha forced them aside. Mentally releasing the last tenuous threads of the dream-state, she pushed herself into a sitting position, shocked when she realized some of the damage done to Alexandra's body had been repaired. Ares had touched her, she recalled. In that instant of contact, he had healed the worst of her injuries. She would be able to move, *if* she was able to free herself.

She looked down at her hands. Buffered somewhat from awareness of her pain, she was startled to see that the shackles had been broken. When he'd taken her hands, his power had reached into the mortal world, however fleetingly. He'd given her a chance, however slight, and with renewed hope surging through her, she searched among the fragments and slivers of steel. She chose the sharpest of the jagged pieces of metal, and retrieved a length of the heavy, linked chain.

Then she waited.

After what felt like an eternity, Amarantha heard the sound she had been waiting to hear, the scrape of a heavy door opening, followed by footsteps. Part of her hoped that it would be Renata himself who came to her, but she knew that was a fruitless wish. He wouldn't risk coming alone, until he felt she was no longer even a weak threat to him.

The robed figure came closer, and she crouched in the darkest corner of the cell, eyes peering through a stringy curtain of ebony hair. A second clanking bang reverberated through the stony chamber, then the stranger entered. She saw it was the last boy who'd tortured her, and she waited for him to get closer. He was leering at her, and laughing softly. She felt a second of pity for the wretched creature; Renata would never allow this one to live past his usefulness, she knew. He was vicious, cruel, violent, and unpredictable in the way that only a true sadistic lunatic could be. The would-be-God could never control this one's perversions and twisted desires.

He reached for her, and she swung the chain, aim precise as the icy links looped around the boy's neck. She yanked, pulled him off balance, and when he fell near her feet, choking and cursing, she caught a handful of blond hair and hauled his head back to expose his throat. The serrated edge of steel ripped across his vulnerable flesh, and she winced when his blood gushed over her in warm, sticky spurts.

She ignored the inhuman sounds of suffering he made as his life poured from him. A quick search of the robe gave her the keys to the dungeon. She grabbed the ring and quickly left the cell. Knowing she was probably being watched, she ran, choosing speed over stealth as she burst into the hallway at the top of the flight of stairs that led to the basement. Two of the robed acolytes stared at her, and started to back away.

They had never expected to see the prisoner freed from her chains. When the others had dragged Doctor Alexandra Christophi into the haven, she had been simply a woman who had defied and challenged the Order. Staring at her now, they saw little of the anthropologist. Behind the spill of inky dark hair, a shimmer of silver could be discerned. Dark eyes flared with shifting light and fire. They knew, in those lightning seconds, that there was God-power among them, and they had been the defilers of it, not the harbingers of the New Order. They began to move, small, pitiful whimpers of fright slipping from mouths that were poised to scream warnings and terror throughout the old monastery.

Before they could get more than a few steps into their flight, Amarantha reached them. The first person, a young girl who looked utterly petrified, was thrown into a wall with careless ease. She groaned once, and was silent. The second, a boy, tried to fight back. She landed a solid blow beneath his chin, and he crumpled as quietly as his companion had.

Amarantha stopped long enough to strip the robe off the boy, pull it over her own head, then she was running again.

The stone building was huge and the corridors a maze that reminded her of the labyrinth of Minos. A lethal smile flitted across her features when she considered that at the center of this maze, too, was a monster. Voices warned her an instant before she turned another corner, and she halted her headlong rush long enough to listen to the orders being issued by Renata's second in command. Even with the distance, Amarantha heard the doubt in this one's voice. He was afraid. His faith not merely shaken, but broken. Still, he gave the directive to send half the

Order's trained killers to the Temple of Zeus, while the rest of them met Renata on the Hill of Ares.

Again, she smiled. She would reach the Temple of Zeus after the madman's assassins, but she knew the hidden passages of the ancient temple. She also knew where to find the weapon she needed, and, she suspected, the legendary Ambrosia of the Gods.

Ignoring the aches and occasionally lancing pains that assailed her borrowed body, the Champion escaped with little impediment. They were preoccupied with the excitement of the impending arrival of their *'True God'*.

♈ ♈ ♈

The Temple of Zeus had changed much since she had walked its corridors. Amarantha was finding it all but impossible to recall the entrance to the secret vaults within the vast stone structure. Frustrated, she went to the main chamber and knelt at the altar. The sounds of others searching was dim, they still hadn't reached the deepest rooms of the building. She looked up into the faces of the King of the Gods and his wife.

"I know you have no wish to help me, but my failure will cost you much."

She trembled, a reactive shudder to another presence within her head. She calmed her heartbeat and listened with her spirit's intuitiveness. The meditative trance was swift, and stable.

She smiled minutes later, satisfied and confident once more.

Andrei Adonidas had known every inch of his domain, and Zeus had permitted him to speak. She went to the chamber that had been his, and quickly located the mechanism hidden in a deep recess within the mini-altar in a corner of the room. The scrape of stone shifting made her look down and she leaped back just in time to avoid falling into the pitch blackness of the hole that was suddenly revealed in the middle of the floor. She rummaged in a desk drawer, found a flashlight, and descended into a darkness that felt like an entity waiting to claim her. Her fingers skimmed the rim of the opening, found the trigger that would slide the stone back into place, and she shivered as the aged rock once again covered the secret vault.

The descent was long and arduous, the light illuminating meager space. The blackness was so complete, it seemed to smother the flickering beam from the flashlight. She was beginning to think she'd made a mistake until she finally came to an open area she had last visited hundreds of years in the past. Relief made her knees wobble for a few seconds, then she forced her body to move forward.

It took precious moments to locate the treasure she sought. From the bottom chamber of an ancient chest, she lifted the sword that belonged to the God of War in another life. Fire and fury pulsed within the shining metals of Hephaestus' work; the vibrations of Ares' very nature forged into the mystical weapon he had so often wielded. She took several deep, calming breaths, absorbing the reverberations of her Master's spirit and strength. Then, steady once again, she walked to a small anteroom. A plain, engraved box stood atop a slightly raised stand. She went to it, flipped back the lid, and grasped the object within its velvet-covered depths. She laughed softly as she stared at the lump of gray stone in her palm. Dropping it into a pocket of the robe, she spun on her heel and headed back.

Getting out of the underground vault was achieved much more quickly than getting into it had been. She knew the paths now that she had located the center of the maze. The distant rumble of many feet searching above her was welcome. It meant that she would not have to face all of Renata's followers at once. Death awaited her on the Areopagus, but she was now slightly more at ease with the eventuality than she had been hours earlier.

ϒ ϒ ϒ

The night had turned stormy in the brief space of time that she had been below the Temple of Zeus. She stepped into the dark, damp air and smelled rain and the near palpable tang of lightning. Thunder rumbled loudly in the heavens. The Gods had gathered above Athens to witness this pivotal contest. The Champion knew in her soul that this would be her last battle on their behalf, and she offered them a prayer of obeisance and respect as she accepted the merging of time that had brought her to her final death.

Rain began, a gentle but steady stream of water that washed some of the dirt of captivity from her aching and wounded body. Amarantha walked, steady and sure, heading for the one place that might give her the added power she needed to survive this latest challenge. As she moved, people backed away from her, seeing Alexandra Christophi, but sensing something vastly more ancient and powerful than the pretty Historian.

Amarantha paid them no heed as she continued uninterrupted to the Hill of Ares.

The force of the rain increased, chilling her flesh. Wind swept up in gusts of icy air, swirling in unleashed frenzy, battering the woman who strode proudly and unflinchingly through the torrents. The Areopagus came into view and she paused for only a moment, gathering courage and strength before she stepped onto the path that would take her to the summit of the antediluvian Hill.

Men ringed the clear crown of the hill, and parted to permit her access to the center of their circle. In the middle of the assembled crowd of worshipers stood Renata, robed in white, smiling benevolently.

"So, you've finally seen sense and brought me what I asked for," he noted with sly satisfaction.

"I've brought your death, madman," she replied casually. "As I granted death to your ancestor, Lyaeus, betrayer of my king." Thunder split the night, rended the sky with sound so immense she thought herself deaf for a few instants. It was followed by a bolt of lightning so intense it blinded, and struck the ancient hill only a few feet from where the self-made God of a modern world faced the timeless Champion of the mythical Gods of Olympus. Acrid smoke rose from the scarred surface, and the pelting rain quickly extinguished the flames that the strike had sparked.

"A sword is hardly a match for what you face here, Champion," Renata said quietly. He gestured and numerous men and women stepped forward, all armed with automatic weapons. "You've been witness to the destructive power of these weapons before, Lady," he mocked. "What do you think they will do to your body if I tell my children to destroy you?"

Amarantha's attention was divided, in spite of the potentially lethal situation she was presently facing. Underlying the force of the storm that raged around them was another kind of energy, the familiar tingling shimmer of God-power. Somehow, despite the impossibility of it, Amarantha knew that Ares was bridging the temporal planes and dimensions that separated them. She waited, heart and soul attuned to the subtle shifts and resonances of building power that were enshrouding the Areopagus.

Renata watched her with wary eyes, unnerved by the complete lack of fear in her stance and expression. He had the upper hand, was in the winning position, yet he felt control and success slipping from his grasp with each thundering pulse of the sky.

"Surround her," he ordered suddenly, "but do not kill her."

Amarantha laughed lightly and watched the confused acolytes form a circle around her.

"You fear me now," she observed, tone smooth with contempt and macabre humor. "Perhaps you are not such a fool, after all," she added, her head tilted to one side as she contemplated him. "Not like your ancestor, who died a more honorable death than his betrayal deserved."

"I want the Ambrosia," Renata growled, his eyes darting everywhere as he tried to grasp what was happening around him, and within him.

She reached into a pocket and produced the shriveled lump of clayish stone. Without hesitation, she tossed it to him.

"That is what you have spent half a lifetime searching for, Leksi Mylonas," she hissed. "Yet you have not the power to use it. You are *not* a God, you are a mortal infidel with delusions of Godhood."

He flung the substance away from him and howled his rage. And, in the instant of distraction his frustrated fury created, Amarantha drove Ares' sword deep into the soil of the Areopagus. She dropped to her knees and clung to the hilt of the weapon as the hill began to quake. A low, keening groan began deep within the earth itself, and terror lit the faces of Renata's young followers. Lightning strikes intensified, coming in continuous bolts as the roiling clouds crashed about in the sky in a chaotic cacophony of deafening noise.

Amarantha felt each quaking crash of thunder rattling her bones, and she expected a barrage of gunfire to tear her apart at any second. The Areopagus quivered with contained fury, and she was shocked into stillness minutes later when Renata's followers started to scream and throw down their weapons.

She stared in uncomprehending wonder as the metal of the weaponry slowly glowed the red of coals. Shrieks of pain and anguish overrode the booming thunder as hands were charred and burned, limbs rendered as useless as the guns they'd carried moments before. A flash of movement caught her eye and she resisted the need to laugh when Renata made a lunge for the discarded Ambrosia. His fingers closed over the lump of stone, and he stared, mouth agape as the brightest bolt of lightning to yet illuminate the night struck close to him. He screamed when the smoke cleared and a figure loomed over him, dark eyes glowing with rage, and unmistakable power.

Dazzling, awesome, and terrifying, none present doubted that they gazed upon the God of War. Ares remained unmoving, his eyes surveying the destruction, missing nothing despite no outward motion of his body. In those precious, eternal pulses of time, the God of War reached outward, his soul seeking and finding the turmoil that dominated so much of the planet. The hatred that drove terrorism to such devastating levels poured into him, the shock of violence and intolerance cascading through his veins as a searing flame of mindless wrath. Pain and loss was the underlay for more suffering, and that too, touched his ancient heart, was absorbed, then dismissed. There was no part of the planet that wasn't examined and understood in those instants while time itself hung suspended. Then he drew back and looked around him with the vast scope of his acquired knowledge blazing from his fiery gaze.

In desperate madness, Renata shouted to those men and women who hadn't fled.

"Take her," he screeched, pointing to the frozen Champion who still gripped the War God's sword.

A few of the braver disciples of the dying Order started toward her. And died as they walked. Ares began to close the distance between himself and Amarantha, casually knocking aside anyone insane enough to stand in his way. A single touch and they died, cast aside like broken puppets. Only one body remained to block his path, and before either he or the Champion could anticipate Renata's move, he flung himself at her, knife in hand. The silver blade, razor-edged, slid past ribs and cut deep. Over his shoulder, she watched Ares' handsome features distort with a rage unlike any she had ever before witnessed. He bellowed his hatred to the very heavens and the hill quaked in the aftershock of it. Those unfortunate enough to be breathing were quickly dispatched in the wake of the War God's roar.

Only Renata continued to breathe when the Heavens quieted. The stillness was eerie, wholly unnatural. Ares glowered down at him, and he whimpered piteously before fear was replaced in his eyes by the glitter of total dementia. The God bent, grabbed his robes and hauled him to his feet.

"The Gods have seen all you have wrought, human," Ares intoned, voice low and alive with the scope of his fury. His very presence rippled the air around them, charged it with power and danger. His voice, rich and soft, shook the souls of those few who still breathed, and they died knowing deeper truths than any their broken leader had ever proffered.

"The Gods are mine to command!" Renata ranted, holding the blood-coated Ambrosia before him in triumph.

Ares struck his hand, knocked the Ambrosia aside without a glance.

"Godhood is a sacred trust," Ares hissed. "Not the domain of maniacs."

"You will bow before me and beg my forgiveness before this is over," Renata raved.

Ares' laughter rang out, and he dropped the mortal into a heap at his feet.

"Hades will enjoy every moment of your agony, and he will undoubtedly be most creative in choosing the means of that suffering," the God of War intoned. He waved his hand, the gesture dismissive, and Renata's shriek of horror seemed to linger on long after he'd been consumed by flame and turned to dust.

Ares paused only long enough to look upon the modern world and its destruction of his monument, then he turned away. He went to Amarantha and knelt next to her.

"It is over, little one," he murmured gently, gathering her into his arms.

Her eyes fluttered open and she stared up into the fierce visage of the God she adored. Through the pain that was stealing life from her, she tried to smile for him.

"Your timing is a little off, Master..."

Some of the anger left Ares' handsome features and he cradled her close to his chest. With a beckoning gesture, the petrified lump of Ambrosia sailed from the ground and settled in the God's outstretched palm.

"I've failed, Ares," she whispered, voice choked with anguish and death. "I've betrayed you, and I have failed you."

He shook his head and closed his fingers around the rock he held. Slowly, as he spread open his hand, she saw the glow begin. The Ambrosia, lifeless in mortal hands, now shimmered and metamorphosed in the hands of a true, full-blooded God.

She raised her trembling fingers to his wrist, stopped him when he would have placed the warm, life-giving food of the Gods to her lips.

"You are free, Ares," she murmured. "Do this, and they will make you pay a terrible price for interfering."

He laughed, bitter irony in the low sound. "Take the Ambrosia, Am."

Life was fading rapidly, and if she had intended to argue, Ares' next actions stopped the words from ever being uttered. He was thoughtful and serious for indeterminate minutes, then he rose with her in his arms, decision clearly made, and looked heavenward.

"Father! Return us!"

She swallowed the Ambrosia, felt its power coursing through her veins as the Areopagus was engulfed in a blaze of pure, white brilliance. As it had so many centuries past, the food of the Gods exploded in her system. The body of Alexandra Christophi trembled with the mutation, burned and peeled away, leaving bare the spirit and form of Amarantha. As the human host of Ares' Champion turned to dust, Amarantha's soul and body merged again into their true form and substance. Long minutes later, the blinding light abated, and she saw they were still on the small Hill.

In a different world and time.

They were home.

"Ares?"

He set her on her feet and smiled, eyes drinking in the well-known silver eyes and shining white hair of his lover. As he bent to kiss her, she whispered; "Why?"

"Because that world could destroy even me," he stated with firm conviction, then silenced her with the passion that had bound them as eternally as the vow she'd made to the Fates so long ago.

EPILOGUE

The Elysian Fields spread out before them in glorious perfection and peace. Colors so varied and rich they couldn't be named by mortal words covered the Underworld paradise ruled by mighty Hades. Flowers, rich with indescribable and intoxicating scents lay as a carpet beneath the feet of those granted entrance to the utopia of the Gods.

Amid the beauty and splendor of the Fields, two figures walked, one dark as night, the other a pale wraith at his side. Neither bore the arms that were customary, parts of their natural being. It was forbidden, even to the Gods themselves.

"I've never understood this," Ares noted with real amusement. He was happy for the moment, and content to have Amarantha next to him again, safe and whole. It made him magnanimous, as it always did.

"I simply want to know that they are together," Amarantha answered and kissed him impulsively. She wrapped her arms around him and sighed softly, enjoying the solid feel of him so close to her.

"I often think you are hoping to see him," Ares stated, with less gentleness than he'd spoken with only seconds before.

"I know the terms of our bargain, my Master," she replied quietly, steel beneath the soft words. "You allow me to see those who have served us, but I know Iphicles is one I will never be permitted to touch again."

And, as always, the sadness that suddenly emanated from her cast shadows over the perfection around them.

"This way," Ares said, irritated and eager to leave the Fields now.

They crested a small rise in the landscape, and Amarantha saw the couple she had known so recently in another Athens. They walked hand in hand, laughing and embracing, so completely happy that their joy surrounded them and touched all who were witness to their love. She smiled, her heart lighter in spite of her own lingering sense of loss.

"Thank you, Ares," she whispered, and turned shining eyes to the God she served and loved.

"I should have sent him to Tartarus with Mylonas," Ares growled, still angered that his lover had lain willingly in Nickolas Stefanos' arms, and had shared his passions.

Amarantha watched the fire of rage begin to burn anew in Ares' dark eyes. She reached up and touched his cheek, turning his gaze from the couple they watched until his look met hers.

"My weakness is not something for which they deserve punishment," she murmured. "I am honored that you have forgiven me. Why make them suffer further separation when we are together again, beloved?"

"Hades did this, little one," he intoned dangerously. "Not me."

"But *you* did not stop it," she insisted. "You, my proud War God, are not without compassion, despite what history has said about you."

"History is more right than you, Am," he snorted, but there was laughter in his expression again.

As they walked away from the young lovers, Amarantha grew quiet. Ares observed, but said nothing until they had left the Fields and were again outside his temple in Thrace.

"Do you think this could be the last time they take me from you, Ares?"

He smiled.

"You live as Fate decrees, Amarantha," he answered. "Only they know the answer to that."

Her eyes closed, and she walked into his arms, holding tightly to him for whatever time they were to be given before duty once more took her from his side.

Author's Note

The geography of this novel is a mixture of fact and fiction, both ancient and modern. I've taken clear liberties with the layout of present day Athens, for reasons that are purely to serve the plot, and I hope I'll be forgiven any glaring errors that people who know the city are going to find herein.

Mythology is varied about all things associated with the Gods of Olympus and their mortal entanglements. Heracles, or Hercules as he is known to most, is a figure of legendary status, and his life and exploits offer numerous inconsistencies of the adventures he had, and those he shared with his mortal twin brother, Iphicles. As with the geography, I've used what is expedient to this rendition of "history". I've long been fascinated with the lesser known of Alcmene's sons, and was lucky enough a long time ago to be given a book that featured him equally with his demi-god brother. It left a lasting impression, needless to say.

The stories of the Gods are as divergent as life itself, so I've chosen one of the twelve to be the principal presence of my story. Ares, perhaps more than any of his counterparts, never goes out of fashion. An unfortunate truth of our time. The God of War is an enigma I enjoyed getting to know throughout the story, and I think he'll linger in the memory for a long time to come. War often brings out the best in men, as it does the worst. I was inclined to think it would be the same for a God like Ares.

I've had fun with this story, from the hours of research reading, to the actual construction of the plot and subplots. I hope you enjoy the results as much as I enjoyed the creation of this variation of the "Eternal Champion".

My love and thanks to the numerous people who've not only been supportive and enthusiastic from the beginning, but who also pushed me onward when I would have given up.

Denysé Bridger,
Dartmouth, NS
Summer 2006

**Our titles are available at major book stores
and local independent resellers who support
Science Fiction and Fantasy readers like you.**

EDGE Science Fiction
and Fantasy Publishing

Tesseract Books

Dragon Moon Press

www.edgewebsite.com
www.dragonmoonpress.com

Our titles are available at major book stores and local independent resellers who support Science Fiction and Fantasy readers like you.

Alien Deception by Tony Ruggiero -(tp) - ISBN-13: 978-1-896944-34-0
Alien Revelation by Tony Ruggiero (tp) - ISBN-13: 978-1-896944-34-8
Alphanauts by J. Brian Clarke (tp) - ISBN-13: 978-1-894063-14-2
Ancestor by Scott Sigler (tp) - ISBN-13: 978-1-896944-73-9
Apparition Trail, The by Lisa Smedman (tp) - ISBN-13: 978-1-894063-22-7
As Fate Decrees by Denysé Bridger (tp) - ISBN-13: 978-1-894063-41-8

Billibub Baddings and The Case of the Singing Sword by Tee Morris (tp)
   - ISBN-13: 978-1-896944-18-0
Black Chalice, The by Marie Jakober (hb) - ISBN-13: 978-1-894063-00-5
Blue Apes by Phyllis Gotlieb (pb) - ISBN-13: 978-1-895836-13-4
Blue Apes by Phyllis Gotlieb (hb) - ISBN-13: 978-1-895836-14-1

Chalice of Life, The by Anne Webb (tp) - ISBN-13: 978-1-896944-33-3
Chasing The Bard by Philippa Ballantine (tp) - ISBN-13: 978-1-896944-08-1
Children of Atwar, The by Heather Spears (pb) - ISBN-13: 978-0-88878-335-6
Claus Effect by David Nickle & Karl Schroeder, The (pb) - ISBN-13: 978-1-895836-34-9
Claus Effect by David Nickle & Karl Schroeder, The (hb) - ISBN-13: 978-1-895836-35-6
Complete Guide to Writing Fantasy, The - Volume 1: Alchemy with Words
   - edited by Darin Park and Tom Dullemond (tp)
   - ISBN-13: 978-1-896944-09-8
Complete Guide to Writing Fantasy, The - Volume 2: Opus Magus
   - edited by Tee Morris and Valerie Griswold-Ford (tp)
   - ISBN-13: 978-1-896944-15-9
Complete Guide to Writing Fantasy, The - Volume 3: The Author's Grimoire
   - edited by Valerie Griswold-Ford & Lai Zhao (tp)
   - ISBN-13: 978-1-896944-38-8
Complete Guide to Writing Science Fiction, The - Volume 1: First Contact
   - edited by Dave A. Law & Darin Park (tp)
   - ISBN-13: 978-1-896944-39-5
Courtesan Prince, The by Lynda Williams (tp) - ISBN-13: 978-1-894063-28-9

Dark Earth Dreams by Candas Dorsey & Roger Deegan (comes with a CD)
   - ISBN-13: 978-1-895836-05-9
Darkling Band, The by Jason Henderson (tp) - ISBN-13: 978-1-896944-36-4
Darkness of the God by Amber Hayward (tp) - ISBN-13: 978-1-894063-44-9
Darwin's Paradox by Nina Munteanu (tp) - ISBN-13: 978-1-896944-68-5
Daughter of Dragons by Kathleen Nelson - (tp) - ISBN-13: 978-1-896944-00-5
Distant Signals by Andrew Weiner (tp) - ISBN-13: 978-0-88878-284-7
Dominion by J. Y. T. Kennedy (tp) - ISBN-13: 978-1-896944-28-9
Dragon Reborn, The by Kathleen H. Nelson - (tp) - ISBN-13: 978-1-896944-05-0
Dragon's Fire, Wizard's Flame by Michael R. Mennenga (tp)
   - ISBN-13: 978-1-896944-13-5
Dreams of an Unseen Planet by Teresa Plowright (tp) - ISBN-13: 978-0-88878-282-3
Dreams of the Sea by Élisabeth Vonarburg (tp) - ISBN-13: 978-1-895836-96-7
Dreams of the Sea by Élisabeth Vonarburg (hb) - ISBN-13: 978-1-895836-98-1

EarthCore by Scott Sigler (tp) ISBN-13: 978-1-896944-32-6
Eclipse by K. A. Bedford (tp) - ISBN-13: 978-1-894063-30-2
Even The Stones by Marie Jakober (tp) - ISBN-13: 978-1-894063-18-0

Fires of the Kindred by Robin Skelton (tp) - ISBN-13: 978-0-88878-271-7
Forbidden Cargo by Rebecca Rowe (tp) - ISBN-13: 978-1-894063-16-6

Game of Perfection, A by Élisabeth Vonarburg (tp)
   - ISBN-13: 978-1-894063-32-6
Green Music by Ursula Pflug (tp) - ISBN-13: 978-1-895836-75-2
Green Music by Ursula Pflug (hb) - ISBN-13: 978-1-895836-77-6
Gryphon Highlord, The by Connie Ward (tp) - ISBN-13: 978-1-896944-38-8

Healer, The by Amber Hayward (tp) - ISBN-13: 978-1-895836-89-9
Healer, The by Amber Hayward (hb) - ISBN-13: 978-1-895836-91-2
Human Thing, The by Kathleen H. Nelson - (hb) - ISBN-13: 978-1-896944-03-6
Hydrogen Steel by K. A. Bedford (tp) - ISBN-13: 978-1-894063-20-3

i-ROBOT Poetry by Jason Christie (tp) - ISBN-13: 978-1-894063-24-1

Jackal Bird by Michael Barley (pb) - ISBN-13: 978-1-895836-07-3
Jackal Bird by Michael Barley (hb) - ISBN-13: 978-1-895836-11-0

Keaen by Till Noever (tp) - ISBN-13: 978-1-894063-08-1
Keeper's Child by Leslie Davis (tp) - ISBN-13: 978-1-894063-01-2

Land/Space edited by Candas Jane Dorsey and Judy McCrosky (tp)
   - ISBN-13: 978-1-895836-90-5
Land/Space edited by Candas Jane Dorsey and Judy McCrosky (hb)
   - ISBN-13: 978-1-895836-92-9
Legacy of Morevi by Tee Morris (tp) - ISBN-13: 978-1-896944-29-6
Legends of the Serai by J.C. Hall - (tp) - ISBN-13: 978-1-896944-04-3
Longevity Thesis by Jennifer Tahn (tp) - ISBN-13: 978-1-896944-37-1
Lyskarion: The Song of the Wind by J.A. Cullum (tp)
   - ISBN-13: 978-1-894063-02-9

Machine Sex and other stories by Candas Jane Dorsey (tp)
   - ISBN-13: 978-0-88878-278-6
Maërlande Chronicles, The by Élisabeth Vonarburg (pb)
   - ISBN-13: 978-0-88878-294-6
Magister's Mask, The by Deby Fredericks (tp) - ISBN-13: 978-1-896944-16-6
Moonfall by Heather Spears (pb) - ISBN-13: 978-0-88878-306-6
Morevi: The Chronicles of Rafe and Askana by Lisa Lee & Tee Morris
   - (tp) - ISBN-13: 978-1-896944-07-4

Not Your Father's Horseman by Valorie Griswold-Ford (tp)
   - ISBN-13: 978-1-896944-27-2

On Spec: The First Five Years edited by On Spec (pb)
   - ISBN-13: 978-1-895836-08-0
On Spec: The First Five Years edited by On Spec (hb)
   - ISBN-13: 978-1-895836-12-7

Operation Immortal Servitude by Tony Ruggerio (tp)
- ISBN-13: 978-1-896944-56-2
Orbital Burn by K. A. Bedford (tp) - ISBN-13: 978-1-894063-10-4
Orbital Burn by K. A. Bedford (hb) - ISBN-13: 978-1-894063-12-8

Pallahaxi Tide by Michael Coney (pb) - ISBN-13: 978-0-88878-293-9
Passion Play by Sean Stewart (pb) - ISBN-13: 978-0-88878-314-1
Plague Saint by Rita Donovan, The (tp) - ISBN-13: 978-1-895836-28-8
Plague Saint by Rita Donovan, The (hb) - ISBN-13: 978-1-895836-29-5

Reluctant Voyagers by Élisabeth Vonarburg (pb) - ISBN-13: 978-1-895836-09-7
Reluctant Voyagers by Élisabeth Vonarburg (hb) - ISBN-13: 978-1-895836-15-8
Resisting Adonis by Timothy J. Anderson (tp) - ISBN-13: 978-1-895836-84-4
Resisting Adonis by Timothy J. Anderson (hb) - ISBN-13: 978-1-895836-83-7
Righteous Anger by Lynda Williams (tp) - ISBN-13: 897-1-894063-38-8

Shadebinder's Oath by Jeanette Cottrell - (tp) - ISBN-13: 978-1-896944-31-9
Silent City, The by Élisabeth Vonarburg (tp) - ISBN-13: 978-1-894063-07-4
Slow Engines of Time, The by Élisabeth Vonarburg (tp) - ISBN-13: 978-1-895836-30-1
Slow Engines of Time, The by Élisabeth Vonarburg (hb) - ISBN-13: 978-1-895836-31-8
Small Magics by Erik Buchanan (tp) - ISBN-13: 978-1-896944-38-8
Sojourn by Jana Oliver - (pb) - ISBN-13: 978-1-896944-30-2
Stealing Magic by Tanya Huff (tp) - ISBN-13: 978-1-894063-34-0
Strange Attractors by Tom Henighan (pb) - ISBN-13: 978-0-88878-312-7

Taming, The by Heather Spears (pb) - ISBN-13: 978-1-895836-23-3
Taming, The by Heather Spears (hb) - ISBN-13: 978-1-895836-24-0
Teacher's Guide to Dragon's Fire, Wizard's Flame by Unwin & Mennenga - (pb)
- ISBN-13: 978-1-896944-19-7
Ten Monkeys, Ten Minutes by Peter Watts (tp) - ISBN-13: 978-1-895836-74-5
Ten Monkeys, Ten Minutes by Peter Watts (hb) - ISBN-13: 978-1-895836-76-9
Tesseracts 1 edited by Judith Merril (pb) - ISBN-13: 978-0-88878-279-3
Tesseracts 2 edited by Phyllis Gotlieb & Douglas Barbour (pb)
- ISBN-13: 978-0-88878-270-0
Tesseracts 3 edited by Candas Jane Dorsey & Gerry Truscott (pb)
- ISBN-13: 978-0-88878-290-8
Tesseracts 4 edited by Lorna Toolis & Michael Skeet (pb)
- ISBN-13: 978-0-88878-322-6
Tesseracts 5 edited by Robert Runté & Yves Maynard (pb)
- ISBN-13: 978-1-895836-25-7
Tesseracts 5 edited by Robert Runté & Yves Maynard (hb)
- ISBN-13: 978-1-895836-26-4
Tesseracts 6 edited by Robert J. Sawyer & Carolyn Clink (pb)
- ISBN-13: 978-1-895836-32-5
Tesseracts 6 edited by Robert J. Sawyer & Carolyn Clink (hb)
- ISBN-13: 978-1-895836-33-2
Tesseracts 7 edited by Paula Johanson & Jean-Louis Trudel (tp)
- ISBN-13: 978-1-895836-58-5
Tesseracts 7 edited by Paula Johanson & Jean-Louis Trudel (hb)
- ISBN-13: 978-1-895836-59-2
Tesseracts 8 edited by John Clute & Candas Jane Dorsey (tp)
- ISBN-13: 978-1-895836-61-5

Tesseracts 8 edited by John Clute & Candas Jane Dorsey (hb)
  - ISBN-13: 978-1-895836-62-2
Tesseracts Nine edited by Nalo Hopkinson and Geoff Ryman (tp)
  - ISBN-13: 978-1-894063-26-5
Tesseracts Ten edited by Robert Charles Wilson and Edo van Belkom (tp)
  - ISBN-13: 978-1-894063-36-4
Tesseracts Eleven edited by Cory Doctorow and Holly Phillips (tp)
  - ISBN-13: 978-1-894063-03-6
Tesseracts Q edited by Élisabeth Vonarburg & Jane Brierley (pb)
  - ISBN-13: 978-1-895836-21-9
Tesseracts Q edited by Élisabeth Vonarburg & Jane Brierley (hb)
  - ISBN-13: 978-1-895836-22-6
Throne Price by Lynda Williams and Alison Sinclair (tp)
  - ISBN-13: 978-1-894063-06-7
Too Many Princes by Deby Fredricks (tp) - ISBN-13: 978-1-896944-36-4
Twilight of the Fifth Sun by David Sakmyster - (tp)
  - ISBN-13: 978-1-896944-01-02

Virtual Evil by Jana Oliver (tp) - ISBN-13: 978-1-896944-76-0

DENYSÉ BRIDGER

Denysé is a native of Atlantic Canada, born in the country's Easternmost province, Newfoundland, and raised in Nova Scotia. A lifelong dreamer, she began writing at an early age and can't recall a time when she wasn't creating in some artistic form. An active interest in the American West, and to a lesser extent the American Civil War, has been a lifelong obsession. Cowboys have been a love-affair that began at the tender age of three, and eventually expanded to encompass an equally timeless passion for pirates, Greek Gods, and Ancient Egypt. The other side of the Old West intrigue is an affinity for Victorian England, particularly the 1885-1895 part of the century.

Denysé's first major fantasy novel is **As Fate Decrees**. The novel relies heavily on Greek Mythology, and is set in Ancient Greece and modern Athens. If you enjoy a tale of Gods, Destiny, and the battles of an Eternal Champion, this is the book for you! Not surprisingly, there's a touch of romance throughout, of course! "It's what I do best, after all!" The next fantasy novel, already in the works, is about pirates, parallel worlds, and sorcery.

At this point in her career, Denyse has had published in the vicinity of 400 stories and novellas, in almost any genre you can name. "The only thing I haven't tried yet is hard-core science fiction, and horror. Since I don't consider vampires as I write them to be the fodder of horror, I classify those stories as Dark Fantasy." Many of her vampire stories have appeared in Margaret L. Carter's anthology, *The Vampire's Crypt*, and *Night To Dawn*, published and edited by Dawn Callahan for the first two years, and now published by author/editor Barbara A. Custer.

Denysé's poetry has been published internationally, as well. She has also been the recipient of numerous awards, most notably the Fan Quality Award, which is given annually for excellence in fan-written fictions based on film and television. As of May 2004, there are four awards in her collection, and no less than a dozen nominations to her credit.

Also in 2004, Denysé was chosen as a winner in the Amber Heat Wave, an annual contest held by ePublishing company Amber Quill Press. One of the novellas published by AQP, Mirage, was included in the anthology collection *Suits, Ties, and the Water Cooler*, which was a finalist for the 2006 EPPIE Award, a prestigious award given for excellence in electronic publishing.

In 2006, Denysé formed a partnership with actor/producer/singer Branscombe Richmond to create and write a serial that is best described as a modern day western. (Think motorcycles in place of horses!) Installments of the book have begun appearing on the American Motorcycle Company website, (www.amc1902.com) the first episode appeared in April 2006. The serial is available for free, and can found at the company's Home Page. A new project with Mr. Richmond will be officially announced shortly. It is a second serial story, this one a romance novel posted in chapters, will be featured on the website of Good Morning, Hawaii. (www.goodmorninghawaiitv.com)

Simply The Best was the title of Denysé's first full-length erotic romance novel, and was her debut title with Liquid Silver Books (www.LSBooks.com). Upcoming projects include a new Historical/Western romance, an adventure/fantasy, and possibly a sequel to *As Fate Decrees* in the near future. In the erotic romance genre there is also lots to explore, including the Victorian mystery series set in and around the infamous Ripper murders; and soon a set of tales that take place at a Venetian Masquerade Ball; as well as many other stories set in a variety of genres.

Denysé also writes an erotic serial for the FREE eZine, *Wicked Escapes*, published bi-monthly. The series is called *Stranded!*, and is comprised of six stories, with all available installments on the website.

The short Action/Thriller *Silent Death* marks Denysé's debut with New Concepts Publishing, a new contemporary vampire thriller with Forbidden Publications, and new titles in future with Samhain Publishing are also in the works. Also, new publisher Twilight Fantasies, will feature a contemporary romance in their anthology *Summer Flings*, in August of 2007. The collection was an invitation only project and the story is based on the music of Italian superstar Patrizio Buanne.

To stay current with all these projects, or to just say hello, visit Denysé's website: http://denysebridger.com Or, sign up for the monthly newsletter *Romance and Fantasy*.

If you prefer to chat with Denysé and other readers, the newsgroup is open to everyone. Denysé Bridger News. MySpace at: http://www.myspace.com/denysebridger.